He knew the grand sweep of history, but he also knew the small tales; the intrigues and petty jealousies, heroism and cowardice, honor and betrayals.

This, I think, is why his stories have such a ring of truth . . . He was a story teller; a man who could keep you up all night with his books and tales . . . He was a cavalier.

—Jerry Pournelle,

EMPIRE

H. BEAM PIPER

SF

ace books

A Division of Charter Communications Inc.
A GROSSET & DUNLAP COMPANY
51 Madison Avenue
New York, New York 10010

EMPIRE

An ACE Book

First Ace printing: May 1981
Published Simultaneously in Canada

2 4 6 8 0 9 7 5 3 1
Manufactured in the United States of America

TABLE OF CONTENTS

TERRO-HUMAN FUTURE HISTORY CHRONOLOGY*

(1942) 1 A.E. Year One of the Atomic Era, which begins when the first atomic pile goes into operation under the direction of Enrico Fermi at the University of Chicago.

29 The first unmanned rocket, the Kilroy, is launched.

32 The first Lunar base is completed.

32 The Thirty Days War; the First Terran Federation is formed.

54 The First Mars Expedition.

92 Contragravity is developed.

108 The Mars Colony is established.

116 The first colony on Venus is started.

144 The first interstellar expedition.

174 Venus secedes from the Terran Federation.

*(*The following dates are approximations suggested by data in H. Beam Piper's short stories and novels.)*

183	The First Terran Federation is dissolved and the Second Terran Federation is established.
377	The Uller Uprising, a revolt against the Federation by the natives of Uller.
390	The Chartered Fenris Company goes bust.
603	The Gartner Trisystem is settled.
629	Zarathustra is found and colonized.
782	Foxx Travis is born.
809	Native revolt on Kwann.
812	Aditya is discovered.
842—854	The System States War, starts when the System States Alliance tries to break away from Federation control.
854	Ten thousand refugees from Abigor flee with the remnants of the System States Navy to found a new civilization. They colonize Excalibur, the first Sword-World.
894	Merlin, the great Federation battle computer is located on Poictesme.
1000—1399	The Interstellar Wars, a series of revolts and wars that lead to the collapse of the Terran Federation.
1359	Aditya is occupied by Morglay.
1473	Skathi is deserted by the Space Vikings.

1503   Six Space Viking ships from Haulteclere raid Aton; four of their ships are destroyed and two others limp home. After this failure the Space Vikings no longer raid civilized worlds.

1548   During a war between Aton and Baldur, the Planetary Nationalist Party on Aton takes power and forms a dictatorship.

1604   The *Nemesis* spaceship is built and Lucas Trask leaves Gram for Tanith in the Old Federation.

1611   The Battle of Audhumla

1613   Omfray of Glaspyth, with a fleet of eight Space Viking ships, lands on Gram.

1613   The Battle of Marduk.

1848   King Steven IV becomes the first Galactic Emperor.

1904   The Sword-Worlds are added to the Empire.

1936   Emperor Paul II begins building the Imperial palace on Odin.

2162   Rodrik VI completes the consolidation of the First Galactic Empire.

2936   Paul XXII tries to move the Empire out of its complacent rut.

INTRODUCTION

John F. Carr

EX-BEATLE JOHN LENNON IS SHOT TO DEATH IN NEW YORK reads the headline of the Los Angeles *Times* as I write this article. Hundreds of distraught fans are already gathering at the famed Dakota Building where John Lennon lived and died. Thousands of flowers drape the fence. Tower Records of Hollywood announces they've sold over a thousand copies of Lennon's new, last, record, "Double Fantasy," in less than ten hours. Radio stations across the dial are playing Lennon's songs and Beatle retrospectives.

I think of James Dean, Jim Morrison, Dylan Thomas, Stanley G. Weinbaum, Marilyn Monroe, John F. Kennedy, Martin Luther King, Cordwainer Smith, Brian Jones—H. Beam Piper.

There's very little other than death that gives these people anything in common; a premature death that robbed them of future success and us of the special talents that might have enriched us all. What they all left us was a terrible sense of loss—within the science fiction community, the rock music

community, the literary community, and occasionally the
entire human family.

At the time of his death, H. Beam Piper was writing at
the top of his form and certainly with the best of his contemporaries. "Omnilingual," "Gunpowder God," *Little
Fuzzy, The Cosmic Computer, Space Viking*: these were the
products of Piper's last five years. When he died, Piper was
working on a major historical novel, *Only the Arquebus,* had
recently completed the third, and now lost, "Fuzzy" novel,
and was finishing a new Empire novelet. We can only imagine what Piper, free of debts and worries, might have accomplished during the next ten or twenty years. Jerry Pournelle believes that had Beam lived, he would have been
elevated to the top ranks of the science fiction pantheon.

But we will never know, and that is the greatest tragedy of
all. Piper's death, by his own hand, because he wrongly
believed his career was finished, brought everything to a
premature end. Because of problems over the estate, it also
kept much of his early work out of print for some time.

For over twenty years Piper's short stories have remained
forgotten in past issues of musty old science fiction pulps.
Other than an occasional anthology appearance, few of
Piper's short stories have ever appeared in book form. But
now, thanks to Ace Books, the best of them are being
reissued in thematic collections like this one. Now together
for the first time in *Empire* are the stories that describe and
define the First Galactic Empire and the later times of the
Terro-Human Future History.

* * *

H. Beam Piper is best known to sf readers for his Fuzzy
books and to fans for his Paratime stories, but it is his
Terro-Human Future History that is his greatest and most
imaginative gift. Robert A. Heinlein may or may not have
created the first future history series in science fiction, but he
certainly gave it its modern definition and legitimacy. Isaac
Asimov and Poul Anderson soon followed with their own
unique contributions. Not far behind was H. Beam Piper.
The Terro-Human Future History may not have the evolu-

tionary synthesis of Gordon R. Dickson's Childe Cycle or the breadth of Anderson's Polesotechnic League and Terran Empire, but Piper's history of the future has a historian's attention to sociological and political detail that is unsurpassed.

As related by Jerry Pournelle, Piper's original plan had been to do a story per century throughout the first several thousand years of the Terro-Human Future History. Even had he lived another twenty years it is doubtful that he would have accomplished this goal. The demand for sequels to the Fuzzy books and *Space Viking* made it improbable. Yet, we are all the poorer for his not having had the time to try.

The Terran Federation itself is well mapped out by *Four-Day Planet, Uller Uprising, Little Fuzzy, Fuzzy Sapiens, The Cosmic Computer,* and half-a-dozen short stories; however, only one novel, *Space Viking,* and three short stories exist to describe the next four or five thousand years. Furthermore, since *Space Viking* takes place several hundred years before the First Galactic Empire, there are some large holes indeed.

"A Slave is a Slave" occurs during the consolidation of the First Empire and does illuminate some imperial policy; however, it leaves us with many questions about where the Empire began and how it rose to power. "Ministry of Disturbance" takes place some eight hundred years later when the Empire is at peace and suffering from stagnation. It sheds some light on a few of the previous Emperors, their reigns, and the state of the once mighty Sword-Worlds, but again provides us with nothing concerning the genesis of the Empire.

In order to learn more about the origins of the First Empire we have to look back at the Federation and its fall. In *The Cosmic Computer,* Piper's major late Federation story, we find the Federation in retrenchment. It is no longer expanding and the economy is deteriorating. Although Piper never makes this explicit, it appears that some sense of common purpose and unity was lost during the System States War, an economic war as brutal as the War Between the States. Part of the reason is that Merlin—the super battle-computer that directed the Federation's strategy during the war—had predicted the breakup of the Federation at the end of the war. ". . . the strain of that conflict [the System States War] had started an irreversible breakup. Two centuries for the Federation as such; at most, another century of irregular trade and occasional war between independent planets, in a Galaxy full of human-populated planets as poor as Poictesme at its worst."

The leaders of Poictesme, the world where Merlin has remained hidden since the war, learn of this prophecy when they locate Merlin. They ask Merlin's advice on how to stop the coming dark age; the computer gives them the Merlin Plan, a step by step blueprint on how to save Poictesme from the breakup of the Federation and then begin a revival of civilization. The mystery here is that there is no further mention of Poictesme or Merlin or the Merlin Plan in any of the novels or short stories that follow *The Cosmic Computer*.

In *Space Viking* we learn that the Interstellar Wars arrived just about the time Merlin predicted, as did the breakup of the Federation. Both books were written at about the same time; *The Cosmic Computer* was published in 1963, while *Space Viking* was serialized in *Analog* starting in Nov. 1962. Yet, there is nothing in *Space Viking* that gives any indication that Merlin or Poictesme had any effect at all in the rebirth of civilization. Unfortunately, Piper never wrote any stories that bridge these two novels, leaving a seven-hundred-year gap that includes the fall of the Federation and rise of Neobarbarism.

At the time of *Space Viking*, the fall of civilization is almost complete; only a few worlds such as Marduk, Aton, Baldur, and Odin have retained some degree of Federation culture and interstellar spaceflight. Most of the former Federation planets have regressed to a more primitive state, anywhere from nuclear-power-using civilizations all the way down to the Old Stone Age. Most of these worlds have political and social structures resembling ones out of Terra's past (unsurprising, since one of Piper's major themes throughout the Terro-Human Future History is that the future repeats the past). In "The Edge of the Knife" Piper has his history professor say: "There were so few things, in the history of the past, which did not have their counterparts in the future." In *Space Viking,* as the title indicates, this theme is played over and over again.

The Sword-Worlds do not suffer from the Federation's fall as they are separated from the Federation by culture as well as distance. The Sword-Worlds were settled by refugees from the System States. "Ten thousand men and women on Abigor, refusing to surrender, had taken the remnant of the System States Alliance navy to space, seeking a world the Federation had never heard of and wouldn't find for a long time. That had been the world they had called Excalibur. From it, their grandchildren had colonized Joyeuse and Durendal and Flamberge; Haulteclere had been colonized in the next generation from Joyeuse, and Gram from Haulteclere." Sword-World civilization continues to flourish until a ship from Morglay returns from the Old Federation to tell what has been going on there since the System States War.

The Space Vikings have a hybrid civilization, a mixture of high technology and feudalism. Sword-World men are expected to fight for their freedoms and keep careful rein on those who lead them. When talking to the Mardukan court, Lucas Trask—Prince of Tanith and former Space Viking—describes their political system: "Well, we don't use the word government very much . . . . We talk a lot about authority and sovereignty, and I'm afraid we burn entirely too much powder over it, but government always seems to us like sovereignty interfering in matters that don't concern it. As long as sovereignty maintains a reasonable semblance of good public order and makes the more serious forms of crime fairly hazardous for the criminals, we're satisfied."

Sword-World civilization, by the time of *Space Viking,* is already on the decline; far too many trained and needed men are being drawn to the Federation for plunder and are then staying. When the Space Vikings do return home, their ships are loaded with stolen goods which can be sold at discounted prices unfairly competing with Sword-World-made products. The result is unemployment and runaway inflation which ruin the local economy. Historically, the same thing happened in Spain after the discovery of the New World; galleons brought load after load of Inca and Aztec gold and silver into the country, driving local artisans out of business and devaluing the currency. The final result was a rigid and unsympathetic aristocracy and a lower class locked into subjugation. "Nothing on Gram, nothing on any of the Sword-Worlds was done as efficiently as three centuries ago. The whole level of Sword-World life was sinking, like the east coastline of this continent, so slowly as to be evident only from the records and monuments of the past."

By the end of *Space Viking*, Lucas Trask has given up hope that civilization will be rekindled by the Space Vikings. "Sooner or later, civilization in the Old Federation would drive them [the Space Vikings] home to loot the planets that had sent them out." The dynastic wars that will bring an end to Sword-World pre-eminence have already begun, some generations ago. Another is about to begin on Gram, Trask's home world.

Trask, however, has a dream of his own—the League of Civilized Worlds. The League will start as a series of treaties and trade alliances with Tanith's neighbors, one that will grow until it pushes back the long night of ignorance and savagery. But, like Poictesme and Merlin, Trask and his League of Civilized Worlds slip into the murky waters of Piper's future history and are never mentioned again.

If the League of Civilized Worlds is not the seed from which the Empire springs, where does it come from? In a "Slave is a Slave" the planet Odin is identified as the Imperial capital. While Odin is briefly mentioned in *Four-Day Planet* and *Space Viking*, there is no indication that it will one day become the capital of the First Empire.

Later in "A Slave is a Slave" we read: "He showed them planet after planet—Marduk, where the Empire had begun . . ." *Space Viking* is the only novel in which Marduk figures predominantly; there it is described as one of the *few* civilized worlds. Marduk, population two billion, never passes through a period of decline or barbarism after the fall of the Federation. At the time of *Space Viking,* Marduk has a British-style monarchy and prime minister with a fairly powerful aristocracy. Although Marduk has about a dozen colonies and client worlds, she shows no sign of becoming the start of the First Empire. Near the end of the book there is a Hitler-type take over of the government; most of the royal family is forced to flee or is murdered. A few escape to Tanith. There Lucas Trask recruits a large space navy and returns to Marduk to free her from the tyranny of Zaspar Mekann and Andray Dunnan.

Simon Bentrik, member of the royal family and friend of Lucas Trask, looks as though he will be the regent for Princess Myrna, who is still a child. Bentrik's son, Steven—a natural leader even as a boy—is her escort when Marduk is reoccupied. Trask advises his father: "You know, the girl will be Queen in a few years, if she isn't now. Queens need Prince Consorts. Your son's a good boy; I liked him the first moment I saw him, and I've liked him better ever since. He'd be a good man on the Throne beside Queen Myrna."

Simon Bentrik doesn't take to Trask's idea right away, but it's obvious that Lucas means to press it. It's in "Ministry of Disturbance" that we learn that it is Steven IV (almost certainly the great-grandson of Steven Bentrik) who is the Emperor who proclaimed Odin the Imperial Planet. The irony here, of course, is that Lucas Trask, by convincing Simon to help his son to the throne of Marduk, has undone his own dream of the League of Civilized Worlds before it even had a chance to begin.

But why did Steven IV move the capital from Marduk to Odin, when both are major worlds? The most likely answer is that Odin is much closer to Terra and the other major civilized worlds. We know Marduk is close to the frontier of the Old Federation; it is only five hundred light-years from Tanith, which was one of the last planets to be colonized by the Federation. In *Four-Day Planet* we learn about a Terra-Odin-Baldur interstellar milk run, which places Odin close to

the center of human worlds. It certainly wouldn't be the first
time in history that a capital was moved for political or
economic reasons; Alexander the Great moved his capital
from Macedonia to Persia for similar reasons.

We can only piece together the details of how the Empire
began and the date when the Mardukan King became Emperor. Piper does give us a few clues; in "Ministry of Disturbance" we learn that a thousand years before, "the Empire
was blazing into being out of the long night of hammering
back the Neobarbarians from world to world." Some two
hundred years later the Empire was consolidated by Rodrick
VI. "A Slave is a Slave" takes place while the Empire was
still expanding under the reign of Rodrick III.

When the Imperial expeditionary force, a seven ship
battle-line unit, reaches Aditya, it's obvious they mean to
bring Aditya into the Empire either peacefully or feet first.
The Empire may appear benevolent on the surface, but its
policies are stamped with hobnailed boots: "The Galaxy is
not big enough for any competition of sovereignty. There
must be one and only one completely sovereign power. The
Terran Federation was once such a power. It failed and
vanished, you know what followed. Darkness and anarchy.
We are clawing our way up out of that darkness. We will not
fail. We will create a peaceful and unified Galaxy." The
Empire has learned from the errors of the long gone Federation and is determined not to repeat its mistakes. ". . . I
think your constitution (for Aditya) . . . will be nothing
short of political disaster, but it will insure some political
stability, which is all that matters from the Imperial point of
view. An Empire statesman must always guard against sympathizing with local factions and interests . . ."

Yet, despite all its power and resolve, the First Galactic
Empire comes crashing down just as the Terran Federation
before it. In "The Edge of the Knife" the professor who
"sees" into the future has this revelation about the First
Empire: "He was struck by the parallel between the buccaneers of the West Indies and the space-pirates in the days of
the dissolution of the First Galactic Empire . . ." Piper, like

Arnold Toynbee—the great British historian who wrote A STUDY OF HISTORY—saw history as a cyclical process, civilizations growing Phoenix-like out of the ashes of previous ones. Later in "The Edge of the Knife" the professor says, "History follows certain patterns. I'm not a Toynbean, by any matter of means, but any historian can see that certain forces generally tend to produce similar effects." Piper also incorporated Toynbee's phases of history; Toynbee's *universal state* is found in Piper's Terran Federation; at the end of *The Cosmic Computer* the Federation is entering a *time of troubles*; and in *Space Viking* we see the *interregnum* before the emergence of the First Galactic Empire.

So, despite Paul the Twenty-Second's Ministry of Disturbance, the Empire is destined to fall. Paul's plans to save the Empire—like those of Conn Maxwell in *The Cosmic Computer* and Lucas Trask in *Space Viking*—are destined to failure because of the deterministic forces of history. In each of these stories we have Piper's self-reliant man—out of the same mold as John W. Campbell's "Citizen" and Robert A. Heinlein's competent man—versus the tide of history. At the end of each of these stories it appears as though the self-reliant man has won; however in future stories we learn that while the battle may have been won, the war was lost.

One is left wondering if this battle between man and history was not a mirror image of the war going on inside Piper himself, a man much like his own characters. Because, despite all his planning, hard work, and ingenuity, Piper ended up with a failed marriage, a mountain of bills, and a career that looked as though it was on the rocks. Is it any wonder then that this self-reliant man committed suicide rather than face becoming a burden on the state or asking for charity from his friends? The sad truth is that his career was not over; Campbell was trying to get a check to him for a Lord Kalvin story, the mid-sixties sf boom was right around the corner, and many of his friends would have been glad to provide him with financial aid.

"Keeper" is Piper's last story in the Terro-Human Future History and takes place five to six thousand years after the founding of the Federation. Terra, after several atomic wars and a new ice age, has fallen into barbarism and has even become lost once or twice in the dark periods between galactic civilizations. ''Not more than a thousand years . . . the glaciation (on Terra) hadn't started in the time of the Third Empire, there is no record of this planet during the Fourth, but by the beginning of the Fifth Empire, less than a thousand years ago, things here were very much as they are now.'' Terra is now an outpost of the Fifth Empire, with only a nearby navy base for company. Dremna, a world not mentioned in any other story, is the Fifth Empire's capital. It appears that the worlds of man have grown in number and that the center of civilization has moved since the time of the First Empire. Certainly Terra is a backwater world: ''This world may be old . . . but it is the Mother World, Terra, the world that sent Man to the Stars.''

We learn very little in ''Keeper'' about the Fifth Empire or the empires that preceded it, nor is it likely that we ever will unless Piper's lost notes and file folders reappear someday. Jerry Pournelle has copies of some of the early notes and letters which spell out some details of Piper's history of the future, but none of them mention any time past the First Empire. Like the Unfinished Symphony, Piper's Terro-Human Future History will remain tantalizingly incomplete.

John F. Carr

Introduction to "The Edge of the Knife"

This story is probably the most unusual of all the stories in the Terro-Human Future History in that it bridges two of Piper's most dominant themes, the history of the future and the nature of time. The story is about a history professor who can "see" into the future, with sometimes disastrous results. His future vision allows him not only to see into the immediate future but also into the far future of the First Empire and beyond. The fact that much of the future he sees is not recorded elsewhere makes this story of real importance for an understanding of Piper's history of the future.

Interestingly enough, this is the only story to take place before the creation of the Terran Federation. It is here that we learn how and why the Federation came into being.

THE EDGE OF THE KNIFE

CHALMERS stopped talking abruptly, warned by the sudden attentiveness of the class in front of him. They were all staring; even Guellick, in the fourth row, was almost half awake. Then one of them, taking his silence as an invitation to questions found his voice.

"You say Khalid ib'n Hussein's been assassinated?" he asked incredulously. "When did that happen?"

"In 1973, at Basra." There was a touch of impatience in his voice; surely they ought to know that much. "He was shot, while leaving the Parliament Building, by an Egyptian Arab named Mohammed Noureed, with an old U.S. Army M3 submachine-gun. Noureed killed two of Khalid's guards and wounded another before he was overpowered. He was lynched on the spot by the crowd; stoned to death. Ostensibly, he and his accomplices were religious fanatics; however, there can be no doubt whatever that the murder was inspired, at least indirectly, by the Eastern Axis."

The class stirred like a grain-field in the wind. Some looked at him in blank amazement; some were hastily averting faces red with poorly suppressed laughter. For a moment he was puzzled, and then realization hit him like a blow in the stomach-pit. He'd forgotten, again.

"I didn't see anything in the papers about it," one boy was saying.

"The newscast, last evening, said Khalid was in Ankara, talking to the President of Turkey," another offered.

"Professor Chalmers, would you tell us just what effect Khalid's death had upon the Islamic Caliphate and the Middle Eastern situation in general?" a third voice asked with exaggerated solemnity. That was Kendrick, the class humorist; the question was pure baiting.

"Well, Mr. Kendrick, I'm afraid it's a little too early to assess the full results of a thing like that, if they can ever be fully assessed. For instance, who, in 1911, could have predicted all the consequences of the pistol-shot at Sarajevo? Who, even today, can guess what the history of the world would have been had Zangara not missed Franklin Roosevelt in 1932? There's always that if."

He went on talking safe generalities as he glanced covertly at his watch. Only five minutes to the end of the period; thank heaven he hadn't made that slip at the beginning of the class. "For instance, tomorrow, when we take up the events in India from the First World War to the end of British rule, we will be largely concerned with another victim of the assassin's bullet, Mohandas K. Gandhi. You may ask yourselves, then, by how much that bullet altered the history of the Indian sub-continent. A word of warning, however: The events we will be discussing will be either contemporary with or prior to what was discussed today. I hope that you're all keeping your notes properly dated. It's always easy to become confused in matters of chronology."

He wished, too late, that he hadn't said that. It pointed up the very thing he was trying to play down, and raised a general laugh.

As soon as the room was empty, he hastened to his desk, snatched pencil and notepad. This had been a bad one, the worst yet; he hadn't heard the end of it by any means. He couldn't waste thought on that now, though. This was all new and important; it had welled up suddenly and without warning into his conscious mind, and he must get it down in notes before the ''memory''—even mentally, he always put that word into quotes—was lost. He was still scribbling furiously when the instructor who would use the room for the next period entered, followed by a few of his students. Chalmers finished, crammed the notes into his pocket, and went out into the hall.

Most of his own Modern History IV class had left the building and were on their way across the campus for science classes. A few, however, were joining groups for other classes here in Prescott Hall, and in every group, they were the center of interest. Sometimes, when they saw him, they would fall silent until he had passed; sometimes they didn't, and he caught snatches of conversation.

''Oh, brother! Did Chalmers really blow his jets this time!'' one voice was saying.

''Bet he won't be around next year.''

Another quartet, with their heads together, were talking more seriously.

''Well, I'm not majoring in History, myself, but I think it's an outrage that some people's diplomas are going to depend on grades given by a lunatic!''

''Mine will, and I'm not going to stand for it. My old man's president of the Alumni Association, and . . .''

That was something he had not thought of, before. It gave him an ugly start. He was still thinking about it as he turned into the side hall to the History Department offices and entered the cubicle he shared with a colleague. The colleague, old Pottgeiter, Medieval History, was emerging in a rush; short, rotund, gray-bearded, his arms full of books and papers, oblivious, as usual, to anything that had happened since the Battle of Bosworth or the Fall of Constantinople. Chalmers stepped quickly out of his way and entered behind him. Marjorie Fenner, the secretary they also shared, was tidying up the old man's desk.

"Good morning, Doctor Chalmers." She looked at him keenly for a moment. "They give you a bad time again in Modern Four?"

Good Lord, did he show it that plainly? In any case, it was no use trying to kid Marjorie. She'd hear the whole story before the end of the day.

"Gave myself a bad time."

Marjorie, still fussing with Pottgeiter's desk, was about to say something in reply. Instead, she exclaimed in exasperation.

"Ohhh! That man! He's forgotten his notes again!" She gathered some papers from Pottgeiter's desk, rushing across the room and out the door with them.

For a while, he sat motionless, the books and notes for General European History II untouched in front of him. This was going to raise hell. It hadn't been the first slip he'd made, either; that thought kept recurring to him. There had been the time when he had alluded to the colonies on Mars and Venus. There had been the time he'd mentioned the secession of Canada from the British Commonwealth, and the time he'd called the U.N. the Terran Federation. And the time he'd tried to get a copy of Franchard's *Rise and Decline of the System States*, which wouldn't be published until the Twenty-eighth Century, out of the college library. None of those had drawn much comment, beyond a few student jokes about the history professor who lived in the future instead of the past. Now, however, they'd all be remembered, raked up, exaggerated, and added to what had happened this morning.

He sighed and sat down at Marjorie's typewriter and began transcribing his notes. Assassination of Khalid ib'n Hussein, the pro-Western leader of the newly formed Islamic Caliphate; period of anarchy in the Middle East; interfactional power-struggles; Turkish intervention. He wondered how long that would last; Khalid's son, Tallal ib'n Khalid, was at school in England when his father was—would be— killed. He would return, and eventually take his father's place, in time to bring the Caliphate into the Terran Federation when the general war came. There were some notes on that already; the war would result from an attempt by the Indian Communists to seize Bangladesh. The trouble was that he so seldom "remembered" an exact date. His "memory" of the year of Khalid's assassination was an exception.

Nineteen seventy-three—why, that was this year. He looked at the calendar. October 16, 1973. At very most, the Arab statesman had two and a half months to live. Would there be any possible way in which he could give a credible warning? He doubted it. Even if there were, he questioned whether he should—for that matter, whether he *could*—interfere. . . .

He always lunched at the Faculty Club; today was no time to call attention to himself by breaking an established routine. As he entered, trying to avoid either a furtive slink or a chip-on-shoulder swagger, the crowd in the lobby stopped talking abruptly, then began again on an obviously changed subject. The word had gotten around, apparently. Handley, the head of the Latin Department, greeted him with a distantly polite nod. Pompous old owl; regarded himself, for some reason, as a sort of unofficial Dean of the Faculty. Probably didn't want to be seen fraternizing with controversial characters. One of the younger men, with a thin face and a mop of unruly hair, advanced to meet him as he came in, as cordial as Handley was remote.

"Oh, hello, Ed!" he greeted, clapping a hand on Chalmers' shoulder. "I was hoping I'd run into you. Can you have dinner with us this evening?" He was sincere.

"Well, thanks, Leonard. I'd like to, but I have a lot of work. Could you give me a rain-check?"

"Oh, surely. My wife was wishing you'd come around, but I know how it is. Some other evening?"

"Yes, indeed." He guided Fitch toward the dining-room door and nodded toward a table. "This doesn't look too crowded; let's sit here."

After lunch, he stopped in at his office. Marjorie Fenner

was there, taking dictation from Pottgeiter; she nodded to him as he entered, but she had no summons to the president's office.

The summons was waiting for him, the next morning, when he entered the office after Modern History IV, a few minutes past ten.

"Doctor Whitburn just phoned," Marjorie said. "He'd like to see you, as soon as you have a vacant period."

"Which means right away. I shan't keep him waiting."

She started to say something, swallowed it, and then asked if he needed anything typed up for General European II.

"No, I have everything ready." He pocketed the pipe he had filled on entering, and went out.

The president of Blanley College sat hunched forward at his desk; he had rounded shoulders and round, pudgy fists and a round, bald head. He seemed to be expecting his visitor to stand at attention in front of him. Chamlers got the pipe out of his pocket, sat down in the desk-side chair, and snapped his lighter.

"Good morning, Doctor Whitburn," he said very pleasantly.

Whitburn's scowl deepened. "I hope I don't have to tell you why I wanted to see you," he began.

"I have an idea." Chalmers puffed until the pipe was drawing satisfactorily. "It might help you get started if you did, though."

"I don't suppose, at that, that you realize the full effect of your performance, yesterday morning, in Modern History Four," Whitburn replied. "I don't suppose you know, for instance, that I had to intervene at the last moment and suppress an editorial in the *Black and Green*, derisively critical of you and your teaching methods, and, by implication, of the administration of this college. You didn't hear about that, did you? No, living as you do in the future, you wouldn't."

"If the students who edit the *Black and Green* are dissatis-

fied with anything here, I'd imagine they ought to say so,"
Chalmers commented. "Isn't that what they teach in the
journalism classes, that the purpose of journalism is to speak
for the dissatisfied? Why make exception?"

"I should think you'd be grateful to me for trying to keep
your behavior from being made a subject of public ridicule
among your students. Why, this editorial which I suppressed
actually went so far as to question your sanity!"

"I should suppose it might have sounded a good deal like
that, to them. Of course, I have been preoccupied, lately,
with an imaginative projection of present trends into the
future. I'll quite freely admit that I should have kept my
extracurricular work separate from my class and lecture
work, but . . ."

"That's no excuse, even if I were sure it were true! What
you did, while engaged in the serious teaching of history,
was to indulge in a farrago of nonsense, obvious as such to
any child, and damage not only your own standing with your
class but the standing of Blanley College as well. Doctor
Chalmers, if this were the first incident of the kind it would
be bad enough, but it isn't. You've done things like this
before, and I've warned you before. I assumed, then, that
you were merely showing the effects of overwork, and I
offered you a vacation, which you refused to take. Well, this
is the limit. I'm compelled to request your immediate resignation."

Chalmers laughed. "A moment ago, you accused me of
living in the future. It seems you're living in the past. Evidently you haven't heard about the Higher Education Faculty
Tenure Act of 1963, or such things as tenure-contracts. Well,
for your information, I have one; you signed it yourself, in
case you've forgotten. If you want my resignation, you'll
have to show cause, in a court of law, why my contract
should be voided, and I don't think a slip of the tongue is a
reason for voiding a contract that any court would accept."

Whitburn's face reddened. "You don't, don't you? Well,

maybe it isn't, but insanity is. It's a very good reason for voiding a contract voidable on grounds of unfitness or incapacity to teach.''

He had been expecting, and mentally shrinking from, just that. Now that it was out, however, he felt relieved. He gave another short laugh.

"You're willing to go into open court, covered by reporters from papers you can't control as you do this student sheet here, and testify that for the past twelve years you've had an insane professor on your faculty?''

"You're . . . You're trying to blackmail me?'' Whitburn demanded, half rising.

"It isn't blackmail to tell a man that a bomb he's going to throw will blow up in his hand.'' Chalmers glanced quickly at his watch. "Now, Doctor Whitburn, if you have nothing further to discuss, I have a class in a few minutes. If you'll excuse me . . .''

He rose. For a moment, he stood facing Whitburn; when the college president said nothing, he inclined his head politely and turned, going out.

Whitburn's secretary gave the impression of having seated herself hastily at her desk the second before he opened the door. She watched him, round-eyed, as he went out into the hall.

He reached his own office ten minutes before time for the next class. Marjorie was typing something for Pottgeiter; he merely nodded to her, and picked up the phone. The call would have to go through the school exchange, and he had a suspicion that Whitburn kept a check on outside calls. That might not hurt any, he thought, dialing a number.

"Attorney Weill's office,'' the girl who answered said.

"Edward Chalmers. Is Mr. Weill in?''

She'd find out. He was; he answered in a few seconds.

"Hello, Stanley; Ed Chalmers. I think I'm going to need a little help. I'm having some trouble with President Whitburn, here at the college. A matter involving the validity of my tenure-contract. I don't want to go into it over this line. Have you anything on for lunch?''

"No, I haven't. When and where?" the lawyer asked.

He thought for a moment. Nowhere too close the campus, but not too far away.

"How about the Continental; Fontainbleu Room? Say twelve-fifteen."

"That'll be all right. Be seeing you."

Marjorie looked at him curiously as he gathered up the things he needed for the next class.

Stanley Weill had a thin, dark-eyed face. He was frowning as he set down his coffeecup.

"Ed, you ought to know better than to try to kid your lawyer," he said. "You say Whitburn's trying to force you to resign. With your contract, he can't do that, not without good and sufficient cause, and under the Faculty Tenure Law, that means something just an inch short of murder in the first degree. Now what's Whitburn got on you?"

Beat around the bush and try to build a background, or come out with it at once and fill in the details afterward? He debated mentally for a moment, then decided upon the latter course.

"Well, it happens that I have the ability to prehend future events. I can, by concentrating, bring into my mind the history of the world, at least in general outline, for the next five thousand years. Whitburn thinks I'm crazy, mainly because I get confused at times and forget that something I know about hasn't happened yet."

Weill snatched the cigarette from his mouth to keep from swallowing it. As it was, he choked on a mouthful of smoke and coughed violently, then sat back in the boothseat, staring speechlessly.

"It started a little over three years ago," Chalmers continued. "Just after New Year's, 1970. I was getting up a series of seminars for some of my postgraduate students on extrapolation of present social and political trends to the middle of the next century, and I began to find that I was getting some very fixed and definite ideas of what the world of 2050 to 2070 would be like. Completely unified world, abolition of all national states under a single world sovereignty, colonies on Mars and Luna, that sort of thing. Some of these ideas didn't seem quite logical; a number of them were complete reversals of present trends, and a lot seemed to depend on arbitrary and unpredictable factors. Mind, this was before the first rocket landed on the Moon, when the whole lunar-base project was a triple-top secret. But I knew, in the spring of 1970, that the first unmanned rocket would be called the *Kilroy*, and that it would be launched some time in 1971. You remember, when the news was released, it was stated that the rocket hadn't been christened until the day before it was launched, when somebody remembered that old 'Kilroy-was-here' thing from the Second World War. Well, I knew about it over a year in advance.''

Weill had been listening in silence. He had a naturally skeptical face; his present expression mightn't really mean that he didn't believe what he was hearing.

"How'd you get all this stuff? In dreams?''

Chalmers shook his head. "It just came to me. I'd be sitting reading, or eating dinner, or talking to one of my classes, and the first thing I'd know, something out of the future would come bubbling up in me. It just kept pushing up into my conscious mind. I wouldn't have an idea of something one minute, and the next it would just be part of my general historical knowledge; I'd know it as positively as I know that Columbus discovered America in 1492. The only difference is that I can usually remember where I've read something in past history, but my future history I know without knowing how I know it.''

"Ah, that's the question!'' Weill pounced. "You don't know how you know it. Look, Ed, we've both studied psychology, elementary psychology at least. Anybody who has to work with people, these days, has to know some psychology. What makes you sure that these prophetic impressions of yours aren't manufactured in your own subconscious mind?''

"That's what I thought, at first. I thought my subconscious was just building up this stuff to fill the gaps in what I'd produced from logical extrapolation. I've always been a stickler for detail,'' he added, parenthetically. ''It would be natural for me to supply details for the future. But, as I said, a lot of this stuff is based on unpredictable and arbitrary factors that can't be inferred from anything in the present. That left me with the alternatives of delusion or precognition, and if I ever came near going crazy, it was before the *Kilroy* landed and the news was released. After that, I knew which it was.''

''And yet, you can't explain how you can have real knowledge of a thing before it happens. Before it exists,'' Weill said.

''I really don't need to. I'm satisfied with knowing that I know. But if you want me to furnish a theory, let's say that all these things really do exist, in the past or in the future, and that the present is just a moving knife-edge that separates the two. You can't even indicate the present. By the time you make up your mind to say, 'Now!' and transmit the impulse to your vocal organs, and utter the word, the original present moment is part of the past. The knife-edge has gone over it. Most people think they know only the present; what they know is the past, which they have already experienced, or read about. The difference with me is that I can see what's on both sides of the knife-edge.''

Weill put another cigarette in his mouth and bent his head to the flame of his lighter. For a moment, he sat motionless, his thin face rigid.

''What do you want me to do?'' he asked. ''I'm a lawyer, not a psychiatrist.''

''I want a lawyer. This is a legal matter. Whitburn's talking about voiding my tenure contract. You helped draw it up; I have a right to expect you to help defend it.''

''Ed, have you been talking about this to anybody else?'' Weill asked.

''You're the only person I've told. It's not the sort of thing you'd bring up casually, in a conversation.''

''Then how'd Whitburn get hold of it?''

''He didn't, not the way I've given it to you. But I made a

couple of slips, now and then. I made a bad one yesterday
morning.''

He told Weill about it, and about his session with
the president of the college that morning. The lawyer
nodded.

''That was a bad one, but you handled Whitburn the right
way,'' Weill said. ''What he's most afraid of is publicity,
getting the college mixed up in anything controversial, and
above all, the reactions of the trustees and people like that. If
Dacre or anybody else makes any trouble, he'll do his best to
cover for you. Not willingly, of course, but because he'll
know that that's the only way he can cover for himself. I
don't think you'll have any more trouble with him. If you can
keep your own nose clean, that is. Can you do that?''

''I believe so. Yesterday I got careless. I'll not do that
again.''

''You'd better not.'' Weill hesitated for a moment. ''I said
I was a lawyer, not a psychiatrist. I'm going to give you some
psychiatric advice, though. Forget this whole thing. You say
you can bring these impressions into your conscious mind by
concentrating?'' He waited briefly; Chalmers nodded, and he
continued: ''Well, stop it. Stop trying to harbor this stuff. It's
dangerous, Ed. Stop playing around with it.''

''You think I'm crazy, too?''

Weill shook his head impatiently. ''I didn't say that. But
I'll say, now, that you're losing your grip on reality. You are
constructing a system of fantasies, and the first thing you
know, they will become your reality, and the world around
you will be unreal and illusory. And that's a state of mental
incompetence that, as a lawyer, I *can* recognize.

''How about the *Kilroy*?''

Weill looked at him intently. ''Ed, are you sure you did
have that experience?'' he asked. ''I'm not trying to imply
that you're consciously lying to me about that. I am suggest-
ing that you manufactured a memory of that incident in your
subconscious mind, and are deluding yourself into thinking
that you knew about it in advance. False memory is a fairly
common thing, in cases like this. Even with the little
psychology I know, I've heard about that. There's been talk

about rockets to the moon for years. You included something about that in your future-history fantasy, and then, after the event, you convinced yourself that you'd known all about it, including the impromptu christening of the rocket, all along.''

A hot retort rose to his lips; he swallowed it hastily. Instead, he nodded amicably.

''That's a point worth thinking of. But right now, what I want to know is, will you represent me in case Whitburn does take this to court and does try to void my contract?''

''Oh, yes; as you said, I have an obligation to defend the contracts I draw up. But avoid giving him any further reason for trying to void it. Don't make any more of these slips. Watch what you say, in class or out of it. And above all, don't talk about this to anybody. Don't tell anybody that you can foresee the future, or even talk about future probabilities. Your business is with the past; stick to it.''

The afternoon passed quietly enough. Word of his defiance of Whitburn had gotten around among the faculty—Whitburn might have his secretary scared witless in his office, but not gossipless outside it—though it hadn't seemed to have leaked down to the students yet. Handley, the Latin professor, managed to waylay him in a hallway, a hallway Handley didn't normally use.

''The tenure-contract system under which we hold our positions here is one of our most valuable safeguards,'' he said, after exchanging greetings. ''It was only won after a struggle, in a time of public animosity toward all intellectuals, and even now, our professional position would be most insecure without it.''

''Yes. I found that out today, if I hadn't known it when I took part in the struggle you speak of.''

''It should not be jeopardized,'' Handley declared.

''You think I'm jeopardizing it?''

Handley frowned. He didn't like being pushed out of the safety of generalization into specific cases.

''Well, now that you make that point, yes. I do. If Docotor Whitburn tries to make an issue of . . . of what happened yesterday . . . and if the court decides against you, you can see the position all of us will be in.''

"What do you think I should have done? Given him my resignation when he demanded it? We have our tenure-contracts, and the system was instituted to prevent just the sort of arbitrary action Whitburn tried to take with me today. If he wants to go to court, he'll find that out.''

"And if he wins, he'll establish a precedent that will threaten the security of every college and university faculty member in the state. In any state where there's a tenure law.''

Leonard Fitch, the psychologist, took an opposite attitude. As Chalmers was leaving the college at the end of the afternoon, Fitch cut across the campus to intercept him.

"I heard about the way you stood up to Whitburn, this morning, Ed,'' he said. "Glad you did it. I only wish I'd done something like that three years ago . . . Think he's going to give you any real trouble?''

"I doubt it.''

"Well, I'm on your side if he does. I won't be the only one, either.''

"Well, thank you, Leonard. It always helps to know that. I don't think there'll be any more trouble, though.''

He dined alone at his apartment, and sat over his coffee, outlining his work for the next day. When both were finished, he dallied indecisively, Weill's words echoing through his mind and raising doubts. It was possible that he had been manufacturing the whole thing in his subconscious mind. That was, at least, a more plausible theory than any he had constructed to explain an ability to produce real knowledge of the future. Of course, there was that business about the *Kilroy*. That had been too close on too many points to be dismissed as coincidence. Then, again, Weill's words came back to disquiet him. Had he really gotten that before the event, as he believed, or had he only imagined, later, that he had?

There was one way to settle that. He rose quickly and went

to the filing-cabinet where he kept his future-history notes and began pulling out envelopes. There was nothing about the *Kilroy* in the Twentieth Century file, where it should be, although he examined each sheet of notes carefully. The possibility that his notes on that might have been filed out of place by mistake occurred to him; he looked in every other envelope. The notes, as far as they went, were all filed in order, and each one bore, beside the future date of ocurrence, the date on which the knowledge—or must he call it delusion?—had come to him. But there was no note on the landing of the first unmanned rocket on Luna.

He put the notes away and went back to his desk, rummaging through the drawers, and finding nothing. He searched everywhere in the apartment where a sheet of paper could have been mislaid, taking all his books, one by one, from the shelves and leafing through them, even books he knew he had not touched for more than three years. In the end, he sat down again at his desk, defeated. The note on the *Kilroy* simply did not exist.

Of course, that didn't settle it, as finding the note would have. He remembered—or believed he remembered—having gotten that item of knowledge—or delusion—in 1970, shortly before the end of the school term. It hadn't been until after the fall opening of school that he had begun making notes. He could have had the knowledge of the robot rocket in his mind then, and neglected putting it on paper.

He undressed, put on his pajamas, poured himself a drink, and went to bed. Three hours later, still awake, he got up, and poured himself another, bigger, drink. Somehow, eventually, he fell asleep.

The next morning, he searched his desk and bookcase in the office at school. He had never kept a diary; now he was wishing that he had. That might have contained something that would be evidence, one way or the other. All day, he vacillated between conviction of the reality of his future knowledge and resolution to have no more to do with it. Once he decided to destroy all the notes he had made, and thought of making a special study of some facet of history, and writing another book, to occupy his mind.

After lunch, he found that more data on the period immediately before the Thirty Day War was coming into his consciousness. He resolutely suppressed it, knowing as he did that it might never come to him again. That evening, too, he cooked dinner for himself at his apartment, and laid out his class-work for the next day. He'd better not stay in, that evening; too much temptation to settle himself by the living-room fire with his pipe and his note-pad and indulge in the vice he had determined to renounce. After a little debate, he decided upon a movie; he put on again the suit he had taken off on coming home, and went out.

The picture, a random choice among the three shows in the neighborhood, was about Seventeenth Century buccaneers; exciting action and a sound-track loud with shots and cutlass-clashing. He let himself be drawn into it completely, and, until it was finished, he was able to forget both the college and the history of the future. But, as he walked home, he was struck by the parallel between the buccaneers of the West Indies and the space-pirates in the days of the dissolution of the First Galactic Empire, in the Tenth Century of the Interstellar Era. He hadn't been too clear on that period, and he found new data rising in his mind; he hurried his steps, almost running upstairs to his room. It was long after midnight before he had finished the notes he had begun on his return home.

Well, that had been a mistake, but he wouldn't make it again. He determined again to destroy his notes, and began casting about for a subject which would occupy his mind to the exclusion of the future. Not the Spanish Conquistadores; that was too much like the early period of interstellar expansion. He thought for a time of the Sepoy Mutiny, and then rejected it—he could "remember" something much like that on one of the planets of the Beta Hydrae system, in the Fourth Century of the Atomic Era. There were so few things, in the history of the past, which did not have their counterparts in the future. That evening, too, he stayed at home, preparing for his various classes for the rest of the week and making copious notes on what he would talk about to each. He needed more whiskey to get to sleep that night.

Whitburn gave him no more trouble, and if any of the trustees or influential alumni made any protest about what had happened in Modern History IV, he heard nothing about it. He managed to conduct his classes without further incidents, and spent his evenings trying, not always successfully, to avoid drifting into ''memories'' of the future. . . .

He came into his office that morning tired and unrefreshed by the few hours' sleep he had gotten the night before, edgy from the strain, of trying to adjust his mind to the world of Blanley College in mid-April of 1973. Pottgeiter hadn't arrived yet, but Marjorie Fenner was waiting for him; a newspaper in her hand, almost bursting with excitement.

''Here; have you seen it, Doctor Chalmers?'' she asked as he entered.

He shook his head. He ought to read the papers more, to keep track of the advancing knife-edge that divided what he might talk about from what he wasn't supposed to know, but each morning he seemed to have less and less time to get ready for work.

''Well, look! Look at that!''

She thrust the paper into his hands, still folded, the big, black headline where he could see it.

KHALID IB'N HUSSEIN ASSASSINATED

He glanced over the leading paragraphs. Leader of Islamic Chaliphate shot to death in Basra . . . leaving Parliament Building for his palace outside the city . . . fanatic, identified as an Egyptian named Mohammed Noureed . . . old American submachine-gun . . . two guards killed and a third seriously wounded . . . seized by infuriated mob and stoned to death on the spot . . .

For a moment, he felt guilt, until he realized that nothing

he could have done could have altered the event. The death of Khalid ib'n Hussein, and all the millions of other deaths that would follow it, were fixed in the matrix of the spacetime continuum. Including, maybe, the death of an obscure professor of Modern History named Edward Chalmers.

"At least, this'll be the end of that silly flap about what happened a month ago in Modern Four. This is modern history, now; I can talk about it without a lot of fools yelling their heads off."

She was staring at him wide-eyed. No doubt horrified at his cold-blooded attitude toward what was really a shocking and senseless crime.

"Yes, of course; the man's dead. So's Julius Caesar, but we've gotten over being shocked at his murder."

He would have to talk about it in Modern History IV, he supposed; explain why Khalid's death was necessary to the policies of the Eastern Axis, and what the consequences would be. How it would hasten the complete dissolution of the old U. N., already weakened by the crisis over the Eastern demands for the demilitarization and internationalization of the United States Lunar Base, and necessitate the formation of the Terran Federation, and how it would lead, eventually, to the Thirty Days' War. No, he couldn't talk about that; that was on the wrong side of the knife-edge. Have to be careful about the knife-edge; too easy to cut himself on it.

Nobody in Modern History IV was seated when he entered the room; they were all crowded between the door and his desk. He stood blinking, wondering why they were giving him an ovation, and why Kendrick and Dacre were so abjectly apologetic. Great heavens, did it take the murder of the greatest Moslem since Saladin to convince people that he wasn't crazy?

Before the period was over, Whitburn's secretary entered with a note in the college president's hand and over his signature; requesting Chalmers to come to his office immediately and without delay. Just like that; expected him to walk right out of his class. He was protesting as he entered the president's office. Whitburn cut him off short.

"Doctor Chalmers,"—Whitburn had risen behind his desk as the door opened—"I certainly hope that you can realize that there was nothing but the most purely coincidental connection between the event featured in this morning's newspapers and your performance, a month ago, in Modern History Four," he began.

"I realize nothing of the sort. The death of Khalid ib'n Hussein is a fact of history, unalterably set in its proper place in time-sequence. It was a fact of history a month ago no less than today."

"So that's going to be your attitude; that your wild utterances of a month ago have now been vindicated as fullfilled prophesies? And I suppose you intend to exploit this—this coincidence—to the utmost. The involvement of Blanley College in a mess of sensational publicity means nothing to you, I presume."

"I haven't any idea what you're talking about."

"You mean to tell me that you didn't give this story to the *Valley Times*?" Whitburn demanded.

"I did not. I haven't mentioned the subject to anybody connected with the *Times*, or anybody else, for that matter. Except my attorney, a month ago, when you were threatening to repudiate the contract you signed with me."

"I suppose I'm expected to take your word for that?"

"Yes you are. Unless you care to call me a liar in so many words." He moved a step closer. Lloyd Whitburn outweighed him by fifty pounds, but most of the difference was fat. Whitburn must have realized that, too.

"No, no; if you say you haven't talked about it to the *Valley Times*, that's enough," he said hastily. "But somebody did. A reporter was here not twenty minutes ago; he refused to say who had given him the story, but he wanted to question me about it."

"What did you tell him?"

"I refused to make any statement whatever. I also called

Colonel Tighlman, the owner of the paper, and asked him, very reasonably, to suppress the story. I thought that my own position and the importance of Blanley College to this town entitled me to that much consideration." Whitburn's face became almost purple. "He . . . he laughed at me!"

"Newspaper people don't like to be told to kill stories. Not even by college presidents. That's only made things worse. Personally, I don't relish the prospect of having this publicized, any more than you do. I can assure you that I shall be most guarded if any of the *Times* reporters talk to me about it, and if I have time to get back to my class before the end of the period, I shall ask them, as a personal favor, not to discuss the matter outside."

Whitburn didn't take the hint. Instead, he paced back and forth, storming about the reporter, the newspaper owner, whoever had given the story to the paper, and finally Chalmers himself. He was livid with rage.

"You certainly can't imagine that when you made those remarks in class you actually possessed any knowledge of a thing that was still a month in the future," he spluttered. "Why, it's ridiculous! Utterly preposterous!"

"Unusual, I'll admit. But the fact remains that I did. I should, of course, have been more careful, and not confused future with past events. The students didn't understand . . ."

Whitburn half-turned, stopping short.

"My God, man! You *are* crazy!" he cried, horrified.

The period-bell was ringing as he left Whitburn's office; that meant that the twenty-three students were scattering over the campus, talking like mad. He shrugged. Keeping them quiet about a thing like this wouldn't have been possible in any case. When he entered his office, Stanley Weill was waiting for him. The lawyer drew him out into the hallway quickly.

"For God's sake, have you been talking to the papers?" he demanded. "After what I told you . . ."

"No, but somebody has." He told about the call to Whitburn's office, and the latter's behavior. Weill cursed the college president bitterly.

"Any time you want to get a story in the *Valley Times*, just order Frank Tighlman not to print it. Well, if you haven't talked, don't.''

"Suppose somebody asks me?''

"A reporter, no comment. Anybody else, none of his damn business. And above all, don't let anybody finagle you into making any claims about knowing the future. I thought we had this under control; now that it's out in the open, what that fool Whitburn'll do is anybody's guess."

Leonard Fitch met him as he entered the Faculty Club, sizzling with excitement.

"Ed, this has done it!" he began, jubilantly. "This is one nobody can laugh off. It's direct proof of precognition, and because of the prominence of the event, everybody will hear about it. And it simply can't be dismissed as coincidence . . .''

"Whitburn's trying to do that.''

"Whitburn's a fool if he is,'' another man said calmly. Turning, he saw that the speaker was Tom Smith, one of the math professors. "I figured the odds against that being chance. There are a lot of variables that might affect it one way or another, but ten to the fifteenth power is what I get for a sort of median figure.''

"Did you give that story to the *Valley Times*?'' he asked Fitch, suspicion rising and dragging anger up after it.

"Of course, I did,'' Fitch said. "I'll admit, I had to go behind your back and have some of my postgrads get statements from the boys in your history class, but you wouldn't talk about it yourself . . .''

Tom Smith was standing beside him. He was twenty years younger than Chalmers, he was an amateur boxer, and he had good reflexes. He caught Chalmers' arm as it was traveling back for an uppercut, and held it.

"Take it easy, Ed; you don't want to start a slugfest in

here. This is the Faculty Club; remember?''

"I won't, Tom; it wouldn't prove anything if I did." He turned to Fitch. "I won't talk about sending your students to pump mine, but at least you could have told me before you gave that story out."

"I don't know what you're sore about," Fitch defended himself. "I believed in you when everybody else thought you were crazy, and if I hadn't collected signed and dated statements from your boys, there'd have been no substantiation. It happens that extrasensory perception means as much to me as history does to you. I've believed in it ever since I read about Rhine's work, when I was a kid. I worked in ESP for a long time. Then I had a chance to get a full professorship by coming here, and after I did, I found that I couldn't go on with it, because Whitburn's president here, and he's a stupid old bigot with an airlocked mind . . ."

"Yes." His anger died down as Fitch spoke. "I'm glad Tom stopped me from making an ass of myself. I can see your side of it." Maybe that was the curse of the professional intellectual, an ability to see everybody's side of everything. He thought for a moment. "What else did you do, beside hand this story to the *Valley Times*? I'd better hear all about it."

"I phoned the secretary of the American Institute of Psionics and Parapsychology, as soon as I saw this morning's paper. With the time difference to the East Coast, I got him just as he reached his office. He advised me to give the thing the widest possible publicity; he thought that would advance the recognition and study of parapsychology. A case like this can't be ignored; it will demand serious study . . ."

"Well, you got your publicity, all right. I'm up to my neck in it."

There was an uproar outside. The doorman was saying, firmly:

"This is the Faculty Club, gentlemen; it's for members only. I don't care if you gentlemen are the press, you simply cannot come in here."

"We're all up to our necks in it," Smith said. "Leonard, I

don't care what your motives were, you ought to have considered the effect on the rest of us first.''

"This place will be a madhouse,'' Handley complained.
"How we're going to get any of these students to keep their
minds on their work . . .''

"I tell you, I don't know a confounded thing about it,''
Max Pottgeiter's voice rose petulantly at the door. "Are you
trying to tell me that Professor Chalmers murdered some
Arab? Ridiculous!''

He ate hastily and without enjoyment, and slipped through
the kitchen and out the back door, cutting between two
frat-houses and circling back to Prescott Hall. On the way, he
paused momentarily and chuckled. The reporters, unable to
storm the Faculty Club, had gone off in chase of other game
and had cornered Lloyd Whitburn in front of Administration
Center. One of them was carrying TV equipment, and they
were trying to get something for telecast. After gesticulating
angrily, Whitburn broke away from them and dashed up the
steps and into the building. A campus policeman stopped
those who tried to follow.

His only afternoon class was American History III. He got
through it somehow, though the class wasn't able to concentrate on the Reconstruction and the first election of Grover
Cleveland. The halls were free of reporters, at least, and
when it was over he hurried to the Library, going to the
faculty reading room in the rear, where he could smoke.
There was nobody there but old Max Pottgeiter, smoking a
cigar, his head bent over a book. The Medieval History
professor looked up.

"Oh, hello, Chalmers. What the deuce is going on around
here? Has everybody gone suddenly crazy?'' he asked.

"Well, they seem to think I have,'' he said bitterly.

"They do? Stupid of them. What's all this about some
Arab being shot? I didn't know there were any Arabs around
here.''

"Not here. At Basra.'' He told Pottgeiter what had happened.

"Well! I'm sorry to hear about that," the old man said. "I have a friend at Southern California, Bellingham, who knew Khalid very well. Was in the Middle East doing some research on the Byzantine Empire; Khalid was most helpful. Bellingham was quite impressed by him; said he was a wonderful man, and a fine scholar. Why would anybody want to kill a man like that?"

He explained in general terms. Pottgeiter nodded understandingly; assassination was a familiar feature of the medieval political landscape, too. Chalmers went on to elaborate. It was a relief to talk to somebody like Pottgeiter, who wasn't bothered by the present moment, but simply boycotted it. Eventually, the period-bell rang. Pottgeiter looked at his watch, as from conditioned reflex, and then rose, saying that he had a class and excusing himself. He would have carried his cigar with him if Chalmers hadn't taken it away from him.

After Pottgeiter had gone, Chalmers opened a book—he didn't notice what it was—and sat staring unseeing at the pages. So the moving knife-edge had come down on the end of Khalid ib'n Hussein's life; what were the events in the next segment of time, and the segments to follow? There would be general war in the Middle East—with consternation, he remembered that he had been talking about that to Pottgeiter. The Turkish army would move in and try to restore order. There would be more trouble in northern Iran, the Indians would invade Bangladesh, and then the general war, so long dreaded, would come. How far in the future that was he could not "remember". . . . He wished he could "remember" how the events between the murder of Khalid and the Thirty Days' War had been spaced chronologically. Something of that had come to him, after the incident in Modern History IV, and he had driven it from his consciousness.

He didn't dare go home, where the reporters would be sure to find him. He simply left the college, at the end of the school-day, and walked without conscious direction until darkness gathered. This morning, when he had seen the paper, he had said, and had actually believed, that the news of the murder in Basra would put an end to the trouble that had started a month ago in the Modern History class. It hadn't; the trouble, it seemed, was only beginning. And with the newspapers, and Whitburn, and Fitch, it could go on forever . . .

It was fully dark, now; his shadow fell ahead of him on the sidewalk, lengthening as he passed under and beyond a street-light, vanishing as he entered the stronger light of the one ahead. The windows of a cheap cafe reminded him that he was hungry, and he entered, going to a table and ordering something absently. There was a television screen over the combination bar and lunch-counter. Some kind of a comedy programme, at which an invisible studio-audience was laughing immoderately and without apparent cause. The roughly dressed customers along the counter didn't seem to see any more humor in it than he did. Then his food arrived on the table and he began to eat without really tasting it.

After a while, an alteration in the noises from the television penetrated his consciousness; a news-program had come on, and he raised his head. The screen showed a square in an Eastern city; the voice was saying:

". . . Basra, where Khalid ib'n Hussein was assassinated early this morning—early afternoon, local time. This is the scene of the crime; the body of the murderer has been removed, but you can still see the stones with which he was pelted to death by the mob . . ."

A close-up of the square, still littered with torn-up paving-stones. A Caliphate army officer, displaying the weapon—it was an old M3, all right; Chalmers had used one of those things, himself, thirty years before, and he and his contemporaries had called it a "grease-gun." There were some recent pictures of Khalid, including one taken as he left the plane on his return from Ankara. He watched, absorbed; it was all exactly as he had "remembered" a month ago. It gratified him to see that his future "memories" were reliable in detail as well as generality.

"But the most amazing part of the story comes, not from

Basra, but from Blanley College, in California," the commentator was saying, "Where, it is revealed, the murder of Khalid was foretold, with uncanny accuracy, a month ago, by a history professor, Doctor Edward Chalmers . . ."

There was a picture of himself, in hat and overcoat, perfectly motionless, as though a brief moving glimpse were being prolonged. A glance at the background told him when and where it had been taken—a year and a half ago, at a convention at Harvard. These telecast people must save up every inch of footage they ever took. There were views of Blanley campus, and interviews with some of the Modern History IV boys, including Dacre and Kendrick. That was one of the things they'd been doing with that jeep-mounted sound-camera, this afternoon, then. The boys, some brashly, some embarrassedly, were substantiating the fact that he had, a month ago, described yesterday's event in detail. There was an interview with Leonard Fitch; the psychology professor was trying to explain the phenomenon of precognition in layman's terms, and making heavy going of it. And there was the mobbing of Whitburn in front of Administration Center. The college president was shouting denials of every question asked him, and as he turned and fled, the guffaws of the reporters were plainly audible.

An argument broke out along the counter.

"I don't believe it! How could anybody know all that about something before it happened?"

"Well, you heard that-there professor, what was his name. An' you heard all them boys . . ."

"Ah, college-boys; they'll do anything for a joke!"

"After refusing to be interviewed for telecast, the president of Blanley College finally consented to hold a press conference in his office, from which telecast cameras were barred. He denied the whole story categorically and stated that the boys in Professor Chalmers' class had concocted the whole thing as a hoax . . ."

"There! See what I told you!"

". . . stating that Professor Chalmers is mentally unsound, and that he has been trying for years to oust him from

his position on the Blanley faculty but has been unable to do
so because of the provisions of the Faculty Tenure Act of
1963. Most of his remarks were in the nature of a polemic
against this law, generally regarded as the college professors'
bill of rights. Other members of the Blanley faculty have
unconditionally confirmed the fact the Doctor Chalmers did
make the statements attributed to him a month ago, long
before the death of Khalid ib'n Hussein . . .''

"Yah! How about *that*, now? How'ya gonna get around
that?"

Beckoning the waitress, he paid his check and hurried out.
Before he reached the door, he heard a voice, almost stutter-
ing with excitement:

"Hey! Look! That's *him!*"

He began to run. He was two blocks from the cafe before
he slowed to a walk again.

That night, he needed three shots of whiskey before he
could get to sleep.

A delegation from the American Institute of Psionics and
Parapsychology reached Blanley that morning, having taken
a strato-plane from the East Coast. They had academic titles
and degrees that even Lloyd Whitburn couldn't ignore. They
talked with Leonard Fitch, and with the students from Modern History IV, and took statements. It wasn't until after
General European History II that they caught up with
Chalmers—an elderly man, with white hair and a ruddy face;
a young man who looked like a heavyweight boxer; a
middle-aged man in tweeds who smoked a pipe and looked as
though he ought to be more interested in grouse-shooting and
flower-gardening than in clairvoyance and telepathy. The
names of the first two meant nothing to Chalmers. They were
important names in their own field, but it was not his field.
The name of the third, who listened silently, he did not catch.

"You understand, gentlemen, that I'm having some difficulties with the college administration about this," he told
them. "President Whitburn has even gone so far as to chal-
lenge my fitness to hold a position here."

"We've talked to him," the elderly man said. "It was not a very satisfactory discussion."

"President Whitburn's fitness to hold his own position could very easily be challenged," the young man added pugnaciously.

"Well, then, you see what my position is. I've consulted my attorney, Mr. Weill, and he has advised me to make absolutely no statements of any sort about the matter."

"I understand," the eldest of the trio said. "But we're not the press, or anything like that. We can assure you that anything you tell us will be absolutely confidential." He looked inquiringly at the middle-aged man in tweeds, who nodded silently. "We can understand that the students in your modern history class are telling what is substantially the truth?"

"If you're thinking about that hoax statement of Whitburn's, that's drivel!" he said angrily. "I heard some of those boys on the telecast, last night; except for a few details in which they were confused, they all stated exactly what they heard me say in class a month ago."

"And we assume,"—again he glanced at the man in tweeds—"that you had no opportunity of knowing anything, at the time, about any actual plot against Khalid's life?"

The man in tweeds broke silence for the first time. "You can assume that. I don't even think this fellow Noureed knew anything about it, then."

"Well, we'd like to know, as nearly as you're able to tell us, just how you became the percipient of this knowledge of the future event of the death of Khalid ib'n Hussein," the young man began. "Was it through a dream, or a waking experience; did you visualize, or have an auditory impression, or did it simply come into your mind . . ."

"I'm sorry, gentlemen." He looked at his watch. "I have to be going somewhere, at once. In any case, I simply can't discuss the matter with you. I appreciate your position; I know how I'd feel if data of historical importance were being withheld from me. However, I trust that you will appreciate my position and spare me any further questioning."

That was all he allowed them to get out of him. They spent another few minutes being polite to one another; he invited them to lunch at the Faculty Club, and learned that they were lunching there as Fitch's guests. They went away trying to hide their disappointment.

The Psionics and Parapsychology people weren't the only delegation to reach Blanley that day. Enough of the trustees of the college lived in the San Francisco area to muster a quorum for a meeting the evening before; a committee, including James Dacre, the father of the boy in Modern History IV, was appointed to get the facts at first hand; they arrived about noon. They talked to some of the students, spent some time closeted with Whitburn, and were seen crossing the campus with the Parapsychology people. They didn't talk to Chalmers or Fitch. In the afternoon, Marjorie Fenner told Chalmers that his presence at a meeting, to be held that evening in Whitburn's office, was requested. The request, she said, had come from the trustees' committee, not from Whitburn; she also told him that Fitch would be there. Chalmers promptly phoned Stanley Weill.

'I'll be there along with you,'' the lawyer said. ''If this trustees' committee is running it, they'll realize that this is a matter in which you're entitled to legal advice. I'll stop by your place and pick you up . . . You haven't been doing any talking, have you?''

He described the interview with the Psionics and Paraphsychology people.

''That was all right . . . Was there a man with a mustache, in a brown tweed suit, with them?''

''Yes. I didn't catch his name . . .''

''It's Cutler. He's an Army major; Central Intelligence. His crowd's interested in whether you had any real advance information on this. He was in to see me, just a while ago. I have the impression he'd like to see this whole thing played down, so he'll be on our side, more or less and for the time being. I'll be around to your place about eight; in the meantime, don't do any more talking than you have to. I hope we can get this straightened out, this evening. I'll have to go to Reno in a day or so to see a client there. . . .''

The meeting in Whitburn's office had been set for eight-thirty; Weill saw to it that they arrived exactly on time. As they got out of his car at Administration Center and crossed to the steps, Chalmers had the feeling of going to a duel, accompanied by his second. The briefcase Weill was carrying may have given him the idea; it was flat and square-cornered, the size and shape of an old case of dueling pistols. He commented on it.

"Sound recorder," Weill said. "Loaded with a four-hour spool. No matter how long this thing lasts, I'll have a record of it, if I want to produce one in court."

Another party was arriving at the same time—the two Psionics and Parapsychology people and the Intelligence major, who seemed to have formed a working partnership. They all entered together, after a brief and guardedly polite exchange of greetings. There were voices raised in argument inside when they came to Whitburn's office. The college president was trying to keep Handley, Tom Smith, and Max Pottgeiter from entering his private room in the rear.

"It certainly is!" Handley was saying. "As faculty members, any controversy involving establishment of standards of fitness to teach under a tenure-contract concerns all of us, because any action taken in this case may establish a precedent which could affect the validity of our own contracts."

A big man with iron-gray hair appeared in the doorway of the private office behind Whitburn; James Dacre.

"These gentlemen have a substantial interest in this, Doctor Whitburn," he said. "If they're here as representatives of the college faculty, they have every right to be present."

Whitburn stood aside. Handley, Smith and Pottgeitter went through the door; the others followed. The other three members of the trustees' committee were already in the room. A few minutes later, Leonard Fitch arrived, also carrying a briefcase.

"Well, everybody seems to be here," Whitburn said,

starting toward his chair behind the desk. "We might as well get this started."

"Yes. If you'll excuse me, Doctor." Dacre stepped in front of him and sat down at the desk. "I've been selected as chairman of this committee; I believe I'm presiding here. Start the recorder, somebody."

One of the other trustees went to the sound recorder beside the desk—a larger but probably not more efficient instrument than the one Weill had in his briefcase—and flipped a switch. Then he and his companions dragged up chairs to flank Dacre's, and the rest seated themselves around the room. Old Pottgeiter took a seat next to Chalmers.

"What are they trying to do, Ed?" Pottgeiter asked, in a loud whisper. "Throw you off the faculty? They can't do that, can they?"

"I don't know, Max. We'll see . . ."

"This isn't any formal hearing, and nobody's on trial here," Dacre was saying. "Any action will have to be taken by the board of trustees as a whole, at a regularly scheduled meeting. All we're trying to do is find out just what's happened here, and who, if anybody, is responsible . . ."

"Well, there's the man who's responsible!" Whitburn cried, pointing at Chalmers. "This whole thing grew out of his behavior in class a month ago, and I'll remind you that at the time I demanded his resignation!"

"I thought it was Doctor Fitch, here, who gave the story to the newspapers," one of the trustees, a man with red hair and a thin, eyeglassed face, objected.

"Doctor Fitch acted as any scientist should, in making public what he believed to be an important scientific discovery," the elder of the two Parapsychology men said. "He believed, and so do we, that he had discovered a significant instance of precognition—a case of real prior knowledge of a future event. He made a careful and systematic record of Professor Chalmers' statements, at least two weeks before the occurrence of the event to which they referred. It is entirely due to him that we know exactly what Professor Chalmers said and when he said it."

"Yes," his younger colleague added, "and in all my experience I've never heard anything more preposterous than this man Whitburn's attempt, yesterday, to deny the fact."

"Well, we're convinced that Doctor Chalmers did in fact say what he's alleged to have said, last month," Dacre began.

"Jim, I think we ought to get that established, for the record," another of the trustees put in. "Doctor Chalmers, is it true that you spoke, in the past tense, about the death of Khalid ib'n Hussein in one of your classes on the sixteenth of last month?"

Chalmers rose. "Yes, it is. And the next day, I was called into this room by Doctor Whitburn, who demanded my resignation from the faculty of this college because of it. Now, what I'd like to know is, why did Doctor Whitburn, in this same room, deny, yesterday, that I'd said anything of the sort, and accuse my students of concocting the story, after the event as a hoax."

"One of them being my son," Dacre added. "I'd like to hear an answer to that, myself."

"So would I," Stanley Weill chimed in. "You know, my client has a good case against Doctor Whitburn for libel."

Chalmers looked around the room. Of the thirteen men around him, only Whitburn was an enemy. Some of the others were on his side, for one reason or another, but none of them were friends. Weill was his lawyer, obeying an obligation to a client which, at bottom, was an obligation to his own conscience. Handley was afraid of the possibility that a precedent might be established which would impair his own tenure-contract. Fitch, and the two men from the Institute of Psionics and Parapsychology, were interested in him as a source of study-material. Dacre resented a slur upon his son; he and the others were interested in Blanley College as an institution, almost an abstraction. And the major in mufti was probably worrying about the consequences to military security of having a prophet at large. Then a hand gripped his shoulder, and a voice whispered in his ear:

"That's good, Ed; don't let them scare you!"

Old Max Pottgeiter, at least, was a friend.

"Doctor Whitburn, I'm asking you, and I expect an answer, why did you make such statements to the press, when you knew perfectly well that they were false?" Dacre demanded sharply.

"I knew nothing of the kind!" Whitburn blustered, showing, under the bluster, fear. "Yes, I demanded this man's resignation on the morning of October Seventeenth, the day after this incident occurred. It had come to my attention on several occasions that he was making wild and unreasonable assertations in class, and subjecting himself, and with himself the whole faculty of this college, to student ridicule. Why, there was actually an editorial about it written by the student editor of the campus paper. I managed to prevent its publication . . ." He went on at some length about that. "If I might be permitted access to the drawers of my own desk," he added with elephantine sarcasm, "I could show you the editorial in question."

"You needn't bother; I have a carbon copy," Dacre told him. "We've all read it. If you did, at the time you suppressed it, you should have known what Doctor Chalmers said in class."

"I knew he'd talked a lot of poppycock about a man who was still living having been shot to death," Whitburn retorted. "And if something of the sort actually happened, what of it? Somebody's always taking a shot at somebody or other, and they can't miss all the time."

"You claim this was pure coincidence?" Fitch demanded. "A ten-point coincidence: Event of assassination, year of the event, place, circumstances, name of assassin, nationality of assassin, manner of killing, exact type of weapon used, guards killed and wounded along with Kahlid, and fate of the assassin. If that's a simple and plausible coincidence, so's dealing ten royal flushes in succession in a poker game. Tom, you figured that out; what did you say the odds against it were?"

"Was all that actually stated by Doctor Chalmers a month ago?" one of the trustees asked, incredulously.

"It absolutely was. Look here, Mr. Dacre, gentlemen."

Fitch came forward, unzipping his briefcase and pulling out papers. "Here are the signed statements of each of Doctor Chalmers' twenty-three Modern History Four students, all made and dated before the assassination. You can refer to them as you please; they're in alphabetical order. And here." He unfolded a sheet of graph paper a yard long and almost as wide. "Here's a tabulated summary of the boys' statements. All agreed on the first point, the fact of the assassination. All agreed that the time was sometime this year. Twenty out of twenty-three agreed on Basra as the place. Why, seven of them even remembered the name of the assassin. That in itself is remarkable; Doctor Chalmers has an extremely intelligent and attentive class."

"They're attentive because they know he's always likely to do something crazy and make a circus out of himself," Whitburn interjected.

"And this isn't the only instance of Doctor Chalmers' precognitive ability," Fitch continued. "There have been a number of other cases . . ."

Chalmers jumped to his feet; Stanley Weill rose beside him, shoved the cased sound-recorder into his hands, and pushed him back into his seat.

"Gentlemen," the lawyer began, quietly but firmly and clearly. "This is getting out of hand. After all, this isn't an investigation of the actuality of precognition as a psychic phenomenon. What I'd like to hear, and what I haven't heard yet, is Doctor Whitburn's explanation of his contradictory statements that he knew about my client's alleged remarks on the evening after they were supposed to have been made and that, at the same time, the whole thing was a hoax concocted by his students."

"Are you implying that I'm a liar?" Whitburn bristled.

"I'm pointing out that you made a pair of contradictory statements, and I'm asking how you could do that knowingly and honestly," Weill retorted.

"What I meant," Whitburn began, with exaggerated slowness, as though speaking to an idiot, "was that yesterday, when those infernal reporters were badgering me, I really thought that some of Professor Chalmers' students had gotten together and given the *Valley Times* an exaggerated story about his insane maunderings a month ago. I hadn't imagined that a member of the faculty had been so lacking in loyalty to the college . . ."

"You couldn't imagine anybody with any more intellectual integrity than you have!" Fitch fairly yelled at him.

"You're as crazy as Chalmers!" Whitburn yelled back. He turned to the trustees. "You see the position I'm in, here, with this infernal Higher Education Faculty Tenure Act? I have a madman on my faculty, and can I get rid of him? No! I demand his resignation, and he laughs at me and goes running for his lawyer! And he is a madman! Nobody but a madman would talk the way he does. You think this Khalid ib'n Hussein business is the only time he's done anything like this? Why, I have a list of a dozen occasions when he's done something just as bad, only he didn't have a lucky coincidence to back him up. Trying to get books that don't exist out of the library, and then insisting that they're standard textbooks. Talking about the revolt of the colonies on Mars and Venus. Talking about something he calls the Terran Federation, some kind of a world empire. Or something he calls Operation Triple Cross, that saved the country during some fantastic war he imagined . . ."

"WHAT!?"

The question cracked out like a string of pistol shots. Everybody turned. The quiet man in the brown tweed suit had spoken; now he looked as though he were very much regretting it.

"Is there such a thing as Operation Triple Cross?" Fitch was asking.

"No, no. I never heard anything about that; that wasn't what I meant. It was this Terran Federation thing," the major said, perhaps a trifle too quickly and too smoothly. He turned to Chalmers. "You never did any work for PSPB; did you ever talk to anybody who did?" he asked.

"I don't even know what the letters mean," Chalmers replied.

"Politico-Strategic Planning Board. It's all pretty hush-hush, but this term Terran Federation is a tentative name for a proposed organization to take the place of the U. N. if that organization breaks up. It's nothing particularly important, and it only exists on paper."

It won't exist only on paper very long, Chalmers thought. He was wondering what Operation Triple Cross was; he had some notes on it, but he had forgotten what they were.

"Maybe he did pick that up from somebody who'd talked indiscreetly," Whitburn conceded. "But the rest of this tommyrot! Why, he was talking about how the city of Reno had been destroyed by an explosion and fire, literally wiped off the map. There's an example for you!"

He'd forgotten about that, too; now he remembered having made a note about it. He was sure that it followed closely after the assassination of Khalid ib'n Hussein. He turned quickly to Weill.

"Didn't you say you had to go to Reno in a day or so?" he asked.

Weill hushed him urgently, pointing with his free hand to the recorder. The exchange prevented him from noticing that Max Pottgeiter had risen, until the old man was speaking.

"Are you trying to tell these people that Professor Chalmers is crazy?" he was demanding. "Why, he has one of the best minds on the campus. I was talking to him only yesterday, in the back room at the Library. You know," he went on apologetically, "my subject is Medieval History; I don't pay much attention to what's going on in the contemporary world, and I didn't understand, really, what all this excitement was about. But he explained the whole thing to me, and did it in terms that I could grasp, drawing some excellent parallels with the Byzantine Empire and the Crusades. All about the revolt at Damascus, and the sack of Beirut, and the war between Jordan and Saudi Arabia, and how the Turkish army intervened, and the invasion of Pakistan . . ."

"When did all this happen?" one of the trustees demanded.

Pottgeiter started to explain; Chalmers realized, sickly, how much of his future history he had poured into the trusting ear of the old medievalist, the day before.

"Good Lord, man; don't you read the papers at all?" another of the trustees asked.

"No! And I don't read inside-dope magazines, or science fiction. I read carefully substantiated facts. And I know when I'm talking to a sane and reasonable man. It isn't a common experience, around here."

Dacre passed a hand over his face. "Doctor Whitburn," he said, "I must admit that I came to this meeting strongly prejudiced against you, and I'll further admit that your own behavior here has done very little to dispel that prejudice. But I'm beginning to get some idea of what you have to contend with, here at Blanley, and I find that I must make a lot of allowances. I had no idea . . . Simply no idea at all!"

"Look, you're getting a completely distorted picture of this, Mr. Dacre," Fitch broke in. "It's precisely as I believed; Doctor Chalmers is an unusually gifted precognitive percipient. You've seen, gentlemen, how his complicated chain of precognitions about the death of Khalid has been proven verdical; I'd stake my life that every one of these precognitions will be similarly verified. And I'll stake my professional reputation that the man is perfectly sane. Of course, abnormal psychology and psychopathology aren't my subjects, but . . ."

"They're not my subjects, either," Whitburn retorted, "but I know a lunatic by his ravings."

"Doctor Fitch is taking an entirely proper attitude," Pottgeiter said, "in pointing out that abnormal psychology is a specialized branch, outside his own field. I wouldn't dream, myself, of trying to offer a decisive opinion on some point of Roman, or Babylonian, history. Well, if the question of Doctor Chalmers' sanity is at issue here, let's consult somebody who specializes in insanity. I don't believe that anybody here is qualified even to express an opinion on that subject, Doctor Whitburn least of all.''

Whitburn turned on him angrily. ''Oh, shut up, you doddering old fool!'' he shouted. ''Look; there's another of them!'' he told the trustees. ''Another deadhead on the faculty that this Tenure Law keeps me from getting rid of. He's as bad as Chalmers, himself. You just heard that string of nonsense he was spouting. Why, his courses have been noted among the students for years as snap courses in which nobody ever has to do any work . . .''

Chalmers was on his feet again, thoroughly angry. Abuse of himself he could take; talking that way about gentle, learned, old Pottgeiter was something else.

''I think Doctor Pottgeiter's said the most reasonable thing I've heard since I came in here,'' he declared. ''If my sanity is to be questioned, I insist that it be questioned by somebody qualified to do so.''

Weill set his recorder on the floor and jumped up beside him, trying to haul him back into his seat.

''For God's sake, man! Sit down and shut up!'' he hissed.

Chalmers shook off his hand. ''No, I won't shut up! This is the only way to settle this, once and for all. And when my sanity's been vindicated, I'm going to sue this fellow . . .''

Whitburn started to make some retort, then stopped short. After a moment, he smiled nastily.

''Do I understand, Doctor Chalmers, that you would be willing to submit to psychiatric examination?'' he asked.

''Don't agree; you're putting your foot in a trap!'' Weill told him urgently.

''Of course, I agree, as long as the examination is conducted by a properly qualified psychiatrist.''

''How about Doctor Hauserman, at Northern State Mental Hospital?'' Whitburn asked quickly. ''Would you agree to an examination by him?''

''Excellent!'' Fitch exclaimed. ''One of the best men in the field. I'd accept his opinion unreservedly.''

Weill started to object again; Chalmers cut him off. ''Doctor Hauserman will be quite satisfactory to me. The only question is, would he be available?''

''I think he would,'' Dacre said, glancing at his watch. ''I wonder if he could be reached now.'' He got to his feet. ''Telephone in your outer office, Doctor Whitburn? Fine. If you gentlemen will excuse me . . .''

It was a good fifteen minutes before he returned, smiling.

''Well, gentlemen, it's all arranged,'' he said. ''Doctor Hauserman is quite willing to examine Doctor Chalmers—with the latter's consent, of course.''

''He'll have it. In writing, if he wishes.''

''Yes. I assured him on that point. He'll be here about noon tomorrow—it's a hundred and fifty miles from the hospital, but the doctor flies his own plane—and the examination can start at two in the afternoon. He seems familiar with the facilities of the psychology department, here; I assured him that they were at his disposal. Will that be satisfactory to you, Doctor Chalmers?''

''I have a class at that time, but one of the instructors can take it over—if holding classes will be possible around here tomorrow,'' he said. ''Now, if you gentlemen will pardon me, I think I'll go home and get some sleep.''

Weill came up to the apartment with him. He mixed a couple of drinks and they went into the living room with them.

''Just in case you don't know what you've gotten yourself into,'' Weill said, ''this Hauserman isn't any ordinary couch-pilot; he's the state psychiatrist. If he gets the idea you aren't sane, he can commit you to a hospital, and I'll bet that's exactly what Whitburn had in mind when he suggested him. And I don't trust this man Dacre. I thought he was on our side, at the start, but that was before your friends got into the act.'' He frowned into his drink. ''And I don't like the way that Intelligence major was acting, toward the last. If he thinks you know something you are not supposed to, a mental hospital may be his idea of a good place to put you away.''

"You don't think this man Hauserman would allow himself to be influenced . . .? No. You just don't think I'm sane. Do you?"

"I know what Hauserman'll think. He'll think this future history business is a classical case of systematized schizoid delusion. I wish I'd never gotten into this case. I wish I'd never even heard of you! And another thing; in case you get past Hauserman all right, you can forget about that damage-suit bluff of mine. You would not stand a chance with it in court."

"In spite of what happened to Khalid?"

"After tomorrow, I won't stay in the same room with anybody who even mentions that name to me. Well, win or lose, it'll be over tomorrow and then I can leave here."

"Did you tell me you were going to Reno?" Chalmers asked. "Don't do it. You remember Whitburn mentioning how I spoke about an explosion there? It happened just a couple of days after the murder of Khalid. There was—will be—a trainload of high explosives in the railroad yard; it'll be the biggest non-nuclear explosion since the *Mont Blanc* blew up in Halifax harbor in World War One . . ."

Weill threw his drink into the fire; he must have avoided throwing the glass in with it by a last-second exercise of self-control.

"Well," he said, after a brief struggle to master himself. "One thing about the legal profession; you do hear the damndest things! . . . Good night, Professor. And try—please try, for the sake of your poor harried lawyer—to keep your mouth shut about things like that, at least till after you get through with Hauserman. And when you're talking to him, don't, don't, for heaven's sake, *don't*, volunteer anything!"

The room was a pleasant, warmly-colored, place. There was a desk, much like the ones in the classrooms, and six or seven wicker armchairs. A lot of apparatus had been pushed back along the walls; the dust-covers were gay cretonne. There was a couch, with more apparatus, similarly covered, beside it. Hauserman was seated at the desk when Chalmers entered.

He rose, and they shook hands. A man of about his own age, smooth-faced, partially bald. Chalmers tried to guess something of the man's nature from his face, but could read nothing. A face well trained to keep its owner's secrets.

"Something to smoke, Professor," he began, offering his cigarette case.

"My pipe, if you don't mind." He got it out and filled it.

"Any of those chairs," Hauserman said, gesturing toward them.

They were all arranged to face the desk. He sat down, lighting his pipe. Hauserman nodded approvingly; he was behaving calmly, and didn't need being put at ease. They talked at random—at least, Hauserman tried to make it seem so—for some time about his work, his book about the French Revolution, current events. He picked his way carefully through the conversation, alert for traps which the psychiatrist might be laying for him. Finally, Hauserman said:

"Would you mind telling me just why you felt it advisable to request a psychiatric examination, Professor?"

"I didn't request it. But when the suggestion was made, by one of my friends, in reply to some aspersions of my sanity, I agreed to it."

"Good distinction. And why was your sanity questioned? I won't deny that I had heard of this affair, here, before Mr. Dacre called me, last evening, but I'd like to hear your version of it."

He went into that, from the original incident in Modern History IV, choosing every word carefully, trying to concentrate on making a good impression upon Hauserman, and at the same time finding that more "memories" of the future were beginning to seep past the barrier of his consciousness. He tried to dam them back; when he could not, he spoke with greater and greater care lest they leak into his speech.

"I can't recall the exact manner in which I blundered into it. The fact that I did make such a blunder was because I was

talking extemporaneously and had wandered ahead of my
text. I was trying to show the results of the collapse of the
Ottoman Empire after the First World War, and the partition
of the Middle East into a loose collection of Arab states, and
the passing of British and other European spheres of influence following the Second. You know, when you consider it,
the Islamic Caliphate was inevitable; the surprising thing is
that it was created by a man like Khalid. . . .''

He was talking to gain time, and he suspected that
Hauserman knew it. The "memories" were coming into his
mind more and more strongly; it was impossible to suppress
them. The period of anarchy following Khalid's death would
be much briefer, and much more violent, than he had previ-
ously thought. Tallal ib'n Khalid would be flying from England even now; perhaps he had already left the plane to take
refuge among the black tents of his father's Bedouins. The
revolt at Damascus would break out before the end of the
month; before the end of the year, the whole of Syria and
Lebanon would be in bloody chaos, and the Turkish army
would be on the march.

"Yes. And you allowed yourself to be carried a little
beyond the present moment, into the future, without realizing it? Is that it?''

"Something like that,'' he replied, wide awake to the trap
Hauserman had set, and fearful that it might be a blind, to
disguise the real trap. "History follows certain patterns. I'm
not a Toynbean, by any manner of means, but any historian
can see that certain forces generally tend to produce similar
effects. For instance, space travel is now a fact; our government has at present a military base on the moon. Within our
lifetimes—certainly within the lifetimes of my students—
there will be explorations and attempts at colonization on
Mars, and serious consideration given to First Terraforming
and the colonizing. You believe that, Doctor?''

"Oh, unreservedly. I'm not supposed to talk about it, but I
did some work on the Philadelphia Project, myself. I'd say
that every major problem of interplanetary flight had been
solved before the first rocket landed on Luna.''

"Yes. And when Mars and Venus are colonized, there will be the same historic situations, at least in general shape, as arose when the European powers were colonizing the New World, or, for that matter, when the Greek city-states were throwing out colonies across the Aegean. That's the sort of thing we call projecting the past into the future through the present."

Hauserman nodded. "But how about the details? Things like the assassination of a specific personage. How can you extrapolate to a thing like that?"

"Well . . ." More "memories" were coming to the surface; he tried to crowd them back. "I do my projecting in what you might call fictionalized form; try to fill in the details from imagination. In the case of Khalid, I was trying to imagine what would happen if his influence were suddenly removed from Near Eastern and Middle Eastern affairs. I suppose I constructed an imaginary scene of his assassination . . ."

He went on at length. Mohammed and Noureed were common enough names. The Middle East was full of old U.S. weapons. Stoning was the traditional method of execution; it diffused responsibility so that no individual could be singled out for blood-feud vengeance.

"You have no idea how disturbed I was when the whole thing happened, exactly as I had described it," he continued. "And worst of all, to me, was this Intelligence officer showing up; I thought I was really in for it!"

"Then you've never really believed that you had real knowledge of the future?"

"I'm beginning to, since I've been talking to these Psionics and Parapsychology people," he laughed. I sounded, he hoped, like a natural and unaffected laugh. "They seem to be convinced that I have."

There would be an Eastern-inspired uprising in Azerbaijan by the middle of the next year; before autumn, the Indian Communists would make their fatal attempt: the Thirty Days' War would be the immediate result. By that time, the

Lunar Base would be completed and ready; the enemy missiles would be aimed primarily at the rocketports from which it was supplied. Delivered without warning, it should have succeeded—except that every rocketport had its secret duplicate and triplicate. That was Operation Triple Cross; no wonder Major Cutler had been so startled at the words, last evening. The enemy would be utterly overwhelmed under the rain of missiles from across space, but until the moon-rockets began to fall, the United States would suffer grievously.

"Honestly, though, I feel sorry for my friend Fitch," he added. "He's going to be frightfully let down when some more of my alleged prophecies misfire on him. But I really haven't been deliberately deceiving him."

And Blanley College was at the center of one of the areas which would receive the worst of the thermonuclear hell to come. And it would be a little under a year . . .

"And that's all there is to it!" Hauserman exclaimed, annoyance in his voice. "I'm amazed that this man Whitburn allowed a thing like this to assume the proportions it did. I must say that I seem to have gotten the story about this business in a very garbled form indeed." He laughed shortly. "I came here convinced that you were mentally unbalanced. I hope you won't take that the wrong way, Professor," he hastened to add. "In my profession, anything can be expected. A good psychiatrist can never afford to forget how sharp and fine is the knife-edge."

"The knife-edge!" The words startled him. He had been thinking, at that moment, of the knife-edge, slicing moment after moment relentlessly away from the future, into the past, at each slice coming closer and closer to the moment when the missiles of the Eastern Axis would fall. "I didn't know they still resorted to surgery, in mental cases," he added, trying to cover his break.

"Oh, no; all that sort of thing is as irrevocably discarded as the whips and shackles of Bedlam. I meant another kind of knife-edge; the thin, almost invisible, line which separates sanity from non-sanity. From madness, to use a deplorable lay expression.'' Hauserman lit another cigarette. ''Most minds are a lot closer to it than their owners suspect, too. In fact, Professor, I was so convinced that your had passed over it that I brought with me a commitment form, made out all but my signature, for you.'' He took it from his pocket and laid it on the desk. ''The modern equivalent of the *lettre-de-cachet*, I suppose the author of a book on the French Revolution would call it. I was all ready to certify you as mentally unsound, and commit you to Northern State Mental Hospital.''

Chalmers sat erect in his chair. He knew where that was; on the other side of the mountains, in the one part of the state completely untouched by the H-bombs of the Thirty Days' War. Why, the town outside which the hospital stood had been a military headquarters during the period immediately after the bombings, and the center from which all the rescue work in the state had been directed.

''And you thought you could commit me to Northern State!'' he demanded, laughing scornfully, and this time he didn't try to make the laugh sound natural and unaffected. ''You—confine *me*, anywhere? Confine a poor old history professor's body, yes, but that isn't me. I'm universal; I exist in all space-time. When this old body I'm wearing now was writing that book on the French Revolution, I was in Paris, watching it happen, from the fall of the Bastille to the Ninth Thermidor. I was in Basra, and saw that crazed tool of the Axis shoot down Khalid ib'n Hussein—and the professor talked about it a month before it happened. I have seen empires rise and stretch from star to star across the Galaxy, and crumble and fall. I have seen . . .''

Doctor Hauserman had gotten his pen out of his pocket and was signing the commitment form with one hand; with the other, he pressed a button on the desk. A door at the rear opened, and a large young man in a white jacket entered.

''You'll have to go away for a while, Professor,'' Hauserman was telling him, much later, after he had allowed himself to become calm again. 'For how long, I don't know. Maybe a year or so.''

"You mean to Northern State Mental?"

"Well . . . Yes, Professor. You've had a bad crack-up. I don't suppose your realize how bad. You've been working too hard; harder than your nervous system could stand. It's been too much for you."

"You mean, I'm nuts?"

"Please, Professor. I deplore that sort of terminology. You've had a severe psychological breakdown . . ."

"Will I be able to have books, and papers, and work a little? I couldn't bear the prospect of complete idleness."

"That would be all right, if you didn't work too hard."

"And could I say good-bye to some of my friends?"

Hauserman nodded and asked, "Who?"

"Well, Professor Pottgeiter . . ."

"He's outside now. He was inquiring about you."

"And Stanley Weill, my attorney. Not business; just to say good-bye."

"Oh, I'm sorry, Professor. He's not in town, now. He left almost immediately after . . . After . . ."

"After he found out I was crazy for sure? Where'd he go?"

"To Reno; he took the plane at five o'clock."

Weill wouldn't have believed, anyhow; no use trying to blame himself for that. But he was as sure that he would never see Stanley Weill alive again as he was that the next morning the sun would rise. He nodded impassively.

"Sorry he couldn't stay. Can I see Max Pottgeiter alone?"

"Yes, of course, Professor."

Old Pottgeiter came in, his face anguished. "Ed! It isn't true," he stammered. "I won't believe that it's true."

"What, Max?"

"That you're crazy. Nobody can make me believe that."

He put his hand on the old man's shoulder. "Confidentially, Max, neither do I. But don't tell anybody I'm not. It's a secret."

Pottgeiter looked troubled. For a moment, he seemed to be wondering if he mightn't be wrong and Hauserman and Whitburn and the others right.

''Max, do you believe in me?'' he asked. ''Do you believe that I knew about Khalid's assassination a month before it happened?''

''It's a horribly hard thing to believe,'' Pottgeiter admitted. ''But, dammit, Ed, you did! I know, medieval history is full of stories about prophecies being fulfilled. I always thought those stories were just legends that grew up after the event. And, of course, he's about a century late for me, but there was Nostradamus. Maybe those old prophecies weren't just *ex post facto* legends, after all. Yes. After Khalid, I'll believe that.''

''All right. I'm saying, now, that in a few days there'll be a bad explosion at Reno, Nevada. Watch the papers and the telecast for it. And you remember what I told you about the Turks annexing Syria and Lebanon?'' The old man nodded. ''When that happens, get away from Blanley. Come up to the town where Northern State Mental Hospital is, and get yourself a place to live, and stay there. And try to bring Marjorie Fenner along with you. Will you do that, Max?''

''If you say so.'' His eyes widened. ''Something bad's going to happen here?''

''Yes, Max. Something very bad. You promise me you will?''

''Of course, Ed. You know, you're the only friend I have around here. You and Marjorie. I'll come, and bring her along.''

''Here's the key to my apartment.'' He got it from his pocket and gave it to Pottgeiter, with instructions. ''Everything in the filing cabinet on the left of my desk. And don't let anybody else see any of it. Keep it safe for me.''

The large young man in the white coat entered.

Introduction to "A Slave is a Slave"

"A Slave is a Slave" takes place in the early days of the Empire when the Imperial Navy is still annexing Old Federation worlds and outposts. Here we learn much about Imperial policy and determination, as well as about the nature of slavery. John W. Campbell once stirred up a hornet's nest of controversy when he suggested in one of his editorials that no man could enslave another without some cooperation or acceptance. In this story Piper not only suggests that some people like slavery, but they will go a long way to ensure its continuation. And that sometimes the difference between a slave and his master is a very slim one indeed.

A SLAVE IS A SLAVE

JURGEN, PRINCE TREVANNION, accepted the coffee cup and lifted it to his lips, then lowered it. These Navy robots always poured coffee too hot; spacemen must have collapsium-lined throats. With the other hand, he punched a button on the robot's keyboard and received a lighted cigarette; turning, he placed the cup on the command-desk in front of him and looked about. The tension was relaxing in Battle-Control, the purposeful pandemonium of the last three hours dying rapidly. Officers of both sexes, in red and blue and yellow and green coveralls, were rising from seats, leaving their stations, gathering in groups. Laughter, a trifle loud; he realized, suddenly, that they had been worried, and wondered if he should not have been a little so himself. No. There would have been nothing he could have done about anything, so worry would not have been useful. He lifted the cup again and sipped cautiously.

"That's everything we can do now," the man beside him said. "Now we just sit and wait for the next move."

Like all the others, Line-Commodore Vann Shatrak wore shipboard battle-dress; his coveralls were black, splashed on

63

breast and between shoulders with the gold insignia of his
rank. His head was completely bald, and almost spherical; a
beaklike nose carried down the curve of his brow, and the
straight lines of mouth and chin chopped under it enhanced
rather than spoiled the effect. He was getting coffee; he
gulped it at once.

"It was very smart work, Commodore. I never saw a
landing operation go so smoothly."

"Too smooth," Shatrak said. "I don't trust it." He
looked suspiciously up at the row of viewscreens.

"It was absolutely unnecessary!"

That was young Obray, Count Erskyll, seated on the
commodore's left. He was a generation younger than Prince
Trevannion, as Shatrak was a generation older; they were
both smooth-faced. It was odd, how beards went in and out of
fashion with alternate generations. He had been worried, too,
during the landing, but for a different reason from the others.
Now he was reacting with anger.

"I told you, from the first, that it was unnecessary. You
see? They weren't even able to defend themselves, let
alone . . ."

His personal communication-screen buzzed; he set down
the coffee and flicked the switch. It was Lanze Degbrend. On
the books, Lanze was carried as Assistant to the Ministerial
Secretary. In practice, Lanze was his chess-opponent, con-
versational foil, right hand, third eye and ear, and, sometimes, trigger-finger. Lanze was now wearing the combat
coveralls of an officer of Navy Landing-Troops; he had a
steel helmet with a transpex visor shoved up, and there was a
carbine slung over his shoulder. He grinned and executed an
exaggeratedly military salute. He chuckled.

"Well, look at you; aren't you the perfect picture of
correct diplomatic dress?"

"You know, sir, I'm afraid I am, for this planet," Degbrend said. "Colonel Ravney insisted on it. He says the
situation downstairs is still fluid, which I take to mean that
everybody is shooting at everybody. He says he has the main

telecast station, in the big building the locals call the Citadel.''

"Oh, good. Get our announcement out as quickly as you can. Number Five. You and Colonel Ravney can decide what interpolations are needed to fit the situation.''

"Number Five; the really tough one,'' Degbrend considered. "I take it that by interpolations you do not mean dilutions?''

"Oh, no; don't water the drink. Spike it.''

Lanze Degbrend grinned at him. Then he snapped down the visor of his helmet, unslung his carbine, and presented it. He was still standing at present arms when Trevannion blanked the screen.

"That still doesn't excuse a wanton and unprovoked aggression!'' Erskyll was telling Shatrak, his thin face flushed and his voice quivering with indignation. "We came here to help these poeple, not to murder them.''

"We didn't come here to do either, Obray,'' he said turning to face the younger man. "We came here to annex their planet to the Galactic Empire, whether they wish it annexed or not. Commodore Shatrak used the quickest and most effective method of doing that. It would have done no good to attempt to parley with them from off-planet. You heard those telecasts of theirs.''

"Authoritarian,'' Shatrak said, then mimicked pompously: "Everybody is commanded to remain calm; the Mastership is taking action. The Convocation of the Lords-Master is in special session; they will decide how to deal with the invaders. The administrators are directed to reassure the supervisors; the overseers will keep the workers at their tasks. Any person disobeying the orders of the Mastership will be dealt with most severely.' ''

"Static, too. No spaceships into this system for the last five hundred years; the Convocation—equals Parliament, I assume—hasn't been in special session for two hundred and fifty.''

"Yes. I've taken over planets with that kind of government before,'' Shatrak said. ''You can't argue with them. You just grab them by the center of authority, quick and hard.''

Count Erskyll said nothing for a moment. He was opposed to the use of force. Force, he believed, was the last resort of incompetence; he had said so frequently enough since this operation had begun. Of course, he was absolutely right, though not in the way he meant. Only the incompetent wait until the last extremity to use force, and by then, it is usually too late to use anything, even prayer.

But, at the same time, he was opposed to authoritarianism, except, of course, when necessary for the real good of the people. And he did not like rulers who called themselves Lords-Master. Good democratic rulers called themselves Servants of the People. So he relapsed into silence and stared at the viewscreens.

One, from an outside pickup on the *Empress Eulalie* herself, showed the surface of the planet, a hundred miles down, the continent under them curving away to a distant sun-reflecting sea; beyond the curved horizon, the black sky was spangled with unwinking stars. Fifty miles down, the sun glinted from the three thousand foot globes of the two transport-cruisers, *Canopus* and *Mizar*.

Another screen, from *Mizar*, gave a clearer if more circumscribed view of the surface—green countryside, veined by rivers and wrinkled with mountains; little towns that were mere dots; a scatter of white clouds. Nothing that looked like roads. There had been no native sapient race on this planet, and in the thirteen centuries since it had been colonized the Terrohuman population had never completely lost the use of contragravity vehicles. In that screen, farther down, the four destroyers, *Irma*, *Irene*, *Isobel* and *Iris*, were tiny twinkles.

From *Irene*, they had a magnified view of the city. On the maps, none later than eight hundred years old, it was called Zeggensburg; it had been built at the time of the first colonization under the old Terran Federation. Tall buildings, rising from wide interspaces of lawns and parks and gardens and, at the very center, widely separated from anything else, the mass of the Citadel, a huge cylindrical tower rising from a cluster of smaller cylinders, with a broad circular landing stage above, topped by the newly raised flag of the Galactic Empire.

There was a second city, a thick crescent, to the south and east. The old maps placed the Zeggensburg spaceport there, but not a trace of that remained. In its place was what was evidently an industrial district, located where the prevailing winds would carry away the dust and smoke. There was quite a bit of both, but the surprising thing was the streets, long curved ones, and shorter ones crossing at regular intervals to form blocks. He had never seen a city with streets before, and he doubted if anybody else on the Empire ships had. Long boulevards to give unobstructed passage to low-level air-traffic, of course, and short winding walkways, but not things like these. Pictures, of course, of native cities on planets colonized at the time of the Federation, and even very ancient ones of cities on pre-Atomic Terra. But these people had contragravity; the towering, wide-spaced city beside this cross-gridded anachronism proved that.

They knew so little about this planet which they had come to bring under Imperial rule. It had been colonized thirteen centuries ago, during the last burst of expansion before the System States War and the disintegration of the Terran Federation, and it had been named Aditya, in the fashion of the times, for some forgotten deity of some obscure and ancient polytheism. A century or so later, it had seceded from or been abandoned by the Federation, then breaking up. That much they had gleaned from old Federation records still existing on Baldur. After that, darkness, lighted only by a brief flicker when more records had turned up on Morglay.

Morglay was one of the Sword-Worlds, settled by refugee rebels from the System States planets. Mostly they had been soldiers and spacemen; there had been many women with them, and many were skilled technicians, engineers, scientists. They had managed to carry off considerable equipment with them, and for three centuries they had lived in isolation, spreading over a dozen hitherto undiscovered planets. Excalibur, Tizona, Gram, Morglay, Durendal, Flamberge, Curtana, Quernbiter; the names were a roll-call of fabulous blades of Old Terran legend.

Then they had erupted, suddenly and calamitously, into what was left of the Terran Federation as the Space Vikings, carrying pillage and destruction, until the newborn Empire rose to vanquish them. In the Sixth Century Pre-Empire, one of their fleets had come from Morglay to Aditya.

The Adityans of that time had been near-barbarians; the descendents of the original settlers had been serfs of other barbarians who had come as mercenaries in the service of one or another of the local chieftains and had remained to loot and rule. Subjugating them had been easy; the Space Vikings had taken Aditya and made it their home. For several centuries, there had been communication between them and their home planet. Then Morglay had become involved in one of the interplanetary dynastic wars that had begun the decadence of the Space Vikings, and again Aditya dropped out of history.

Until this morning, when history returned in the black ships of the Galactic Empire.

He stubbed out the cigarette and summoned the robot to give him another. Shatrak was speaking:

"You see, Count Erskyll, we really had to do it this way, for their own good." He wouldn't have credited the commodore with such guile; anything was justified, according to Obray of Erskyll, if done for somebody else's good. "What we did, we just landed suddenly, knocked out their army, seized the center of government, before anybody could do anything. If we'd landed the way you'd wanted us to, somebody would have resisted, and the next thing, we'd have had to kill about five or six thousand of them and blow down a couple of towns, and we'd have lost a lot of our own people doing it. You might say, we had to do it to save them from themselves."

Obray of Erskyll seemed to have doubts, but before he could articulate them, Shatrak's communication-screen was calling attention to itself. The commodore flicked the switch, and his executive officer, Captain Patrique Morvill, appeared in it.

"We've just gotten reports, sir, that some of Ravney's people have captured a half-dozen missile-launching sites around the city. His air-reconn tells them that that's the lot of them. I have an officer of one of the parties that participated. You ought to hear what he has to say, sir."

"Well, good!" Vann Shatrak whooshed out his breath. "I don't mind admitting, I was a little on edge about that."

"What till you hear what Lieutenant Carmath has to say." Morvill seemed to be strangling a laugh. "Ready for him, Commodore?"

Shatrak nodded; Morvill made a hand-signal and vanished in a flicker of rainbow colors; when the screen cleared, a young Landing-Troop lieutenant in battle-dress was looking out of it. He saluted and gave his name, rank and unit.

"This missile-launching site I'm occupying, sir; it's twenty miles north-west of the city. We took it thirty minutes ago; no resistance whatever. There are four hundred or so people here. Of them, twelve, one dozen, are soldiers. The rest are civilians. Ten enlisted men, a non-com of some sort, and something that appears to be an officer. The officer had a pistol, fully loaded. The non-com had a submachine gun, empty, with two loaded clips on his belt. The privates had rifles, empty, and no ammunition. The officer did not know where the rifle ammunition was stored."

Shatrak swore. The second lieutenant nodded. "Exactly my comment when he told me, sir. But this place is beautifully kept up. Lawns all mowed, trees neatly pruned, everything policed up like inspection morning. And there is a headquarters office building here adequate for an Army division . . ."

"How about the armament, Lieutenant?" Shatrak asked with forced patience.

"Ah, yes; the armament, sir. There are eight big launching cradles for panplanetary or off-planet missiles. They are all polished up like the Crown Jewels. But none, repeat none, of them is operative. And there is not a single missile on the installation."

Shatrak's facial control didn't slip. It merely intensified, which amounted to the same thing.

"Lieutenant Carmath, I am morally certain I heard you correctly, but let's just check. You said . . ."

He repeated the lieutenant back, almost word for word. Carmath nodded.

"That was it, sir. The missile-crypts are stacked full of old photoprints and recording and microfilm spools. The sighting-and-guidance systems for all the launchers are completely missing. The letoff mechanisms all lack major parts. There is an elaborate set of detection equipment, which will detect absolutely nothing. I saw a few pairs of binoculars about; I suspect that that is what we were first observed with."

"This office, now; I suppose all the paperwork is up to the minute in quintuplicate, and initialed by everybody within sight or hearing?"

"I haven't checked on that yet, sir. If you're thinking of betting on it, please don't expect me to cover you, though."

"Well, thank you, Lieutenant Carmath. Stick around; I'm sending down a tech-intelligence crew to look at what's left of the place. While you're waiting, you might sort out whoever seems to be in charge and find out just what in Nifflheim he thinks that launching-station was maintained for."

"I think I can tell you that, now, Commodore," Prince Trevannion said as Shatrak blanked the screen. "We have a petrified authoritarianism. Quite likely some sort of an oligarchy; I'd guess that this Convocation thing they talk about consists of all the ruling class, everybody has equal voice, and nobody will take the responsibility for doing anything. And the actual work of government is probably handled by a corps of bureaucrats entrenched in their jobs, unwilling to exert any effort and afraid to invite any criticism, and living only to retire on their pensions. I've seen

governments like that before.'' He named a few. ''One thing;
once a government like that has been bludgeoned into the
Empire, it rarely makes any trouble later.''

''Just to judge by this missileless non-launching station,''
Shatrak said, ''they couldn't even decide on what kind of
trouble to make, or how to start it. I think you're going to
have a nice easy Proconsulate here, Count Erskyll.''

Count Erskyll started to say something. No doubt he was
about to tell Shatrak, cuttingly, that he didn't want an easy
Proconsulate, but an opportunity to help these people. He
was saved from this by the buzzing of Shatrak's
communication-screen.

It was Colonel Pyairr Ravney, the Navy Landing-Troop
commander. Like everybody else who had gone down to
Zeggensburg, he was in battle-dress and armed; the transpex
visor of his helmet was pushed up. Between Shatrak's generation and Count Erskyll's, he sported a pointed mustache and
a spiky chin-beard, which, on his thin and dark-eyed face,
looked distinctly Metphistophelean. He was grinning.

''Well, sir, I think we can call it a done job,'' he said.
''There's a delegation here who want to talk to the Lords-
Master of the ships on behalf of the Lords-Master of the
Convocation. Two of them, with about a dozen portfolio-
bearers and note-takers. I'm not too good in Lingua Terra,
outside Basic at best, and their brand is far from that. I
gather that they're some kind of civil-servants, personal
representatives of the top Lords-Master.''

''Do we want to talk to them?'' Shatrak asked.

''Well, we should only talk to the actual, titular, heads of
the   government—Mastership,''   Erskyll,   suddenly
protocol-conscious, objected. ''We can't negotiate with
subordinates.''

''Oh, who's talking about negotiating; there isn't anything
to negotiate. Aditya is now a part of the Galactic Empire. If
this present regime assents to that, they can stay in power. If
not, we will toss them out and install a new government. We
will receive this delegation, inform them to that effect, and

send them back to relay the information to their Lords-Master.'' He turned to the Commodore. ''May I speak to Colonel Ravney?''

Shatrak assented. He asked Ravney where these Lords-Master were.

''Here in the Citadel, in what they call the Convocation Chamber. Close to a thousand of them, screaming recriminations at one another. Sounds like feeding time at the Imperial Zoo. I think they all want to surrender, but nobody dares propose it first. I've just put a cordon around it and placed it off limits to everybody. And everything outside off limits to the Convocation.''

''Well thought of, Colonel. I suppose the Citadel teems with bureaucrats and such low life-forms?''

''Bulging with them. Literally thousands. Lanze Degbrend and Commander Douvrin and a few others are trying to get some sensible answers out of some of them.''

''This delegation; how had you thought of sending them up?''

''Landing-craft to *Isobel*; *Isobel* will bring them the rest of the way.''

He looked at his watch. ''Well, don't be in too much of a rush to get them here, Colonel. We don't want them till after lunch. Delay them on *Isobel*; the skipper can see that they have their own lunch aboard. And entertain them with some educational films. Something to convince them that there is slightly more to the Empire than one ship-of-the-line, two cruisers and four destroyers.''

Count Erskyll was dissatisfied about that, too. He wanted to see the delegation at once and make arrangements to talk to their superiors. Count Erskyll, among other things, was zealous, and of this he disapproved. Zealous statesmen perhaps did more mischief than anything in the Galaxy—with the possible exception of procrastinating soldiers. That could indicate the fundamental difference between statecraft and war. He'd have to play with that idea a little.

An Empire ship-of-the-line was almost a mile in diameter.

It was more than a battle-craft; it also had political functions.
The grand salon, on the outer zone where the curvature of the
floors was less disconcerting, was as magnificent as any but a
few of the rooms of the Imperial Palace at Asgard on Odin,
the floor richly carpeted and the walls alternating mirrors and
paintings. The movable furniture varied according to occasion; at present, it consisted of the bare desk at which they
sat, the three chairs they occupied, and the three secretary-
robots, their rectangular black cases blazened with the Sun
and Cogwheel of the Empire. It faced the door, at the far end
of the room; on either side, a rank of spacemen, in dress
uniform and under arms, stood.

In principle, annexing a planet to the Empire was simplicity itself, but like so many things simple in principle, it was
apt to be complicated in practice, and to this, he suspected,
the present instance would be no exception.

In principle, one simply informed the planetary government that it was now subject to the sovereignty of his Imperial Majesty, the Galactic Emperor. This information was
always conveyed by a Ministerial Secretary, directly under
the Prime Minister and only one more step down from the
Emperor, in the present instance Jurgen, Prince Trevannion.
To make sure that the announcement carried conviction, the
presumedly glad tidings were accompanied by the Imperial
Space Navy, at present represented by Commodore Vann
Shatrak and a seven ship battle-line unit, and two thousand
Imperial Landing-Troops.

When the locals had been properly convinced—with as
little bloodshed as necessary, but always beyond any
dispute—an Imperial Proconsul, in this case Obray, Count
Erskyll, would be installed. He would by no means govern
the planet. The Imperial Constitution was definite on that
point; every planetary government should be sovereign as to
intraplanetary affairs. The Proconsul, within certain narrow
and entirely inelastic limits, would merely govern the government.

Unfortunately, Obray, Count Erskyll, appeared not to
understand this completely. It was his impression that he was

a torch-bearer of Imperial civilization, or something equally picturesque and metaphorical. As he conceived it, it was the duty of the Empire, as represented by himself, to make over backward planets like Aditya in the image of Odin or Marduk or Osiris or Baldur or, preferably, his own home world of Aton.

This was Obray of Erskyll's first proconsular appointment, it was due to family influence, and it was a mistake. Mistakes, of course, were inevitable in anything as large and complex as the Galactic Empire, and any institution guided by men was subject to one kind of influence or another, family influence being no worse than any other kind. In this case, the ultra-conservative Erskylls of Aton, from old Errol, Duke of Yorvoy, down, had become alarmed at the political radicalism of young Obray, and had, on his graduation from the University of Nefertiti, persuaded the Prime Minister to appoint him to a Proconsulate as far from Aton as possible, where he would not embarrass them. Just at that time, more important matters having been gotten out of the way, Aditya had come up for annexation, and Obray of Erskyll had been named Proconsul.

That had been the mistake. He should have been sent to some planet which had been under Imperial rule for some time, where the Proconsulate ran itself in a well-worn groove, and where he could at leisure learn the procedures and unlearn some of the unrealisms absorbed at the University from professors too well insulated from the realities of politics.

There was a stir among the guards; helmet-visors were being snapped down; feet scuffed. They stiffened to attention, the great doors at the other end of the grand salon slid open, and the guards presented arms as the Adityan delegation was ushered in.

There were fourteen of them. They all wore ankle-length gowns, and they all had shaven heads. The one in the lead carried a staff and wore a pale green gown; he was apparently a herald. Behind him came two in white gowns, their empty hands folded on their breasts; one was a huge bulk of obesity

with a bulging brow, protuberant eyes and a pursey little
mouth, and the other was thin and cadaverous, with a skull-
like, almost fleshless face. The ones behind, in dark green
and pale blue, carried portfolios and slung sound-recorder
cases. There was a metallic twinkle at each throat; as they
approached, he could see that they all wore large silver
gorgets. They came to a halt twenty feet from the desk. The
herald raised his staff.

"I present the Admirable and Trusty Tchall Hozhet, personal chief-slave of the Lord-Master Olvir Nikkolon, Chairman of the Presidium of the Lords-Master's Convocation,
and Khreggor Chmidd, chief-slave in office to the Lord-
Master Rovard Javasan, Chief of Administration of Management of the Mastership," he said. Then he stopped,
puzzled, looking from one to another of them. When his eyes
fell on Vann Shatrak, he brightened.

"Are you," he asked, "the chief-slave of the chief
Lord-Master of this ship?"

Shatrak's face turned pink; the pink darkened to red. He
used a word; it was a completely unprintable word. So,
except for a few scattered pronouns, conjunctions and prep-
ositions, were the next fifty words he used. The herald
stiffened. The two delegates behind him were aghast. The
subordinate burden-bearers in the rear began looking around
apprehensively.

"I," Shatrak finally managed, "am an officer of his
Imperial Majesty's Space Navy. I am in command of this
battle-line unit. I am *not*,"—he reverted briefly to
obscenity—"a slave."

"You mean, you are a Lord-Master, too?" That seemed
to horrify the herald even more than the things Shatrak had
been calling him. "Forgive me, Lord-Master. I did not
think . . ."

"That's right; you didn't," Shatrak agreed. "And don't
call me Lord-Master again, or I'll . . ."

"Just a moment, Commodore." He waved the herald
aside and addressed the two in white gowns, shifting to
Lingua Terra. "This is a ship of the Galactic Empire," he

told them. "In the Empire, there are no slaves. Can you understand that?"

Evidently not. The huge one, Khreggor Chmidd, turned to the skull-faced Tchall Hozhet, saying: "Then they must all be Lords-Masters." He saw the objection to that at once. "But how can one be a Lord-Master if there are no slaves?"

The horror was not all on the visitors' side of the desk, either. Obray of Erskyll was staring at the delegation and saying, "Slaves!" under his breath. Obray of Erskyll had never, in his not-too-long life, seen a slave before.

"They can't be," Tchall Hozhet replied. "A Lord-Master is one who owns slaves." He gave that a moment's consideration. "But if they aren't Lords-Master, they must be slaves, and . . ." No. That wouldn't do, either. "But a slave is one who belongs to a Lord-Master."

Rule of the Excluded Third; evidently Pre-Atomic formal logic had crept back to Aditya. Chmidd, looking around, saw the ranks of spacemen on either side, now at parade-rest.

"But aren't they slaves?" he asked.

"They are spacemen of the Imperial Navy," Shatrak roared. "Call one a slave to his face and you'll get a rifle-butt in yours. And I shan't lift a finger to stop it." He glared at Chmidd and Hozhet. "Who had the infernal impudence to send slaves to deal with the Empire? He needs to be taught a lesson."

"Why, I was sent by the Lord-Master Olvir Nikkolon, and . . ."

"Tchall!" Chmidd hissed at him. "We cannot speak to Lords-Master. We must speak to their chief-slaves."

"But they have no slaves," Hozhet objected. "Didn't you hear the . . . the one with the small beard . . . say so?"

"But that's ridiculous, Khreggor. Who does the work, and who tells them what to do? Who told these people to come here?"

"Our Emperor sent us. That is his picture, behind me. But we are not his slaves. He is merely the chief man among us. Do your Masters not have one among them who is chief?"

"That's right," Chmidd said to Hozhet. "In the Convocation, your Lord-Master is chief, and in the Mastership, my Lord-Master, Rovard Javasan, is chief.''

"But they don't tell the other Lords-Master what to do. In Convocation, the other Lords-Master tell them . . .''

"That's what I meant about an oligarchy,'' he whispered, in Imperial, to Erskyll.

"Suppose we tell Ravney to herd these Lords-Master onto a couple of landing-craft and bring them up here?'' Shatrak suggested. He made the suggestion in Lingua Terra Basic, and loudly.

"I think we can manage without that.'' He raised his voice, speaking in Lingua Terra Basic:

"It does not matter whether these slaves talk to us or not. This planet is now under the rule of his Imperial Majesty, Rodrik III. If this Mastership wants to govern the planet under the Emperor, they may do so. If not, we will make an end of them and set up a new government here.''

He paused. Chmidd and Hozhet were looking at one another in shocked incredulity.

"Tchall, they mean it,'' Chmidd said. "They can do it, too.''

"We have nothing more to say to you slaves,'' he continued. "Hereafter, we will speak directly to the Lords-Master.''

"But . . . The Lords-Master never do business directly,'' Hozhet said. "It is un-Masterly. Such discussions are between chief-slaves.''

"This thing they call the Convocation,'' Shatrak mentioned. "I wonder if the members have the business done entirely through their slaves.''

"Oh, no!'' That shocked Chmidd into direct address. "No slave is allowed in the Convocation Chamber.''

He wondered how they kept the place swept out. Robots, no doubt. Or else, what happened when the Masters weren't there didn't count.

"Very well. Your people have recorders; are they on?'

Hozhet asked Chmidd; Chmidd asked the herald, who asked one of the menials in the rear, who asked somebody else. The reply came back through the same channels; they were.

"Very well. At this time tomorrow, we will speak to the Convocation of Lords-Master. Commodore Shatrak, see to it that Colonel Ravney has them in the Convocation Chamber, and that preparations in the room are made, so that we may address them in the dignity befitting representatives of his Imperial Majesty." He turned to the Adityan slaves. "That is all. You have permission to go."

They watched the delegation back out, with the honor-guard following. When the doors had closed behind them, Shatrak ran his hand over his bald head and laughed.

"Shaved heads, every one of them. That's probably why they thought I was your slave. Bet those gorgets are servile badges, too." He touched the Knight's Star of the Order of the Empire at his throat. "Probably thought that was what this was. We would have to draw something like this!"

"They simply can't imagine anybody not being either a slave or a slave-owner," Erskyll was saying. "That must mean that there is no free non-slave-holding class at all. Universal slavery! Well, we'll have to do something about that. Proclaim total emancipation, immediately."

"Oh, no; we can't do anything like that. The Constitution won't permit us to. Section Two, Article One: *Every Empire planet shall be self-governed as to its own affairs, in the manner of its own choice, and wihout interference.*"

"But slavery . . . Section Two, Article Six," Erskyll objected. "*There shall be no chattel slavery or serfdom anywhere in the Empire; no sapient being of any race what-soever shall be the property of any being but himself.*"

"That's correct," he agreed. "If this Mastership intends to remain the planetary government under the Empire, they will be obliged to abolish slavery, but they will have to do it by their own act. We cannot do it for them."

"You know what I'd do, Prince Trevannion?" Shatrak said. "I'd just heave this Mastership thing out, and set up a nice tight military dictatorship. We have the planet under

martial rule now; let's just keep it that way for about five
years, till we can train a new government."

That suggestion seemed to pain Count Erskyll almost as
much as the existing situation.

They dined late, in Commodore Shatrak's private dining
room. Beside Shatrak, Erskyll and himself, there were Lanze
Degbrend, and Count Erskyll's charge-d'affaires, Sharll Ernanday, and Patrique Morvill and Pyairr Ravney and the
naval intelligence officer, Commander Andrey Douvrin. Ordinarily, he deplored serious discussion at meals, but under
the circumstances it was unavoidable; nobody could think or
talk of anything else. The discussion which he had hoped
would follow the meal began before the soup-course.

"We have a total population of about twenty million,"
Lanze Degbrend reported. "A trifle over ten thousand Masters, all ages and both sexes. The remainder are all slaves."

"I find that incredible," Erskyll declared promptly.
"Twenty million people, held in slavery by ten thousand!
Why do they stand for it? Why don't they rebel?"

"Well, I can think of three good reasons," Douvrin said.
"Three square meals a day."

"And no responsibilities; no need to make decisions,"
Degbrend added. "They've been slaves for seven and a half
centuries. They don't even know the meaning of freedom,
and it would frighten them if they did."

"Chain of command," Shatrak said. When that seemed
not to convey any meaning to Erskyll, he elaborated: "We
have a lot of dirty-necked working slaves. Over every dozen
of them is an overseer with a big whip and a stungun. Over
every couple of overseers there is a guard with a submachine
gun. Over them is a supervisor, who doesn't need a gun
because he can grab a handphone and call for troops. Over
the supervisors, there are higher supervisors. Everybody has
it just enough better than the level below him that he's afraid
of losing his job and being busted back to fieldhand."

"That's it exactly, Commodore," Degbrend said. "The

whole society is a slave hierarchy. Everybody curries favor
with the echelon above, and keeps his eye on the echelon
below to make sure he isn't being undercut. We have something not too unlike that, ourselves. Any organizational society is, in some ways, like a slave society. And everything is
determined by established routine. The whole thing has simply been running on momentum for at least five centuries,
and if we hadn't come smashing in with a situation none of
the routines covered, it would have kept on running for
another five, till everything wore out and stopped. I heard
about those missile-stations, by the way. They're typical of
everything here."

"That's another thing," Erskyll interrupted. "These
Lords-Master are the descendants of the old Space-Vikings,
and the slaves of the original inhabitants. The Space Vikings
were a technologically advanced people; they had all the old
Terran Federation science and technology, and a lot they
developed for themselves on the Sword-Worlds."

"Well? They still had a lot of it, on the Sword-Worlds,
two centuries ago when we took them over."

"But technology always drives out slavery; that's a fundamental law of socio-economics. Slavery is economically
unsound; it cannot compete with power-industry, let alone
cybernetics and robotics."

He was tempted to remind young Obray of Erskyll that
there were no such things as fundamental laws of socio-
economics; merely usually reliable generalized statements of
what can more or less be depended upon to happen under
most circumstances. He resisted the temptation. Count
Erskyll had had enough shocks, today, without adding to
them by gratuitous blasphemy.

"In this case, Obray, it worked in reverse. The Space
Vikings enslaved the Adityans to hold them in subjugation.
That was a politico-military necessity. Then, being committed to slavery, with a slave population who had to be made to
earn their keep, they found cybernetics and robotics economically unsound."

"And almost at once, they began appointing slave over-seers, and the technicians would begin training slave assistants. Then there would be slave supervisors to direct the overseers, slave administrators to direct them, slave secretaries and bookkeepers, slave technicians and engineers."

"How about the professions, Lanze?"

"All slave. Slave physicians, teachers, everything like that. All the Masters are taught by slaves; the slaves are educated by apprenticeship. The courts are in the hands of slaves; cases are heard by the chief slaves of judges who don't even know where their own courtrooms are; every Master has a team of slave lawyers. Most of the lawsuits are estate-inheritance cases; some of them have been in litigation for generations."

"What do the Lords-Master do?" Shatrak asked.

"Masterly things," Degbrend replied. "I was only down there since noon, but from what I could find out, that consists of feasting, making love to each other's wives, being entertained by slave performers, and feuding for social precedence like wealthy old ladies on Odin."

"You got this from the slaves? How did you get them to talk, Lanze?"

Degbrend and Ravney exchanged amused glances. Ravney said:

"Well, I detailed a sergeant and six privates to accompany Honorable Degbrend," Ravney said. "They . . . How would you put it, Lanze?"

"I asked a slave a question. If he refused to answer, somebody knocked him down with a rifle-butt," Degbrend replied. "I never had to do that more than once in any group, and I only had to do it three times in all. After that, when I asked questions, I was answered promptly and fully. It is surprising how rapidly news gets around the Citadel."

"You mean you had those poor slaves beaten?" Erskyll demanded.

"Oh, no. Beating implies repeated blows. We only gave one to a customer; that was enough."

"Well, how about the army, if that's what those people in the long red-brown coats were?" Shatrak changed the subject by asking Ravney.

"All slave, of course, officers and all. What will we do about them, sir? I have about three thousand, either confined to their barracks or penned up in the Citadel. I requisitioned food for them, paid for it in chits. There were a few isolated companies and platoons that gave us something of a fight; most of them just threw away their weapons and bawled for quarter. I've segregated the former; with your approval, I'll put them under Imperial officers and noncoms for a quickie training in our tactics, and then use them to train the rest."

"Do that, Pyairr. We only have two thousand men of our own, and that's not enough. Do you think you can make soldiers out of any of them?"

"Yes, I believe so, sir. They are trained, organized and armed for civil-order work, which is what we'll need them for ourselves. In the entire history of this army, all they have done has been to overawe unarmed slaves; I am sure they have never been in combat with regular troops. They have an elaborate set of training and field regulations for the sort of work for which they were intended. What they encountered today was entirely outside those regulations, which is why they behaved as they did."

"Did you have any trouble getting cooperation from the native officers?" Shatrak asked.

"Not in the least. They cooperated quite willingly, if not always too intelligently. I simply told them that they were now the personal property of his Imperial Majesty, Rodrik III. They were quite flattered by the change of ownership. If ordered to, I believe that they would fire on their former Lords-Master without hesitation."

"You told those slaves that they . . . *belonged* . . . to the *Emperor?*"

Count Erskyll was aghast. He stared at Ravney for an instant, then snatched up his brandy-glass—the meal had gotten to that point—and drained it at a gulp. The others watched solicitously while he coughed and spluttered over it.

"Commodore Shatrak," he said sternly. "I hope that you will take severe disciplinary action; this is the most outrageous . . ."

"I'll do nothing of the sort," Shatrak retorted. "The colonel is to be commended; did the best thing he could, under the circumstances. What are you going to do when slavery is abolished here, Colonel?"

"Oh, tell them that they have been given their freedom as a special reward for meritorious service, and then sign them up for a five-year enlistment."

"That might work. Again, it might not."

"I think, Colonel, that before you do that, you had better disarm them again. You might possibly have some trouble, otherwise."

Ravney looked at him sharply. "They might not want to be free? I'd thought of that."

"Nonsense!" Erskyll declared. "Who ever heard of slaves rebelling against freedom?"

Freedom was a Good Thing. It was a Good Thing for everybody, everywhere and all the time. Count Erskyll knew it, because freedom was a Good Thing for him.

He thought, suddenly, of an old tomcat belonging to a lady of his acquaintance at Paris-on-Baldur, a most affectionate cat, who insisted on catching mice and bringing them as presents to all his human friends. To this cat's mind, it was inconceivable that anybody would not be most happy to receive a nice fresh-killed mouse.

"Too bad we have to set any of them free," Vann Shatrak said. "Too bad we can't just issue everybody new servile gorgets marked, *Personal Property of his Imperial Majesty* and let it go at that. But I guess we can't."

"Commodore Shatrak, you are joking," Erskyll began.

"I hope I am," Shatrak replied grimly.

The top landing-stage of the Citadel grew and filled the forward viewscreen of the ship's launch. It was only when he realized that the tiny specks were people, and the larger, birdseed-sized, specks vehicles, that the real size of the thing was apparent. Obray of Erskyll, beside him, had been silent. He had been looking at the crescent-shaped industrial city, like a servile gorget around Zeggensburg's neck.

"The way they've been crowded together!" he said. "And the buildings; no space between. And all that smoke! They must be using fossil fuel!"

"It's probably too hard to process fissionables in large quantities, with what they have."

"You were right, last evening. These people have deliberately halted progress, even retrogressed, rather than give up slavery."

Halting progress, to say nothing of retrogression, was an unthinkable crime to him. Like freedom, progress was a Good Thing, anywhere, at all times, and without regard to direction.

Colonel Ravney met them when they left the launch. The top landing-stage was swarming with Imperial troops.

"Convocation Chamber's three stages down," he said. "About two thousand of them there now; been coming in all morning. We have everything set up." He laughed. "They tell me slaves are never permitted to enter it. Maybe, but they have the place bugged to the ceiling all around."

"Bugged? What with?" Shatrak asked, and Erskyll was wanting to know what he meant. No doubt he thought Ravney was talking about things crawling out of the woodwork.

"Screen pickups, radio pickups, wired microphones; you name it and it's there. I'll bet every slave in the Citadel knows everything that happens in there while it's happening."

Shatrak wanted to know if he had done anything about them. Ravney shook his head.

"If that's how they want to run a government, that's how they have a right to run it. Commander Douvrin put in a few of our own, a little better camouflaged than theirs."

There were more troops on the third stage down. They formed a procession down a long empty hallway, a few scared-looking slaves peeping from doorways at them. There were more troops where the corridor ended in great double

doors, emblazoned with a straight broadsword diagonally
across an eight-pointed star. Emblematology of planets conquered by the Space Vikings always included swords and
stars. An officer gave a signal; the doors started to slide apart,
and within, from a screen-speaker, came a fanfare of trumpets.

At first, all he could see was the projection-screen, far
ahead, and the tessallated aisle stretching toward it. The
trumpets stopped, and they advanced, and then he saw the
Lords-Master.

They were massed, standing among benches on either
side, and if anything Pyairr Ravney had understated their
numbers. They all wore black, trimmed with gold; he wondered if the coincidence that these were also the Imperial
colors might be useful. Queer garments, tightly fitted tunics
at the top which became flowing robes below the waist,
deeply scalloped at the edges. The sleeves were exaggeratedly wide; a knife or a pistol, and not necessarily a
small one, could be concealed in every one. He was sure that
thought had entered Vann Shatrak's mind. They were armed,
not with dress-daggers, but with swords; long, straight
cross-hilted broadswords. They were the first actual swords
he had ever seen, except in museums or on the stage.

There was a bench of gold and onyx at the front, where,
normally the seven-man Presidium sat, and in front of it were
thronelike seats for the Chiefs of Managements, equivalent
to the Imperial Council of Ministers. Because of the projection screen that had been installed, they had all been moved
to an improvised dais on the left. There was another dais on
the right, under a canopy of black and gold velvet,
emblazoned with the gold sun and superimposed black cogwheel of the Empire. There were three thrones, for himself,
Shatrak, and Erskyll, and a number of lesser but still impos-
ing chairs for their staffs.

They took their seats. He slipped the earplug of his
memophone into his left ear and pressed the stud in the
middle of his Grand Star of the Order of Odin. The

memophone began giving him the names of the Presidium
and of the Chiefs of Managements. He wondered how many
upper-slaves had been gunbutted to produce them.

"Lords and Gentlemen," he said, after he had greeted
them and introduced himself and the others, "I speak to you
in the name of his Imperial Majesty, Rodrik III. His Majesty
will now greet you in his own voice, by recording."

He pressed a button on the arm of his chair. The screen
lighted, flickered, and steadied, and the trumpets blared
again. When the fanfare ended, a voice thundered:

"The Emperor speaks!"

Rodrik III compromised on the beard question with a small
mustache. He wore the stern but kindly expression the best
theatrical directors in Asgard had taught him; Public Face
Number Three. He inclined his head slightly and stiffly, as a
man wearing a seven-pound crown must.

"We greet our subjects of Aditya to the fellowship of the
Empire. We have long had good reports of you, and we are
happy now to speak to you. Deserve well of us, and prosper
under the Sun and Cogwheel."

Another fanfare, as the image vanished. Before any of the
Lords-Master could find voice, he was speaking to them:

"Well, Lords and Gentlemen, you have been welcomed
into the Empire by his Majesty. I know, there hasn't been a
ship in or out of this system for five centuries, and I suppose
you have a great many question to ask about the Galactic
Empire. Members of the Presidium and Chief of Managements may address me directly; others will please address the
chairman."

Olvir Nikkolon, the owner of Tchall Hozhet, was on his
feet at once. He had a loose-lipped mouth and a not entirely
straight nose and pale eyes that were never entirely still.

"What I want to know is; why did you people have to
come here to take our planet away from us? Isn't the rest of
the galaxy big enough for you?"

"No, Lord Nikkolon. The Galaxy is not big enough for
any competition of sovereignty. There must be one and only
one completely sovereign power. The Terran Federation was

once such a power. It failed, and vanished; you know what followed. Darkness and anarchy. We are clawing our way up out of that darkness. We will not fail. We will create a peaceful and unified Galaxy.''

He talked to them, about the collapse of the old Federation, about the interstellar wars, about the Neobarbarians, about the long night. He told them how the Empire had risen on a few planets five thousand lightyears away, and how it had spread.

''We will not repeat the mistakes of the Terran Federation. We will not attempt to force every planetary government into a common pattern, or dictate the ways in which they govern themselves. We will foster in every way peaceful trade and communication. But we will not again permit the plague of competing sovereignties, the condition under which war is inevitable. The first attempt to set up such a sovereignty in competition with the Empire will be crushed mercilessly, and no planet inhabited by any sapient race will be permitted to remain outside the Empire.

''Lords and Gentlemen, permit me to show you a little that we have already accomplished, in the past three hundred years.''

He pressed another button. The screen flickered, and the show started. It lasted for almost two hours; he used a handphone to interject comments and explanations. He showed them planet after planet—Marduk, where the Empire had begun, Baldur, Vishnu, Belphegor, Morglay, whence their ancestors had come, Amaterasu, Irminsul, Fafnir, finally Odin, the Imperial Planet. He showed towering cities swarming with aircars; spaceports where the huge globes of interstellar ships landed and lifted out; farms and industries; vast crowds at public celebrations; troop-reviews and naval bases and fleet-maneuvers; historical views of the battles that had created Imperial power.

''That, Lords and Gentlemen, is what you have an opportunity to bring your planet into. If you accept, you will continue to rule Aditya under the Empire. If you refuse, you will only put us to the inconvenience of replacing you with a new planetary government, which will be annoying for us and, probably, fatal for you.''

Nobody said anything for a few minutes. Then Rovard Javasan, the Chief of Administration and the owner of the mountainous Khreggor Chmidd, rose.

"Lords and Gentlemen, we cannot resist anything like this," he said. "We cannot even resist the force they have here; that was tried yesterday, and you all saw what happened. Now, Prince Trevannion; just to what extent will the Mastership retain its sovereignty under the Empire?''

"To practically the same extent as at present. You will, of course, acknowledge the Emperor as your supreme ruler, and will govern subject to the Imperial Constitution. Have you any colonies on any of the other planets of this system?''

"We had a shipyard and docks on the inner moon, and we had mines on the fourth planet of this system, but it is almost airless and the colony was limited to a couple of domecities. Both were abandoned years ago.''

"Both will be reopened before long, I daresay. We'd better make the limits of your sovereignty the orbit of the outer planet of this system. You may have your own normal-space ships, but the Empire will control all hyperdrive craft, and all nuclear weapons. I take it you are the sole government on this planet? Then no other will be permitted to compete with you.''

"Well, what are they taking away from us, then?'' somebody in the rear asked.

"I assume that you are agreed to accept the sovereignty of his Imperial Majesty? Good. As a matter of form, Lord Nikkolon, will you take a vote? His Imperial Majesty would be most gratified if it were unanimous.''

Somebody insisted that the question would have to be debated, which meant that everybody would have to make a speech, all two thousand of them. He informed them that there was nothing to debate; they were confronted with an accomplished fact which they must accept. So Nikkolon made a speech, telling them at what a great moment in Adityan history they stood, and concluded by saying:

''I take it that it is the unanimous will of this Convocation that the sovereignty of the Galactic Emperor be acknowledged, and that we, the 'Mastership of Aditya' do here proclaim our loyal allegiance to his Imperial Majesty, Rodrik the Third. Any dissent? Then it is ordered so recorded.''

Then he had to make another speech, to inform the representatives of his new sovereign of the fact. Prince Trevannion, in the name of the Emperor, delivered the well-worn words of welcome, and Lanze Degbrend got the coronet out of the black velvet bag under his arm and the Imperial Proconsul, Obray, Count Erskyll, was crowned. Erskyll's charge-d'affaires, Sharll Ernanday, produced the scroll of the Imperial Constitution, and Erskyll began to read.

Section One: The universality of the Empire. The absolute powers of the Emperor. The rules of succession. The Emperor also to be Planetary King of Odin.

Section Two: Every planetary government to be sovereign in its own internal affairs . . . Only one sovereign government upon any planet, or within normal-space travel distance . . . All hyperspace ships, and all nuclear weapons . . . No planetary government shall make war . . . enter into any alliance . . . tax, regulate or restrain interstellar trade or communication . . . Every sapient being shall be equally protected . . .

Then he came to Article Six. He cleared his throat, raised his voice, and read:

''There shall be no chattel-slavery or serfdom anywhere in the Empire; no sapient being, of any race whatsoever, shall be the property of any being but himself.''

The Convocation Chamber was silent, like a bomb with a defective fuse, for all of thirty seconds. Then it blew up with a roar. Out of the corner of his eye, he saw the doors slide apart and an airjeep, bristling with machine guns, float in and rise to the ceiling. The first inarticulate roar was followed by a babel of voices, like a tropical cloudburst on a prefab hut. Olvir Nikkolon's mouth was working as he shouted unheard.

He pressed another of the row of buttons on the arm of his chair. Out of the screen-speaker a voice, as loud, by actual sound-meter test, as an antivehicle gun, thundered:

"SILENCE!"

Into the shocked stillness which it produced, he spoke, like a schoolmaster who has returned to find his room in an uproar:

"Lord Nikkolon; what is this nonsense? You are Chairman of the Presidium; is this how you keep order here? What is this, a planetary parliament or a spaceport saloon?"

"You tricked us!" Nikkolon accused. "You didn't tell us about that article when we voted. Why, our whole society is based on slavery!"

Other voices joined in:

"That's all right for you people, you have robots . . ."

"Maybe you don't know it, but there are twenty million slaves on this planet . . ."

"Look, you can't free slaves! That's ridiculous. A slave's a *slave*!"

"Who'll do the work? And who would they belong to? They'd have to belong to somebody!"

"What I want to know," Rovard Javasan made himself heard, is, "*how* are you going to free them?"

There was an ancient word, originating in one of the lost languages of Pre-Atomic Terra—*sixtifor*. It meant, the basic, fundamental, question. Rovard Javasan, he suspected, had just asked the sixtifor. Of course, Obray, Count Erskyll, Planetary Proconsul of Aditya, didn't realize that. He didn't even know what Javasan meant. Just free them. Commodore Vann Shatrak couldn't see much of a problem, either. He would have answered, Just free them, and then shoot down the first two or three thousand who took it seriously. Jurgen, Prince Trevannion, had no intention whatever of attempting to answer the sixtifor.

"My dear Lord Javasan, that is the problem of the Adityan Mastership. They are your slaves; we have neither the intention nor the right to free them. But let me remind you that slavery is specifically prohibited by the Imperial Constitution; if you do not abolish it immediately, the Empire will be forced to intervene. I believe, toward the last of those audiovisuals, you saw some examples of Imperial intervention."

They had. A few looked apprehensively at the ceiling, as though expecting the hellburners and planetbusters and nega-matter-bombs at any moment. Then one of the members among the benches rose.

"We don't know how we are going to do it, Prince Trevannion," he said. "We will do it, since this is the Empire law, but you will have to tell us how."

"Well, the first thing will have to be an Act of Convocation, outlawing the ownership of one being by another. Set some definite date on which the slaves must all be freed; that need not be too immediate. Then, I would suggest that you set up some agency to handle all the details. And, as soon as you have enacted the abolition of slavery, which should be this afternoon, appoint a committee, say a dozen of you, to confer with Count Erskyll and myself. Say you have your committee aboard the *Empress Eulalie* in six hours. We'll have transportation arranged by then. And let me point out, I hope for the last time, that we discuss matters directly, without intermediaries. We don't want any more slaves, pardon, freedmen, coming aboard to talk for you, as happened yesterday."

Obray, Count Erskyll, was unhappy about it. He did not think that the Lords-Master were to be trusted to abolish slavery; he said so, on the launch, returning to the ship. Jurgen, Prince Trevannion was inclined to agree. He doubted if any of the Lords-Master he had seen were to be trusted, unassisted, to fix a broken mouse-trap.

Line-Commodore Vann Shatrak was also worried. He was wondering how long it would take for Pyairr Ravney to make useful troops out of the newly-surrendered slave soldiers, and where he was going to find contragravity to shift them expeditiously from trouble-spot to trouble-spot. Erskyll thought he was anticipating resistance on the part of the

Masters, and for once he approved the use of force. Ordinarily, force was a Bad Thing, but this was a Good Cause, which justified any means.

They entertained the committee from the Convocation for dinner, that evening. They came aboard stiffly hostile—most understandably so, under the circumstances—and Prince Trevannion exerted all his copious charm to thaw them out, beginning with the pre-dinner cocktails and continuing through the meal. By the time they retired for coffee and brandy to the parlor where the conference was to be held, the Lords-ex-Masters were almost friendly.

"We've enacted the Emancipation Act," Olvir Nikkolon, who was ex officio chairman of the committee, reported. "Every slave on the planet must be free before the opening of the next Midyear Feasts."

"And when will that be?"

Aditya, he knew, had a three hundred and fifty-eight day year; even if the Midyear Feasts were just past, they were giving themselves very little time. In about a hundred and fifty days, Nikkolon said.

"Good heavens!" Erskyll began, indignantly.

"I should say so, myself," he put in, cutting off anything else the new Proconsul might have said. "You gentlemen are allowing yourselves dangerously little time. A hundred and fifty days will pass quite rapidly, and you have twenty million slaves to deal with. If you start at this moment and work continuously, you'll have a little under a second apiece for each slave."

The Lords-Master looked dismayed. So, he was happy to observe, did Count Erskyll.

"I assume you have some system of slave registration?" he continued.

That was safe. They had a bureaucracy, and bureaucracies tend to have registrations of practically everything.

"Oh, yes, of course," Rovard Javasan assured him. "That's your Management, isn't it, Sesar; Servile Affairs?"

"Yes, we have complete data on every slave on the planet," Sesar Martwynn, the Chief of Servile Management, said. "Of course, I'd have to ask Zhorzh about the details . . ."

Zhorzh was Zhorzh Khouzhik, Martwynn's chief-slave in office.

"At least, he was my chief-slave; now you people have taken him away from me. I don't know what I'm going to do without him. For that matter, I don't know what poor Zhorzh will do, either."

"Have you gentlemen informed your chief-slaves that they are free, yet?"

Nikkolon and Javasan looked at each other. Sesar Martwynn laughed.

"They know," Javasan said. "I must say they are much disturbed."

"Well, reassure them, as soon as you're back at the Citadel," he told them. "Tell them that while they are now free, they need not leave you unless they so desire; that you will provide for them as before."

"You mean, we can keep our chief-slaves?" somebody cried.

"Yes, of course—chief-freedmen, you'll have to call them, now. You'll have to pay them a salary . . ."

"You mean, give them money?" Ranal Valdry, the Lord Provost-Marshal demanded, incredulously. "Pay our own slaves?"

"You idiot," somebody told him, "they aren't our slaves any more. That's the whole point of this discussion."

"But . . . but how can we pay slaves?" one of the committeemen-at-large asked. "Freedmen, I mean?"

"With money. You do have money, haven't you?"

"Of course we have. What do you think we are, savages?"

"What kind of money?"

Why, money; what did he think? The unit was the star-piece, the stelly. When he asked to see some of it, they were indignant. Nobody carried money; wasn't Masterly. A Master never even touched the stuff; that was what slaves were for. He wanted to know how it was secured, and they didn't know what he meant, and when he tried to explain their incomprehension deepened. It seemed that the Mastership issued money to finance itself, and individual Masters issued money on their personal credit, and it was handled through the Mastership Banks.

"That's Fedrig Daffysan's Management; he isn't here," Rovard Javasan said. "I can't explain it, myself."

And without his chief-slave, Fedrig Daffysan probably would not be able to, either.

"Yes, gentlemen. I understand. You have money. Now, the first thing you will have to do is furnish us with a complete list of all the slave-owners on the planet, and a list of all the slaves held by each. This will be sent back to Odin, and will be the basis for the compensation to be paid for the destruction of your property-rights in these slaves. How much is a slave worth, by the way?"

Nobody knew. Slaves were never sold; it wasn't Masterly to sell one's slaves. It wasn't even heard of.

"Well, we'll arrive at some valuation. Now, as soon as you get back to the Citadel, talk at once to your former chief-slaves, and their immediate subordinates, and explain the situation to them. This can be passed down through administrative freedmen to the workers; you must see to it that it is clearly understood, at all levels, that as long as the freedmen remain at their work they will be provided for and paid, but that if they quit your service they will receive nothing. Do you think you can do that?"

"You mean, give them everything we've been giving them now, and then pay them money?" Ranal Valdry almost howled.

"Oh, no. You pay them a fixed wage. You charge them for everything you give them, and deduct that from their wages. It will mean considerable extra bookkeeping, but outside of that I believe you'll find that things will go along much as they always did."

The Masters had begun to relax, and by the time he was finished all of them were smiling in relief. Count Erskyll, on the other hand, was almost writhing in his chair. It must be horrible to be a brilliant young Proconsul of liberal tendencies and to have to sit mute while a cynical old Ministerial Secretary, vastly one's superior in the Imperial Establishment and a distant cousin of the Emperor to boot, calmly bartered away the sacred liberties of twenty million people.

"But would that be legal, under the Imperial Constitution?" Olvir Nikkolon asked.

"I shouldn't have suggested it if it hadn't been. The Constitution only forbids physical ownership of one sapient being by another; it emphatically does not guarantee anyone an unearned livelihood."

The Convocation committee returned to Zeggensburg to start preparing the servile population for freedom, or reasonable facsimile. The chief-slaves would take care of that; each one seemed to have a list of other chief-slaves, and the word would spread from them on an each-one-call-five system. The public announcement would be postponed until the word could be passed out to the upper servile levels. A meeting with the chief-slaves in office of the various Managements was scheduled for the next afternoon.

Count Erskyll chatted with forced affability while the departing committeemen were being seen to the launch that would take them down. When the airlock closed behind them, he drew Prince Trevannion aside out of earshot of their subordinates.

"You know what you're doing?" he raged, in a hoarse whisper. "You're simply substituting peonage for outright slavery!"

"I'd call that something of a step." He motioned Erskyll into one of the small hall-cars, climbed in beside him, and lifted it, starting toward the living-area. "The Convocation has acknowledged the principle that sapient beings should not be property. That's a great deal, for one day."

"But the people will remain in servitude, you know that. The Masters will keep them in debt, and they'll be treated just as brutally . . ."

"Oh, there will be abuses; that's to be expected. This

Freedmen's Management, née Serville Management, will have to take care of that. Better make a memo to talk with this chief-freedman of Martwynn's, what's his name? Zhorzh Khoushik; that's right, let Zhorzh do it. Employment Practices Code, investigation agency, enforcement. If he can't do the job, that's not our fault. The Empire does not guarantee every planet an honest, intelligent and efficient government; just a single one.''

"But . . .''

"It will take two or three generations. At first, the freedmen will be exploited just as they always have been, but in time there will be protests, and disorders, and each time, there will be some small improvement. A society must evolve, Obray. Let these people earn their freedom. Then they will be worthy of it.''

"They should have their freedom now.''

"This present generation? What do you think freedom means to them? *We don't have to work, any more.* So down tools and let everything stop at once. *We can do anything we want to.* Let's kill the overseer. And: *Anything that belongs to the Masters belongs to us; we're Masters too, now.* No, I think it's better, for the present, to tell them that this freedom business is just a lot of Masterly funny-talk, and that things aren't really being changed at all. It will effect a considerable saving of his Imperial Majesty's ammunition, for one thing.''

He dropped Erskyll at his apartment and sent the hall-car back from his own. Lanze Degbrend was waiting for him when he entered.

"Ravney's having trouble. That is the word he used,'' Degbrend said. In Pyairr Ravney's lexicon, trouble meant shooting. "The news of the Emancipation Act is leaking all over the place. Some of the troops in the north who haven't been disarmed yet are mutinying, and there are slave insurrections in a number of places.''

"They think the Masters have forsaken them, and it's every slave for himself.'' He hadn't expected that to start so soon. "The announcement had better go out as quickly as

possible. And I think we're going to have some trouble. You
have information-taps into Count Erskyll's numerous staff?
Use them as much as you can.''

"You think he's going to try to sabotage this employment
programme of yours, sir?''

"Oh, he won't think of it in those terms. He'll be prevent-
ing me from sabotaging the Emancipation. He doesn't want
to wait three generations; he wants to free them at once.
Everything has to be at once for six-month-old puppies,
six-year-old children, and reformers of any age.''

The announcement did not go out until nearly noon the
next day. In terms comprehensible to any lowgrade submo-
ron, it was emphasized that all this meant was that slaves
should henceforth be called freedmen, that they could have
money just like Lords-Master, and that if they worked faith-
fully and obeyed orders they would be given everything they
were now receiving. Ravney had been shuttling troops about,
dealing with the sporadic outbreaks of disorder here and
there; many of these had been put down, and the rest died out
after the telecast explaining the situation.

In addition, some of Commander Douvrin's intelligence
people had discovered that the only source of fissionables
and radioactives for the planet was a complex of uranite
mines, separation plants, refineries and reaction-plants on
the smaller of Aditya's two continents, Austragonia. In spite
of other urgent calls on his resources, Ravney landed troops
to seize these, and a party of engineers followed them down
from the *Empress Eulalie* to make an inspection.

At lunch, Count Erskyll was slightly less intransigent on
the subject of the wage-employment proposals. No doubt
some of his advisors had been telling him what would happen
if any appreciable number of Aditya's labor-force stopped
work suddenly, and the wave of uprisings that had broken out
before any public announcement had been made puzzled
him. He was also concerned about finding a suitable building
for a proconsular palace; the business of the Empire on
Aditya could not be conducted long from shipboard.

Going down to the Citadel that afternoon, they found the chief-freedmen of the non-functional Chiefs of Management assembled in a large room on the fifth level down. There was a cluster of big tables and communication-screens and wired telephones in the middle, with smaller tables around them, at which freedmen in variously colored gowns sat. The ones at the central tables, a dozen and a half, all wore chief-slaves' white gowns.

Trevannion and Erskyll and Patrique Morvill and Lanze Degbrend joined these; subordinates guided the rest of the party—a couple of Ravney's officers and Erskyll's numerous staff of advisors and specialists—to distribute themselves with their opposite numbers in the Mastership. Everybody on the Adityan side seemed uneasy with these strange hermaphrodite creatures who were neither slaves nor Lords-Master.

"Well, gentlemen," Count Erskyll began, "I suppose you have been informed by your former Lords-Master of how relations between them and you will be in the future?"

"Oh, yes, Lord Proconsul," Khreggor Chmidd replied happily. "Everything will be just as before, except that the Lords-Master will be called Lords-Employer, and the slaves will be called freedmen, and any time they want to starve to death, they can leave their Employers if they wish.

Count Erskyll frowned. That wasn't just exactly what he had hoped Emancipation would mean to these people.

"Nobody seems to understand about this money thing, though," Zhorzh Khouzhik, Sesar Martwynn's chief-freedman said. "My Lord-Master—" He slapped himself across the mouth and said, "Lord-Employer!" five times, rapidly. "My Lord-*Employer* tried to explain it to me, but I don't think he understands very clearly, himself."

"None of them do."

The speaker was a small man with pale eyes and a mouth like a rattrap; Yakoop Zhannar, chief-freedman to Ranal Valdry, the Provost-Marshal.

"It's really your idea, Prince Trevannion," Erskyll said. "Perhaps you can explain it."

"Oh, it's very simple. You see . . ."

At least, it had seemed simple when he started. Labor was a commodity, which the worker sold and the employer purchased; a "fair wage" was one which enabled both to operate at a profit. Everybody knew that—except here on Aditya. On Aditya, a slave worked because he was a slave, and a Master provided for him because he was a Master, and that was all there was to it. But now, it seemed, there weren't any more Masters, and there weren't any more slaves.

"That's exactly it," he replied, when somebody said as much. "So now, if the slaves, I mean, freedmen, want to eat, they have to work to earn money to buy food, and if the Employers want work done, they have to pay people to do it."

"Then why go to all the trouble about the money?" That was an elderly chief-freedman, Mykhyl Eschkhaffar, whose Lord-Employer, Oraze Borztall, was Manager of Public Works. "Before your ships came, the slaves worked for the Masters, and the Masters took care of the slaves, and everybody was content. Why not leave it like that?"

"Because the Galactic Emperor, who is the Lord-Master of these people, says that there must be no more slaves. Don't ask me why," Tchall Hozhet snapped at him. "I don't know either. But they are here with ships and guns and soldiers; what can we do?"

"That's very close to it," he admitted. "But there is one thing you haven't considered. A slave only gets what his master gives him. But a free worker for pay gets money which he can spend for whatever he wants, and he can save money, and if he finds that he can make more money working for somebody else, he can quit his employer and get a better job."

"We hadn't thought of that," Khreggor Chmidd said. "A slave, even a chief-slave, was never allowed to have money of his own, and if he got hold of any, he couldn't spend it. But now . . ." A glorious vista seemed to open in front of him. "And he can accumulate money. I don't suppose a common worker could, but an upper slave . . . Especially a chief-slave . . .'' He slapped his mouth, and said, "Freedman!" five times.

"Yes, Khreggor.'' That was Ridgerd Schferts (Fedrig Daffysan; Fiscal Management). "I am sure we could all make quite a lot of money, now that we are freedmen."

Some of them were briefly puzzled; gradually, comprehension dawned. Obray, Count Erskyll, looked distressed; he seemed to be hoping, vainly, that they weren't thinking of what he suspected they were.

"How about the Mastership freedmen?" another asked. "We, here, will be paid by our Lords-Mas- . . . Lords-Employer. But everybody from the green robes down were provided for by the Mastership. Who will pay them, now?"

"Why, the Mastership, of course," Ridgerd Schferts said. "My Management—my Lord-Employer's, I mean—will issue the money to pay them."

"You may need a new printingpress," Lanze Degbrend said. "And an awful lot of paper."

"This planet will need currency acceptable in interstellar trade," Erskyll said.

Everybody looked blankly at him. He changed the subject:

"Mr. Chmidd, could you or Mr. Hozhet tell me what kind of a constitution the Mastership has?"

"You mean, like the paper you read in the Convocation?" Hozhet asked. "Oh, there is nothing at all like that. The former Lords-Master simply ruled."

No. they reigned. This servile *tammanihal*—another ancient Terran word, of uncertain origin—ruled.

"Well, how is the Mastership organized then?" Erskyll persisted. "How did the Lord Nikkolon get to be Chairman of the Presidium, and the Lord Javasan to be Chief of Administration?"

That was very simple. The Convocation, consisting of the heads of all the Masterly families, actually small clans, numbered about twenty-five hundred. They elected the seven members of the Presidium, who drew lots for the Chairmanship. They served for life. Vacancies were filled by election on nomination of the surviving members. The Presidium appointed the Chiefs of Managements, who also served for life.

At least, it had stability. It was self-perpetuating.

"Does the Convocation make the laws?" Erskyll asked.

Hozhet was perplexed. "*Make* laws, Lord Proconsul? Oh, no. We already have laws."

There were planets, here and there through the Empire, where an attitude like that would have been distinctly beneficial; planets with elective parliaments, every member of which felt himself obligated to get as many laws enacted during his term of office as possible.

"But this is dreadful; you *must* have a constitution!" Obray of Erskyll was shocked. "We will have to get one drawn up and adopted."

"We don't know anything about that at all," Khreggor Chmidd admitted. "This is something new. You will have to help us."

"I certainly will, Mr. Chmidd. Suppose you form a committee—yourself, and Mr. Hozhet, and three or four others; select them among yourselves—and we can get together and talk over what will be needed. And another thing. We'll have to stop calling this the Mastership. There are no more Masters."

"The Employership?" Lanze Degbrend dead-panned.

Erskyll looked at him angrily. "This is something," he told the chief-freedmen, "that should not belong to the Employers alone. It should belong to everybody. Let us call it the Commonwealth. That means something everybody owns in common."

"Something everybody owns, nobody owns," Mykhyl Eschkhaffar objected.

"Oh, no, Mykhyl; it will belong to everybody," Khreggor Chmidd told him earnestly. "But somebody will have to take care of it for everybody. That," he added complacently, "will be you and me and the rest of us here."

"I believe," Yakoop Zhannar said, almost smiling, "that this freedom is going to be a wonderful thing. For us."

"I don't like it!" Mykhyl Eschkhaffar said stubbornly.
"Too many new things, and too much changing names. We
have to call slaves freedmen; we have to call Lords-Master
Lords-Employer; we have to call the Management of Servile
Affairs the Management for Freedmen. Now we have to call
the Mastership this new name, Commonwealth. And all
these new things, for which we have no routine procedures
and no directives. I wish these people had never heard of this
planet."

"That makes at least two of us," Patrique Morvill said,
sotto voce.

"Well, the planetary constitution can wait just a bit,"
Prince Trevannion suggested. "We have a great many items
on the agenda which must be taken care of immediately. For
instance, there's this thing about finding a proconsular palace . . .

A surprising amount of work had been done at the small
tables where Erskyll's staff of political and economic and
technological experts had been conferring with the subordinate upper-freedmen. It began coming out during the pre-
dinner cocktails aboard the *Empress Eulalie*, continued
through the meal, and was fully detailed during the formal
debriefing session afterward.

Finding a suitable building for the Proconsular Palace
would present difficulties. Real estate was not sold on
Aditya, any more than slaves were. It was not only un-
Masterly but illegal; estates were all entailed and the inalien-
able property of Masterly families. What was wanted was
one of the isolated residential towers in Zeggensburg, far
enough from the Citadel to avoid an appearance of too close
supervision. The last thing anybody wanted was to establish
the Proconsul in the Citadel itself. The Management of
Business of the Mastership, however, had promised to do
something about it. That would mean no doubt, that the
Empress Eulalie would be hanging over Zeggensburg, serving as Proconsular Palace, for the next year or so.

The Servile Management, rechristened Freedmen's Management, would undertake to safeguard the rights of the newly emancipated slaves. There would be an Employment Code—Count Erskyll was invited to draw that up—and a force of investigators, and an enforcement agency, under Zhorzh Khouzhik.

One of Commander Douvrin's men, who had been at the Austragonia nuclear-industries establishment, was present and reported:

"Great Ghu, you ought to see that place! They've people working in places I wouldn't send an unshielded robot, and the hospital there is bulging with radiation-sickness cases. The equipment must have been brought here by the Space Vikings. What's left of it is the damnedest mess of goldbergery I ever saw. The whole thing ought to be shut down and completely rebuilt."

Erskyll wanted to know who owned it. The Mastership, he was told.

"That's right," one of his economics men agreed. "Management of Public Works." That would be Mykhyl Eschkhaffar, who had so bitterly objected to the new nomenclature. "If anybody needs fissionables for a power-reactor or radioactives for nuclear-electric conversion, his chief business slave gets what's needed. Furthermore, doesn't even have to sign for it."

"Don't they sell it for revenue?"

"Nifflheim, no! This government doesn't need revenue. This government supports itself by counterfeiting. When the Mastership needs money, they just have Ridgerd Schferts print up another batch. Like everybody else."

"Then the money simply isn't worth anything!" Erskyll was horrified, which was rapidly becoming his normal state.

"Who cares about money, Obray," he said. "Didn't you hear them, last evening? It's un-Masterly to bother about things like money. Of course, everybody owes everybody for everything, but it's all in the family."

"Well, something will have to be done about that!"

That was at least the tenth time he had said that, this evening.

It came practically as a thunderbolt when Khreggor
Chmidd screened the ship the next afternoon to report that a
Proconsular Palace had been found, and would be ready for
occupancy in a day or so. The chief-freedmen of the Management of Business of the Mastership and of the Lord Chief
Justiciar had found one, the Elegry Palace, which had been
unoccupied except for what he described as a small caretaking staff for years, while two Masterly families disputed
inheritance rights and slave lawyers quibbled endlessly before a slave judge. The chief freedman of the Lord Chief
Justiciar had simply summoned judge and lawyers into his
office and ordered them to settle the suit at once. The settle-
ment had consissted of paying both litigants the full value of
the building; this came to fifty million stellies apiece. Ar-
bitrarily, the stelly was assigned a value in Imperial crowns
of a hundred for one. A million crowns was about what the
building would be worth, with contents, on Odin. It would be
paid for with a draft on the Imperial Exchequer.

"Well, you have some hard currency on the planet, now."
he told Count Erskyll, while they were having a pre-dinner
drink together that evening. "I hope it doesn't touch off an
inflation, if the term is permissible when applied to Adityan
currency."

Erskyll snapped his fingers. "Yes! And there's the money
we've been spending for supplies. And when we start compensation payments . . . Excuse me for a moment."

He dashed off, his drink in his hand. After a long interval,
he was back, carrying a fresh one he had gotten from a
bartending robot en route.

"Well, that's taken care of," he said. "My fiscal man's
getting in touch with Ridgerd Schferts; the Elegry heirs will
be paid in Adityan stellies, and the Imperial crowns will be
held in the Commonwealth Bank, or, better, banked in Asgard, to give Aditya some off-planet credit. And we'll do the
same with our other expenditures, and with the slave-
compensation. This is going to be wonderful; this planet
needs everything in the way of industrial equipment; this is
how they're going to get it."

"But, Obray; the compensations are owing to the individual Masters. They should be paid in crowns. You know as well as I do that this hundred-for-one rate is purely a local fiction. On the interstellar exchange, these stellies have a crown value of precisely zero-point-zero."

"You know what would happen if these ci-devant Masters got hold of Imperial crowns," Erskyll said. "They'd only squander them back again for useless imported luxuries. This planet needs a complete modernization, and this is the only way the money to pay for it can be gotten." He was gesturing excitedly with the almost-full glass in his hand; Prince Trevannion stepped back out of the way of the splash he anticipated. "I have no sympathy for these ci-devant Masters. They own every stick and stone and pinch of dust on this planet, as it is. Is that fair?"

"Possibly not. But neither is what you're proposing to do."

Obray, Count Erskyll, couldn't see that. He was proposing to secure the Greatest Good for the Greatest Number, and to Nifflheim with any minorities who happened to be in the way.

The Navy took over the Elegry Palace the next morning, ran up the Imperial Sun and Cogwheel flag, and began transmitting views of its interior up to the *Empress Eulalie*. It was considerably smaller than the Imperial Palace at Asgard on Odin, but room for room the furnishings were rather more ornate and expensive. By the next afternoon, the counterespionage team that had gone down reported the Masterly living quarters clear of pickups, microphones, and other apparatus of servile snooping, of which they had found many. The *Canopus* was recalled from her station over the northern end of the continent and began sending down the proconsulate furnishings stowed aboard, including several hundred domestic robots.

The skeleton caretaking staff Chmidd had mentioned proved to number five hundred.

"What are we going to do about them?" Erskyll wanted to

know. "There's a limit to the upkeep allowance for a proconsulate, and we can't pay five hundred useless servants. The chief-freedman, and about a dozen assistants, and a few to operate the robots, when we train them, but five hundred . . . !"

"Let Zhorzh do it," Prince Trevannion suggested. "Isn't that what this Freedmen's Management is for; to find employment for emancipated slaves? Just emancipate them and turn them over to Khouzhik."

Khouzhik promptly placed all of them on the payroll of his Management. Khouzhik was having his hands full. He had all his top mathematical experts, some of whom even understood the use of the slide-rule, trying to work up a scale of wages. Erskyll loaned him a few of his staff. None of the ideas any of them developed proved workable. Khouzhik had also organized a corps of investigators, and he was beginning to annex the private guard-companies of the Lords-ex-Master, whom he was organizing into a police force.

The nuclear works on Austragonia were closed down. Mykhyl Eschkhaffar ordered a programme of rationing and priorities to conserve the stock of plutonium and radioactive isotopes on hand, and he decided that henceforth nuclear-energy materials would be sold instead of furnished freely. He simply found out what the market quotations on Odin were, translated that into stellies, and adopted it. This was just a base price; there would have to be bribes for priority allocations, rakeoffs for the under-freedmen, and graft for the business-freedmen of the Lords-ex-Masters who bought the stuff. The latter were completely unconcerned; none of them even knew about it.

The Convocation adjourned until the next regular session, at the Mid-year Feasts, an eight-day intercalary period which permitted dividing the 358-day Adityan year into ten months of thirty-five days each. Count Erskyll was satisfied to see them go. He was working on a constitution for the Commonwealth of Aditya, and was making very little progress with it.

"It's one of these elaborate check-and-balance things," Lanze Degbrend reported. "To begin with, it was the constitution of Aton, with an elective president substituted for a hereditary king. Of course, there are a lot of added gadgets; Atonian Radical Democrat stuff. Chmidd and Hozhet and the other chief-slaves don't like it, either."

"Slap your mouth and say, 'Freedmen,' five times."

"Nuts," his subordinate retorted insubordinately. "I know a slave when I see one. A slave is a slave, with or without a gorget; if he doesn't wear it around his neck, he has it tattoed on his soul. It takes at least three generations to rub it off."

"I could wish that Count Erskyll . . ." he began. "What else is our Proconsul doing?"

"Well, I'm afraid he's trying to set up some kind of a scheme for the complete nationalization of all farms, factories, transport facilites, and other means of production and distribution," Degbrend said.

"He's not going to try to do that himself, is he?" He was, he discovered, speaking sharply, and modified his tone. "He won't do it with Imperial authority, or with Imperial troops. Not as long as I'm here. And when we go back to Odin, I'll see to it that Vann Shatrak understands that."

"Oh, no. The Commonwealth of Aditya will do that," Degbrend said. "Chmidd and Hozhet and Yakoop Zhannar and Zhorzh Khouzhik and the rest of them, that is. He wants it done legitimately and legally. That means, he'll have to wait till the Midyear Feasts, when the Convocation assembles, and he can get his constitution enacted. If he can get it written by then."

Vann Shatrak sent two of the destroyers off to explore the moons of Aditya, of which there were two. The outer moon, Aditya-*Ba'*, was an irregular chunk of rock fifty miles in diameter, barely visible to the naked eye. The inner, Aditya-*Alif*, however, was an eight-hundred-mile sphere; it had once been the planetary ship-station and shipyard-base. It seemed to have been abandoned when the Adityan technology and economy had begun sagging under the

weight of the slave system. Most of the installations remained, badly run down but repairable. Shatrak transferred
as many of his technicians as he could spare to the *Mizar* and
sent her to recondition the shipyard and render the underground city habitable again so that the satellite could be
used as a base for his ships. He decided, then, to send the
Irma back to Odin with reports of the annexation of Aditya, a
proposal that Aditya-*Alif* be made a permanent Imperial
naval-base, and a request for more troops.

Prince Trevannion taped up his own reports, describing
the general situation on the newly annexed planet, and doing
nothing to minimize the problems facing its Proconsul.

"Count Erskyll" he finished, "is doing the best possible
under circumstances from which I myself would feel inclined
to shrink. If not carried to excess, perhaps youthful idealism
is not without value in Empire statecraft. I understand that
Commodore Shatrak, who is also coping with some very
trying problems, is requesting troop reenforcements. I believe this request amply justified, and would recommend that
they be gotten here as speedily as possible.

"I understand that he is also recommending a permanent
naval base on the larger of this planet's two satellites. This I
also endorse unreservedly. It would have a most salutory
effect on the local government. I would further recommend
that Commodore Shatrak be placed in command of it, with
suitable promotion, which he has long ago earned."

Erskyll was surprised that he was not himself returning to
Odin on the destroyer, and evidently disturbed. He mentioned it during pre-dinner cocktails that evening.

"I know, my own work here is finished; was the moment
the Convocation voted acknowledgment of Imperial rule."
Prince Trevannion replied. "I would like to stay on for the
Midyear Feasts, though. The Convocation will vote on your
constitution, and I would like to be able to report their action
to the Prime Minister. How is it progressing, by the way?"

"Well, we have a rough draft. I don't care much for it,
myself, but Citizen Hozhet and Citizen Chmidd and Citizen

Zhannar and the others are most enthusiastic, and, after all, they are the ones who will have to operate under it.''

The Masterly estates would be the representative units; from each, the freedmen would elect representatives to regional elective councils, and these in turn would elect representatives to a central electoral council which would elect a Supreme People's Legislative Council. This would not only function as the legislative body, but would also elect a Manager-in-Chief, who would appoint the Chiefs of Management, who, in turn, would appoint their own subordinates.

''I don't like it, myself,'' Erskyll said. ''It's not democratic enough. There should be a direct vote by the people. Well,'' he grudged, ''I suppose it will take a little time for them to learn democracy.'' This was the first time he had come out and admitted that. ''There is to be a Constituent Convention in five years, to draw up a new consititution.''

''How about the Convocation? You don't expect them to vote themselves out of existence, do you?''

''Oh, we're keeping the Convocation, in the present constitution, but they won't have any power. Five years from now, we'll be rid of them entirely. Look here; you're not going to work against this, are you? You won't advise these ci-devant Lords-Master to vote against it, when it comes up?''

''Certainly not. I think your constitution—Khreggor Chmidd's and Tchall Hozhet's, to be exact—will be nothing short of a political disaster, but it will insure some political stability, which is all that matters from the Imperial point of view. An Empire statesman must always guard against sympathizing with local factions and interests, and I can think of no planet on which I could be safer from any such temptation. If these Lords-Master want to vote their throats cut, and the slaves want to re-enslave themselves, they may all do so with my complete blessing.''

If he had been at all given to dramatic gestures he would then have sent for water and washed his hands.

Metaphorically, he did so at that moment; thereafter his interest in Adityan affairs was that of a spectator at a boring and stupid show, watching only because there is nothing else to watch, and wishing that it had been possible to have returned to Odin on the *Irma*. The Prime Minister, however, was entitled to a full and impartial report, which he would scarcely get from Count Erskyll, on this new jewel in the Imperial Crown. To be able to furnish that, he would have to remain until the Midyear Feasts, when the Convocation would act on the new constitution. Whether the constitution was adopted or rejected was, in itself, unimportant; in either case, Aditya would have a government recognizable as such by the Empire, which was already recognizing some fairly unlikely-looking governments. In either case, too, Aditya would make nobody on any other planet any trouble. It wouldn't have, at least for a long time, even if it had been left unannexed, but no planet inhabited by Terro-humans could be trusted to remain permanently peaceful and isolated. There is a spark of aggressive ambition in every Terro-human people, no matter how debased, which may smoulder for centuries or even millennia and then burst, fanned by some wind, into flame. To shift the metaphor slightly, the Empire could afford to leave no unwatched pots around to boil over unexpectedly.

Occasionally, he did warn young Erskyll of the dangers of overwork and emotional over-involvement. Each time, the Proconsul would pour out some tale of bickering and rivalry among the chief-freedmen of the Managements. Citizen Khouzhik and Citizen Eschkhaffar—they were all calling each other Citizen, now—were contesting overlapping juris-dictions. Khouzhik wanted to change the name of his Management—he no longer bothered mentioning Sesar Martwynn—to Labor and Industry. To this, Mykhyl Es-chkhaffar objected vehemently; any Industry that was going to be managed would be managed by his—Oraze Borztall was similarly left unmentioned—management of Public Works. And they were also feuding about the robotic and remote-controlled equipment that had been sent down from the *Empress Eulalie* to the Austragonia nuclear-power works.

Khouzhik was also in controversy with Yakoop Zhannar, who was already calling himself People's Provost-Marshal. Khouzhik had taken over all the private armed-guards on the Masterly farms and in the factories, and assimilated them into something he was calling the People's Labor Police, ostensibly to enforce the new Code of Employment Practice. Zhannar insisted that they should be under his Management; when Chmidd and Hozhet supported Khouzhik, he began clamoring for the return of the regular army to his control.

Commodore Shatrak was more than glad to get rid of the Adityan army, and so was Pyairr Ravney, who was in immediate command of them. The Adityans didn't care one way or the other. Zhannar was delighted, and so were Chmidd and Hozhet. So, oddly, was Zhorzh Khouzhik. At the same time, the state of martial law proclaimed on the day of the landing was terminated.

The days slipped by. There were entertainments at the new Proconsular Palace for the Masterly residents of Zeggensburg, and Erskyll and his staff were entertained at Masterly palaces. The latter affairs pained Prince Trevannion excessively—hours on end of gorging uninspired cooking and guzzling too-sweet wine and watching ex-slave performers whose acts were either brutal or obscene and frequently both, and, more unforgivable, stupidly so. The Masterly conversation was simply stupid.

He borrowed a reconn-car from Ravney; he and Lanze Degbrend and, usually, one or another of Ravney's young officers, took long trips of exploration. They fished in mountain streams, and hunted the small deerlike game, and he found himself enjoying these excursions more than anything he had done in recent years; certainly anything since Aditya had come into the viewscreens of the *Empress Eulalie*. Once in a while, they claimed and received Masterly hospitality at some large farming estate. They were always greeted

with fulsome cordiality, and there was always surprise that
persons of their rank and consequence should travel unac-
companied by a retinue of servants.

He found things the same wherever he stopped. None of
the farms were producing more than a quarter of the potential
yield per acre, and all depleting the soil outrageously. Ten
slaves—he didn't bother to think of them as freedmen—
doing the work of one, and a hundred of them taking all day
to do what one robot would have done before noon. White-
gowned chief-slaves lording it over green and orange
gowned supervisors and clerks; overseers still carrying and
frequently using whips and knouts and sandbag flails.

Once or twice, when a Masterly back was turned, he
caught a look of murderous hatred flickering into the eyes of
some upper-slave. Once or twice, when a Master thought his
was turned, he caught the same look in Masterly eyes,
directed at him or at Lanze.

The Midyear Feasts approached; each time he returned to
the city he found more excitement as preparations went on.
Mykhyl Eschkhaffar's Management of Public Works was
giving top priority to redecorating the Convocation Chamber
and the lounges and dining-rooms around it in which the
Masters would relax during recesses. More and more Masterly families flocked in from outlying estates, with
contragravity-flotillas and retinues of attendants, to be entertained at the city palaces. There were more and gaudier
banquets and balls and entertainments. By the time the Feasts
began, every Masterly man, woman and child would be in
the city.

There were long columns of military contragravity coming
in, too; troop-carriers and combat-vehicles. Yakoop Zhannar
was bringing in all his newly recovered army, and Zhorzh
Khouzhik his newly organized People's Labor Police. Vann
Shatrak, who was now commanding his battle-line unit by
screen from the Proconsular Palace, began fretting.

"I wish I hadn't been in such a hurry to terminate martial
rule," he said, once. "And I wish Pyairr hadn't been so

confoundedly efficient in retraining those troops. That may cost us a few extra casualties, before we're through.''

Count Erskyll laughed at his worries.

"It's just this rivalry between Citizen Khouzhik and Citizen Zhannar," he said. "They're like a couple of ci-devant Lords-Master competing to give more extravagant feasts. Zhannar's going to hold a review of his troops, and of course, Khouzhik intends to hold a review of his police. That's all there is to it.''

"Well, just the same, I wish some reinforcements would get here from Odin," Shatrak said.

Erskyll was busy, in the days before the Midyear Feasts, either conferring at the Citadel with the ex-slaves who were the functional heads of the Managements or at the Proconsular Palace with Hozhet and Chmidd and the chief-freedmen of the influential Convocation leaders and Presidium members. Everybody was extremely optimistic about the constitution.

He couldn't quite understand the optimism, himself.

"If I were one of these Lords-Master, I wouldn't even consider the thing," he told Erskyll. "I know, they're stupid, but I can't believe they're stupid enough to commit suicide, and that's what this amounts to.''

"Yes, it does," Erskyll agreed, cheerfully. "As soon as they enact it, they'll be of no more consequence than the Assemblage of Peers on Aton; they'll have no voice in the operation of the Commonwealth, and none in the new constitution that will be drawn up five years from now. And that will be the end of them. All the big estates, and the factories and mines and contragravity-ship lines will be nationalized.''

"And they'll have nothing at all, except a hamper-full of repudiated paper stellies," he finished. "That's what I mean. What makes you think they'll be willing to vote for that?''

"They don't know they're voting for it. They'll think they're voting to keep control of the Mastership. People like

Olvir Nikkolon and Rovard Javasan and Ranal Valdry and
Sesar Martwynn think they still own their chief-freedmen;
they think Hozhet and Chmidd and Zhannar and Khouzhik
will do exactly what they tell them. And they believe anything the Hozhets and Chmidds and Zhannars tell them. And
every chief-freedman is telling his Lord-Employer that the
only way they can keep control is by adopting the constitution; that they can control the elections on their estates, and
handpick the People's Legislative Council. I tell you, Prince
Trevannion, the constitution is as good as enacted."

Two days before the opening of the Convocation, the *Irma*
came into radio-range, five light-hours away, and began
transmitting in taped matter at sixty-speed. Erskyll's report
and his own acknowledged; a routine "well done" for the
successful annexation. Commendation for Shatrak's handling of the landing operation. Orders to take over Aditya-
Alif and begin construction of a permanent naval base. Noti-
fication of promotion to base-admiral, and blank commission
as line-commodore; that would be Patrique Morvill. And
advice that one transport-cruiser, *Algol,* with an Army contragravity brigade aboard, and two engineering ships, would
leave Odin for Aditya in fifteen days. The last two words
erased much of the new base-admiral's pleasure.

"Fifteen days, great Ghu! And those tubs won't make near
the speed of *Irma*, getting here. We'll be lucky to see them in
twenty. And Beelzebub only knows what'll be going on here
then."

Four times, the big screen failed to respond. They were all
crowded into one of the executive conference-rooms at the
Proconsular Palace, the batteries of communication and recording equipment incongruously functional among the
gold-encrusted luxury of the original Masterly furnishings.
Shatrak swore.

"Andrey, I thought your people had planted those pickups
where they couldn't be found," he said to Commander
Douvrin.

"There is no such place, sir," the intelligence officer
replied. "Just places where things are hard to find."

"Did you mention our pickups to Chmidd or Hozhet or any of the rest of the shaveheads?" Shatrak asked Erskyll.

"No. I didn't even know where they were. And it was the freedmen who found them," Erskyll said. "I don't know why they wouldn't want us looking in."

Lanze Degbrend, at the screen, twisted the dial again, and this time the screen flickered and cleared, and they were looking into the Convocation Chamber from the extreme rear, above the double doors. Far away, in front, Olvir Nikkolon was rising behind the gold and onyx bench, and from the speaker the call bell tolled slowly, and the buzz of over two thousand whispering voices diminished. Nikkolon began to speak:

"Seven and a half centuries ago, our fathers went forth from Morglay to plant upon this planet a new banner . . ."

It was evidently a set speech, one he had recited year after year, and every Lord Chairman of the Presidium before him. The spendid traditions. The glories of the Masterly race. The all-conquering Space Vikings. The proud heritage of the Sword-Worlds. Lanze was fiddling with the control knobs, stepping up magnification and focusing on the speaker's head and shoulders. Then everybody laughed; Nikkolon had a small plug in one ear, with a fine wire running down to vanish under his collar. Degbrend brought back the full view of the Convocation Chamber.

Nikkolon went on and on. Vann Shatrak summoned a robot to furnish him with a cold beer and another cigar. Erskyll was drumming an impatient devil's tattoo with his fingernails on the gold-encrusted table in front of him. Lanze Degbrend began interpolating sarcastic comments. And finally, Pyairr Ravney, who came from Lugaluru, reverted to the idiom of his planet's favorite sport:

"Come on, come on; turn out the bull! What's the matter, is the gate stuck?"

If so, it came quickly unstuck, and the bull emerged, pawing and snorting.

"This year, other conquerors have come to Aditya, here to plant another banner, and Sun and Cogwheel of the Galactic

Empire, and I blush to say it, we are as helpless against these conquerors as were the miserable barbarians and their wretched serfs whom our fathers conquered seven hundred and sixty-two years ago, whose descendants, until this black day, had been our slaves.''

He continued, his voice growing more impassioned and more belligerent. Count Erskyll fidgeted. This wasn't the way the Chmidd-Hozhet Constitution ought to be introduced.

"So, perforce, we accepted the sovereignty of this alien Empire. We are now the subject of his Imperial Majesty, Rodrik III. We must govern Aditya subject to the Imperial Constitution.'' (Groans, boos; catcalls, if the Adityan equivalent of cats made noises like that.) ''At one stroke, this Constitution has abolished our peculiar institution, upon which is based our entire social structure. This I know. But this same Imperial Constitution is a collapsium-strong shielding; let me call your attention to Article One, Section Two: *Every Empire planet shall be self-governed as to its own affairs, in the manner of its own choice and without interference.* Mark this well, for it is our guarantee that this government, of the Masters, by the Masters, and for the Masters, shall not perish from Aidtya.'' (Prolonged cheering.)

''Now, these arrogant conquerors have overstepped their own supreme law. They have written for this Mastership a constitution, designed for the sole purpose of accomplishing the liquidation of the Masterly class and race. They have endeavored to force this planetary constitution upon us by threats of force, and by a shameful attempt to pervert the fidelity of our chief-slaves—I will not insult these loyal servitors with this disgusting new name, freedmen—so that we might, a second time, be tricked into voting assent to our own undoing. But in this, they have failed. Our chief-slaves have warned us of the trap concealed in this constitution written by the Proconsul, Count Erskyll. My faithful Tchall Hozhet has shown me all the pitfalls in this infamous document . . .''

Obray, Count Erskyll, was staring in dismay at the screen.

Then he began cursing blasphemously, the first time he had ever been heard to do so, and, as he was at least nominally a Pantheist, this meant blaspheming the entire infinite universe.

"The rats! The dirty treacherous rats! We came here to help them, and look; they've betrayed us . . . !" He lost his voice in a wheezing sob, and then asked: "Why did they do it? Do they want to go on being slaves?"

Perhaps they did. It wasn't for love of their Lords-Master; he was sure of that. Even from the beginning, they had found it impossible to disguise their contempt . . .

Then they saw Olvir Nikkolon stop short and thrust out his arm, pointing directly below the pickup, and as he watched, something green-gray, a remote-control contragravity lorry, came floating into the field of the screen. One of the vehicles that had been sent down from the *Empress Eulalie* for use at the uranium mines. As it lifted and advanced toward the center of the room, the other Lords-Master were springing to their feet.

Vann Shatrak also sprang to his feet, reaching the controls of the screen and cutting the sound. He was just in time to save them from being, at least temporarily, deafened, for no sooner had he silenced the speaker than the lorry vanished in a flash that filled the entire room.

When the dazzle left their eyes, and the smoke and dust began to clear, they saw the Convocation Chamber in wreckage, showers of plaster and bits of plastiboard still falling from above. The gold and onyx bench was broken in a number of places; the Chiefs of Management in front of it, and the Presidium above, had vanished. Among the benches lay black-clad bodies, a few still moving. Smoke rose from burning clothing. Admiral Shatrak put on the sound again; from the screen came screams and cries of pain and fright.

Then the doors on the two long sides opened, and red-brown uniforms appeared. The soldiers advanced into the Chamber, unslinging rifles and submachine guns. Unheeding the still falling plaster, they moved forward, firing as they came. A few of them slung their firearms and picked up

Masterly dress swords, using them to finish the wounded among the benches. The screams grew fewer, and then stopped.

Count Erskyll sat frozen, staring white-faced and horror-sick into screen. Some of the others had begun to recover and were babbling excitedly. Vann Shatrak was at a communication-screen, talking to Commodore Patrique Morvill, aboard the *Empress Eulalie:*

"All the Landing-Troops, and all the crewmen you can spare and arm. And every vehicle you have. This is only the start of it; there'll be a general massacre of Masters next. I don't doubt it's started already."

At another screen, Pyairr Ravney was saying, to the officer of the day of the Palace Guard: "No, there's no telling what they'll do next. Whatever it is, be ready for it ten minutes ago."

He stubbed out his cigarette and rose, and as he did, Erskyll came out of his daze and onto his feet.

"Commodore Shatrak! I mean, Admiral," he corrected himself. "We must re-impose martial rule. I wish I'd never talked you into terminating it. Look at that!" He pointed at the screen; big dump-lorries were already coming in the doors under the pickup, with a mob of gowned civil-service people crowding in under them. They and the soldiers began dragging bodies out from among the seats to be loaded and hauled away. "There's the planetary government, murdered to the last man!"

"I'm afraid we can't do anything like that," he said. "This seems to be a simple transfer of power by *coup d' etat* rather more extreme than usual, but normal political practice on this sort of planet. The Empire has no right to interfere."

Erskyll turned on him indignantly. "But it's mass murder!"

"It's an accomplished fact. Whoever ordered this, Citizen Chmidd and Citizen Hozhet and Citizen Zhannar and the rest of your good democratic citizens, are now the planetary government of Aditya. As long as they don't attack us, or repudiate the sovereignty of the Emperor, you'll have to recognize them as such.''

"A bloody-handed gang of murderers; recognize them?''

"All governments have a little blood here and there on their hands; you've seen this by screen instead of reading about it in a history book, but that shouldn't make any difference. And you've said, yourself, that the Masters would have to be eliminated. You've told Chmidd and Hozhet and the others that, repeatedly. Of course, you meant legally, by constitutional and democratic means, but that seemed just a bit too tedious to them. They had them all together in one room, where they could be eliminated easily, and . . . Lanze; see if you can get anything on the Citadel telecast.''

Degbrend put on another communication-screen and fiddled for a moment. What came on was a view, from another angle, of the Convocation Chamber. A voice was saying:

". . . not one left alive. The People's Labor Police, acting on orders of People's Manager of Labor Zhorzh Khouzhik and People's Provost-Marshal Yakoop Zhannar, are now eliminating the rest of the ci-devant Masterly class, all of whom are here in Zeggensburg. The people are directed to cooperate; kill them all, men, women and children. We must allow none of these foul exploiters of the people live to see today's sun go down . . .''

"You mean, we sit here while those animals butcher women and children?'' Shatrak demanded, looking from the Proconsul to the Ministerial Secretary. "Well, by Ghu, I won't! If I have to face a court for it, all well and good, but . . .''

"You won't, Admiral. I seem to recall, some years ago, a Commodore Hastings, who got a baronetcy for stopping a pogrom on Anath . . .''

"And broadcast an announcement that any of the Masterly class may find asylum here at the Proconsular Palace. They're political fugitives; scores of precedents for that,'' Erskyll added.

Shatrak was back at the screen to the *Empress Eulalie*.

"Patrique, get a jam-beam focussed on that telecast station at the Citadel; get it off the air. Then broadcast on the same wavelength; announce that anybody claiming sanctuary at the Pronconsular Palace will be taken in and protected. And start getting troops down, and all the spacemen you can spare."

At the same time, Ravney was saying, into his own screen:

"Plan Four, Variation H-3; this is a rescue operation. This is not, repeat, underscore, *not* an intervention in planetary government. You are to protect members of the Masterly class in danger from mob violence. That's anybody with hair on his head. Stay away from the Citadel; the ones there are all dead. Start with the four buildings closest to us, and get them cleared out. If the shaveheads give you any trouble, don't argue with them, just shoot them . . ."

Erskyll, after his brief moment of decisiveness, was staring at the screen to the Convocation Chamber, where bodies were still being heaved into the lorries like black sacks of grain. Lanze Degbrend summoned a robot, had it pour a highball, and gave it to the Proconsul.

"Go ahead, Count Erskyll; drink it down. Medicinal," he was saying. "Believe me you certainly need it."

Erskyll gulped it down. "I think I could use another, if you please," he said, handing the glass back to Lanze. "And a cigarette." After he had tasted his second drink and puffed on the cigarette, he said: "I was so proud. I thought they were learning democracy."

"We don't, any of us, have too much to be proud about," Degbrend told him. "They must have been planning and preparing this for a couple of months, and we never caught a whisper of it."

That was correct. They had deluded Erskyll into thinking that they were going to let the Masters vote themselves out of power and set up a representative government. They had deluded the Masters into believing that they were in favor of the *status quo*, and opposed to Erskyll's democratization and socialization. There must be only a few of them in the conspiracy. Chmidd and Hozhet and Zhannar and Khouzhik and Schferts and the rest of the Citadel chief-slave clique. Among them, they controlled all the armed force. The bickering and rivalries must have been part of the camouflage. He supposed that a few of the upper army commanders had been in on it, too.

A communication-screen began making noises. Somebody flipped the switch, and Khreggor Chmidd appeared in it. Erskyll swore softly, and went to face the screen-image of the elephantine ex-slave of the ex-Lord Master, the late Rovard Javasan.

"Citizen Proconsul; why is our telecast station, which is vitally needed to give information to the people, jammed off the air, and why are you broadcasting, on our wavelength, advice to the criminals of the ci-devant Masterly class to take refuge in your Proconsular Palace from the just vengeance of the outraged victims of their centuries-long exploitation?" he began. "This is a flagrant violation of the Imperial Constitution; our Emperor will not be pleased at this unjustified intervention in the affairs, and this interference with the planetary authority, of the People's Commonwealth of Aditya!"

Obray of Erskyll must have realized, for the first time, that he was still holding a highball glass in one hand and a cigarette in the other. He flung both of them away.

"If the Imperial troops we are sending into the city to rescue women and children in danger from your hoodlums meet with the least resistance, you won't be in a position to find out what his Majesty thinks about it, because Admiral Shatrak will have you and your accomplices shot in the Convocation Chamber, where you massacred the legitimate government of this planet," he barked.

So the real Obray, Count Erskyll, had at last emerged. All the liberalism and socialism and egalitarianism, all the Helping-Hand, Torch-of-Democracy, idealism, was merely a surface stucco applied at the university during the last six years. For twenty-four years before that, from the day of his birth, he had been taught, by his parents, his nurse, his governess, his tutors, what it meant to be an Erskyll of Aton and a grandson of Errol, Duke of Yorvoy. As he watched Khreggor Chmidd in the screen, he grew angrier, if possible.

"Do you know what you blood-thirsty imbeciles have done?" he demanded. "You have just murdered, along with two thousand men, some five billion crowns, the money needed to finance all these fine modernization and industrialization plans. Or are you crazy enough to think that the Empire is going to idemnify you for being emancipated and pay that money over to you?"

"But, Citizen Proconsul . . ."

"And don't call me Citizen Proconsul! I am a noble of the Galactic Empire, and on this pigpen of a planet I represent his Imperial Majesty. You will respect, and address, me accordingly."

Khreggor Chmidd no longer wore the gorget of servility, but, as Lanze Degbrend had once remarked, it was still tattooed on his soul. He gulped.

"Y-yes, Lord-Master Proconsul!"

They were together again in the big conference-room, which Vann Shatrak had been using, through the day, as an extemporised Battle-Control. They slumped wearily in chairs; they smoked and drank coffee; they anxiously looked from viewscreen to viewscreen, wondering when, and how soon, the trouble would break out again. It was dark, outside, now. Floodlights threw a white dazzle from the top of the Proconsular Palace and from the tops of the four buildings around it that Imperial troops had cleared and occupied, and from contragravity vehicles above. There was light and activity at the Citadel, and in the Servile City to the south-east; the rest of Zeggensburg was dark and quiet.

"I don't think we'll have any more trouble," Admiral Shatrak was saying. "They won't be fools enough to attack us here, and all the Masters are dead, except for the ones we're sheltering."

"How many did we save?" Count Erskyll asked.

Eight hundred odd, Shatrak told him. Erskyll caught his breath.

"So few! Why, there were almost twelve thousand of them in the city this morning."

"I'm surprised we saved so many," Lanze Degbrend said. He still wore combat coveralls, and a pistol-belt lay beside his chair. "Most of them were killed in the first hour."

And that had been before the landing-craft from the ships had gotten down, and there had only been seven hundred men and forty vehicles available. He had gone out with them, himself; it had been the first time he had worn battle-dress and helmet or carried a weapon except for sport in almost thirty years. It had been an ugly, bloody, business; one he wanted to forget as speedily as possible. There had been times, after seeing the mutilated bodies of Masterly women and children, when he had been forced to remind himself that he had come out to prevent, not to participate in, a massacre. Some of Ravney's men hadn't even tried. Atrocity has a horrible facility for begetting atrocity.

"What'll we do with them?" Erskyll asked. "We can't turn them loose; they'd all be murdered in a matter of hours, and in any case, they'd have nowhere to go. The Commonwealth,"—he pronounced the name he had himself selected as though it were an obscenity—"has nationalized all the Masterly property."

That had been announced almost as soon as the Citadel telecast-station had been unjammed, and shortly thereafter they had begun encountering units of Yakoop Zhannar's soldiers and Zhorzh Khouzhik's police who had been sent out to stop looting and vandalism and occupy the Masterly palaces. There had been considerable shooting in the Servile City; evidently the ex-slaves had to be convinced that they must not pillage or destroy their places of employment.

"Evacuate them off-planet," Shatrak said. "As soon as *Algol* gets here, we'll load the lot of them onto *Mizar* or *Canopus* and haul them somewhere. Ghu only knows how they'll live, but . . ."

"Oh, they won't be paupers, or public charges, Admiral," he said. "You know, there's an estimated five billion crowns in slave-compensation, and when I return to Odin I shall represent most strongly that these survivors be paid the whole sum. But I shall emphatically not recommend that they be resettled on Odin. They won't be at all grateful to us for today's business, and on Odin they could easily stir up some very adverse public sentiment.''

"My resignation will answer any criticism of the Establishment the public may make,'' Erskyll began.

"Oh, rubbish; don't talk about resigning, Obray. You made a few mistakes here, though I can't think of a better planet in the Galaxy on which you could have made them. But no matter what you did or did not do, this would have happened eventually.''

"You really think so?'' Obray, Count Erskyll, was desperately anxious to be assured of that. "Perhaps if I hadn't been so insistent on this constitution . . .''

"That wouldn't have made a particle of difference. We all made this inevitable simply by coming here. Before we came, it would have been impossible. No slave would have been able even to imagine a society without Lords-Master; you heard Chmidd and Hozhet, the first day, aboard the *Empress Eulalie*. A slave had to have a Master; he simply couldn't belong to nobody at all. And until you started talking socialization, nobody could have imagined property without a Masterly property-owning class. And a massacre like this would have been impossible to organize or execute. For one thing, it required an elaborate conspiratorial organization, and until we emancipated them, no slave would have dared trust any other slave; every one would have betrayed any other to curry favor with his Lord-Master. We taught them that they didn't need Lords-Master, or Masterly favor, any more. And we presented them with a situation their established routines didn't cover, and forced them into doing some original thinking, which must have hurt like Nifflheim at first. And we retrained the army and handed it over to Yakoop Zhannar, and inspired Zhorzh Khouzhik to organize the Labor Police, and fundamentally, no government is anything but armed force. Really, Obray, I can't see that you can be blamed for anything but speeding up an inevitable process slightly.''

"You think they'll see it that way at Asgard?''

"You mean the Prime Minister and His Majesty? That will be the way I shall present it to them. That was another reason I wanted to stay on here. I anticipated that you might want a credible witness to what was going to happen,'' he said. "Now, you'll be here for not more than five years before you're promoted elsewhere. Nobody remains longer than that on a first Proconsular appointment. Just keep your eyes and ears and, especially, your mind, open while you are here. You will learn many things undreamed-of by the political-science faculty at the University of Nefertiti.''

"You said I made mistakes,'' Erskyll mentioned, ready to start learning immediately.

"Yes. I pointed one of them out to you some time ago: emotional involvement with local groups. You began sympathizing with the servile class here almost immediately. I don't think either of us learned anything about them that the other didn't, yet I found them despicable, one and all. Why did you think them worthy of your sympathy?''

"Why, because . . .'' For a moment, that was as far as he could get. His motivation had been thalamic rather than cortical and he was having trouble verbalizing it. "They were *slaves*. They were being exploited and oppressed . . .''

"And, of course, their exploiters were a lot of heartless villains, so that made the slaves good and virtuous innocents. That was your real, fundamental, mistake. You know, Obray, the downtrodden and long-suffering proletariat aren't at all good or innocent or virtuous. They are just incompetent; they lack the abilities necessary for overt villainy. You saw, this afternoon, what they were capable of doing when they were given an opportunity. You know, it's quite all right to give the underdog a hand, but only one hand. Keep the other hand on your pistol—or he'll try to eat the one you gave him! As you may have noticed, today, when underdogs get up, they tend to act like wolves.''

"What do you think this Commonwealth will develop into, under Chmidd and Hozhet and Khouzhik and the rest?'' Lanze Degbrend asked, to keep the lecture going.

"Oh, a slave-state, of course; look who's running it, and whom it will govern. Not the kind of a slave-state we can do anything about,'' he hastened to add. "The Commonwealth will be very definite about recognizing that sapient beings cannot be property. But all the rest of the property will belong to the Commonweatlh. Remember that remark of Chmidd's: 'It will belong to everybody, but somebody will have to take care of it for everybody. That will be you and me.' ''

Erskyll frowned. "I remember that. I didn't like it, at the time. It sounded . . .''

Out of character, for a good and virtuous proletarian; almost Masterly, in fact. He continued:

"The Commonwealth will be sole employer as well as sole property-owner, and anybody who wants to eat will have to work for the Commonwealth on the Commonwealth's terms. Chmidd's and Hozhet's and Khouzhik's, that is. If that isn't substitution of peonage for chattel slavery, I don't know what the word peonage means. But you'll do nothing to interfere. You will see to it that Aditya stays in the empire and adheres to the Constitution and makes no trouble for anybody off-planet. I fancy you won't find that too difficult. They'll be good, as long as you deny them the means to be anything else. And make sure that they continue to call you Lord-Master Proconsul.''

Lecturing, he found, was dry work. He summoned a bartending robot:

"Ho, slave! Attend your Lord-Master!''

Then he had to use his ultraviolet pencil-light to bring it to him, and dial for the brandy-and-soda he wanted. As long as that was necessary, there really wasn't anything to worry about. But some of these days, they'd build robots that would anticipate orders, and robots to operate robots, and robots to supervise them, and . . .

No. It wouldn't quite come to that. A slave is a slave, but a robot is only a robot. As long as they stuck to robots, they were reasonably safe.

Introduction to "Ministry of Disturbance"

This is the final story about the First Empire, and it takes place in a distant time when the Empire's greatest problem is her own success. The population and economy have become too static, and as everyone knows nature abhors a vacuum . . . So Imperial Majesty Paul the XXII decides to make some changes, but not even he can foresee the future that will follow the Ministry of Disturbance.

MINISTRY OF DISTURBANCE

THE SYMPHONY was ending, the final triumphant paean soaring up and up, beyond the limit of audibility. For a moment, after the last notes had gone away, Paul sat motionless, as though some part of him had followed. Then he roused himself and finished his coffee and cigarette, looking out the wide window across the city below—treetops and towers, roofs and domes and arching skyways, busy swarms of aircars glinting in the early sunlight. Not many people cared for João Coelho's music, now, and least of all for the Eighth Symphony. It was the music of another time, a thousand years ago, when the Empire was blazing into being out of the long night and hammering back the Neo-barbarians from world after world. Today people found it perturbing.

He smiled faintly at the vacant chair opposite him, and lit another cigarette before putting the breakfast dishes on the serving-robot's tray, and, after a while, realized that the robot was still beside his chair, waiting for dismissal. He gave it an instruction to summon the cleaning robots and sent it away. He could as easily have summoned them himself, or let the guards who would be in checking the room do it for him, but maybe it made a robot feel trusted and important to relay orders to other robots.

Then he smiled again, this time in self-derision. A robot couldn't feel important, or anything else. A robot was nothing but steel and plastic and magnetized tape and photo-micropositronic circuits, whereas a man—His Imperial Majesty Paul XXII, for instance—was nothing but tissues and cells and colloids and electro-neuronic circuits. There was a difference; anybody knew that. The trouble was that he had never met anybody—which included physicists, biologists, psychologists, psionicists, philosophers and theologians—who could define the difference in satisfactorily exact terms. He watched the robot pivot on its treads and glide away, trailing steam from its coffee pot. It might be silly to treat robots like people, but that wasn't as bad as treating people like robots, an attitude which was becoming entirely too prevalent. If only so many people didn't act like robots!

He crossed to the elevator and stood in front of it until a tiny electroencephalograph inside recognized his distinctive brain-wave pattern. Across the room, another door was popping open in response to the robot's distinctive wave pattern. He stepped inside and flipped a switch—there were still a few things around that had to be manually operated—and the door closed behind him and the elevator gave him an instant's weightlessness as it started to drop forty floors.

When it opened, Captain-General Dorflay of the Household Guard was waiting for him, with a captain and ten privates. General Dorflay was human. The captain and his ten soldiers weren't. They wore helmets, emblazoned with the golden sun and superimposed black cogwheel of the Empire, and red kilts and black ankle boots and weapons belts, and the captain had a narrow gold-laced cape over his shoulders, but for the rest, their bodies were covered with a stiff mat of black hair, and their faces were slightly like terriers'. (For all his humanity, Captain-General Dorflay's face was more like a bulldog's.) They were hillmen from the southern hemisphere of Thor, and as a people they made excellent mercenaries. They were crack shots, brave and crafty fighters, totally uninterested in politics off their own planet, and, because they had grown up in a patriarchial-clan society, they were fanatically loyal to anybody whom they accepted as their chieftain. Paul stepped out and gave them an inclusive nod.

"Good morning, gentlemen."

"Good morning, Your Imperial Majesty," General Dorflay said, bowing the couple of inches consistent with military dignity. The Thoran captain saluted by touching his forehead, his heart, which was on the right side, and the butt of his pistol. Paul complimented him on the smart appearance of his detail, and the captain asked how it could be otherwise, with the example and inspiration of his imperial majesty. Compliment and response could have been a playback from every morning of the ten years of his reign. So could Dorflay's question: "Your Majesty will proceed to his study?"

He wanted to say, "No, to Nifflheim with it; let's get an aircar and fly a million miles somewhere," and watch the look of shocked incomprehension on the captain-general's face. He couldn't do that, though; poor old Harv Dorflay might have a heart attack. He nodded slowly.

"If you please, General."

Dorflay nodded to the Thoran captain, who nodded to his men. Four of them took two paces forward; the rest, unslinging weapons, went scurrying up the corridor, some posting themselves along the way and the rest continuing to the main hallway. The captain and two of his men started forward slowly; after they had gone twenty feet, Paul and General Dorflay fell in behind them, and the other two brought up the rear.

"Your Majesty," Dorflay said, in a low voice, "let me beg you to be most cautious. I have just discovered that there exists a treasonous plot against your life."

Paul nodded. Dorflay was more than due to discover another treasonous plot; it had been ten days since the last one.

"I believe you mentioned it, General. Something about planting loose strontium-90 in the upholstery of the Audience Throne, wasn't it?"

And before that, somebody had been trying to smuggle a fission bomb into the Palace in a wine cask, and before that, it was a booby trap in the elevator, and before that, somebody was planning to build a submachine gun into the viewscreen in the study, and—

"Oh, no, Your Majesty; that was—Well, the persons involved in that plot became alarmed and fled the planet before I could arrest them. This is something different, Your Majesty. I have learned that unauthorized alterations have been made on one of the cooking-robots in your private kitchen, and I am positive that the object is to poison Your Majesty."

They were turning into the main hallway, between the rows of portraits of past emperors, Paul and Rodrik, Paul and Rodrik, alternating over and over on both walls. He felt a smile growing on his face, and banished it.

"The robot for the meat sauces, wasn't it?" he asked.

"Why—! Yes, Your Majesty."

"I'm sorry, general. I should have warned you. Those alterations were made by roboticists from the Ministry of Security; they were installing an adaptation of a device used in the criminalistics-labs, to insure more uniform measurements. They'd done that already for Prince Travann, the Minister, and he'd recommended it to me."

That was a shame, spoiling poor Harv Dorflay's murder plot. It had been such a nice little plot, too; he must have had a lot of fun inventing it. But a line had to be drawn somewhere. Let him turn the Palace upside down hunting for bombs; harass ladies-in-waiting whose lovers he suspected of being hired assassins; hound musicians into whose instruments he imagined firearms had been built; the emperor's private kitchen would have to be off limits.

Dorflay, who should have been looking crestfallen but relieved, stopped short—shocking breach of Court etiquette—and was staring in horror.

"Your Majesty! Prince Travann did that openly and with your consent? But, Your Majesty, I am convinced that it is Prince Travann himself who is the instigator of every one of these diabolical schemes. In the case of the elevator, I became suspicious of a man named Samml Ganner, one of Prince Travann's secret police agents. In the case of the gun in the viewscreen, it was a technician whose sister is a member of the household of Countess Yirzy, Prince Travann's mistress. In the case of the fission bomb—"

The two Thorans and their captain had kept on for some distance before they had discovered that they were no longer being followed, and were returning. He put his hand on General Dorflay's shoulder and urged him forward.

"Have you mentioned this to anybody?"

"Not a word, Your Majesty. This Court is so full of treachery that I can trust no one, and we must never warn the villain that he is suspected—"

"Good. Say nothing to anybody." They had reached the door of the study now. "I think I'll be here until noon. If I leave earlier, I'll flash you a signal."

He entered the big oval room, lighted from overhead by the great star-map in the ceiling, and crossed to his desk, with the viewscreens and reading screens and communications screens around it, and as he sat down, he cursed angrily, first at Harv Dorflay and then, after a moment's reflection, at himself. He was the one to blame; he'd known Dorflay's paranoid condition for years. Have to do something about it. Any psycho-medic would certify him; be no problem at all to have him put away. But be blasted if he'd do that. That was no way to repay loyalty, even insane loyalty. Well, he'd find a way.

He lit a cigarette and leaned back, looking up at the glowing swirl of billions of billions of tiny lights in the ceiling. At least, there were supposed to be billions of billions of them; he'd never counted them, and neither had any of the seventeen Rodriks and sixteen Pauls before him who had sat under them. His hand moved to a control button on his chair arm, and a red patch, roughly the shape of a pork shop, appeared on the western side.

That was the Empire. Every one of the thousand three hundred and sixty-five inhabited worlds, a trillion and a half intelligent beings, fourteen races—fifteen if you counted the Zarathustran Fuzzies, who were almost able to qualify under the talk-and-build-a-fire rule. And that had been the Empire when Rodrik VI had seen the map completed, and when Paul II had built the Palace, and when Stevan IV, the grandfather of Paul I, had proclaimed Odin the Imperial planet and Asgard the capital city. There had been some excuse for staying inside that patch of stars then; a newly-won Empire must be consolidated within before it can safely be expanded. But that had been over eight centuries ago.

He looked at the Daily Schedule, beautifully embossed and neatly slipped under his desk glass. Luncheon on the South Upper Terrace, with the Prime Minister and the Bench of Imperial Counselors. Yes, it was time for that again; that happened as inevitably and regularly as Harv Dorflay's murder plots. And in the afternoon, a Plenary Session, Cabinet and Counselors. Was he going to have to endure the Bench of Counselors twice in the same day? Then the vexation was washed out of his face by a spreading grin. Bench of Counselors; that was the answer! Elevate Harv Dorflay to the Bench. That was what the Bench was for, a gold-plated dustbin for the disposal of superannuated dignitaries. He'd do no harm there, and a touch of outright lunacy might enliven and even improve the Bench.

And in the evening, a banquet, and a reception and ball, in honor of His Majesty Ranulf XIV, Planetary King of Durendal, and First Citizen Zhorzh Yaggo, People's Manager-in-Chief of and for the Planetary Commonwealth of Aditya. Bargain day; two planetary chiefs of state in one big combination deal. He wondered what sort of prizes he had drawn this time, and closed his eyes, trying to remember. Durendal, of course, was one of the Sword-Worlds, settled by refugees from the losing side of the System States War in the time of the old Terran Federation, who had reappeared in Galactic history a few centuries later as the Space Vikings. They all had monarchial and rather picturesque governments; Durendal, he seemed to recall, was a sort of quasi-feudalism. About Aditya he was less sure. Something unpleasant, he thought; the titles of the government and its head were suggestive.

He lit another cigarette and snapped on the reading screen to see what they had piled onto him this morning, and then swore when a graph chart, with jiggling red and blue and green lines, appeared. Chart day, too. Everything happens at once.

It was the interstellar trade situation chart from Economics. Red line for production, green line for exports, blue for imports, sectioned vertically for the ten Viceroyalties and subsectioned for the Prefectures, and with the magnification and focus controls he could even get data for individual planets. He didn't bother with that, and wondered why he bothered with the charts at all. The stuff was all at least twenty days behind date, and not uniformly so, which accounted for much of the jiggling. It had been transmitted from Planetary Proconsulate to Prefecture, and from Prefecture to Viceroyalty, and from there to Odin, all by ship. A ship on hyperdrive could log lightyears an hour, but radio waves still had to travel 186,000 mps. The supplementary chart for the past five centuries told the real story—three perfectly level and perfectly parallel lines.

It was the same on all the other charts. Population fluctuating slightly at the moment, completely static for the past five centuries. A slight decrease in agriculture, matched by an increase in synthetic food production. A slight population movement toward the more urban planets and the more densely populated centers. A trend downward in employment—nonworking population increasing by about .0001 per cent annually. Not that they were building better robots; they were just building them faster than they wore out. They all told the same story—a stable economy, a static population, a peaceful and undisturbed Empire; eight centuries, five at least, of historyless tranquility. Well, that was what everybody wanted, wasn't it?

He flipped through the rest of the charts, and began getting summarized Ministry reports. Economics had denied a request from the Mining Cartel to authorize operations on a couple of uninhabited planets; danger of local market gluts and overstimulation of manufacturing. Permission granted to Robotics Cartel to—Request from planetary government of Durendal for increase of cereal export quotas under consideration—they wouldn't want to turn that down while King Ranulf was here. Impulsively, he punched out a combination on the communication screen and got Count Duklass, Minister of Economics.

Count Duklass had thinning red hair and a plump, agreeable, extrovert's face. He smiled and waited to be addressed.

"Sorry to bother Your Lordship," Paul greeted him. "What's the story on this export quota request from Durendal? We have their king here, now. Think he's come to lobby for it?"

Count Duklass chuckled. "He's not doing anything about it, himself. Have you met him yet, sir?"

"Not yet. He's to be presented this evening."

"Well, when you see him—I think the masculine pronoun is permissible—you'll see what I mean, sir. It's this Lord Koreff, the Marshal. He came here on business, and had to bring the king along, for fear somebody else would grab him while he was gone. The whole object of Durendalian politics, as I understand, is to get possession of the person of the king. Koreff was on my screen for half an hour; I just got rid of him. Planet's pretty heavily agricultural, they had a couple of very good crop years in a row, and now they have grain running out their ears, and they want to export it and cash in."

"Well?"

"Can't let them do it, Your Majesty. They're not suffering any hardship; they're just not making as much money as they think they ought to. If they start dumping their surplus into interstellar trade, they'll cause all kinds of dislocations on other agricultural planets. At least, that's what our computers all say.''

And that, of course, was gospel. He nodded.

"Why don't they turn their surplus into whisky? Age it five or six years and it'd be on the luxury goods schedule and they could sell it anywhere.''

Count Duklass' eyes widened. "I never thought of that, Your Majesty. Just a microsec; I want to make a note of that. Pass it down to somebody who could deal with it. That's a wonderful idea, Your Majesty!''

He finally got the conversation to an end, and went back to the reports. Security, as usual, had a few items above the dead level of bureaucratic procedure. The planetary king of Excalibur had been assassinated by his brother and two nephews, all three of whom were now fighting among themselves. As nobody had anything to fight with except small arms and a few light cannon, there would be no intervention. There had been intervention on Behemoth, however, where a whole continent had tried to secede from the planetary republic and the Imperial Navy had been requested to send a task force. That was all right, in both cases. No interference with anything that passed for a planetary government, but only one sovereignty on any planet with nuclear weapons, and only one supreme sovereignty in a galaxy with hyperdrive ships.

And there was rioting on Amaterasu, because of public indignation over a fraudulent election. He looked at that in incredulous delight. Why, here on Odin there hadn't been an election in the past six centuries that hadn't been utterly fraudulent. Nobody voted except the nonworkers, whose votes were bought and sold wholesale, by gangster bosses to pressure groups, and no decent person would be caught within a hundred yards of a polling place on an election day. He called the Minister of Security.

Prince Travann was a man of his own age—they had been classmates at the University—but he looked older. His thin face was lined, and his hair was almost completely white. He was at his desk, with the Sun and Cogwheel of the Empire on the wall behind him, but on the breast of his black tunic he wore the badge of his family, a silver planet with three silver moons. Unlike Count Duklass, he didn't wait to be spoken to.

"Good morning, Your Majesty."

"Good morning, Your Highness; sorry to bother you. I just caught an interesting item in your report. This business on Amaterasu. What sort of a planet is it, politically? I don't seem to recall."

"Why, they have a republican government, sir; a very complicated setup. Really, it's a junk heap. When anything goes badly, they always build something new into the government, but they never abolish anything. They have a president, a premier, and an executive cabinet, and a tricameral legislature, and two complete and distinct judiciaries. The premier is always the presidential candidate getting the next highest number of votes. In the present instance, the president, who controls the planetary militia, is accusing the premier, who controls the police, of fraud in the election of the middle house of the legislature. Each is supported by the judiciary he controls. Practically every citizen belongs either to the militia or the police auxiliaries. I am looking forward to further reports from Amaterasu," he added dryly.

"I daresay they'll be interesting. Send them to me in full, and redstar them, if you please, Prince Travann."

He went back to the reports. The Ministry of Science and Technology had sent up a lengthy one. The only trouble with it was that everything reported was duplication of work that had been done centuries before. Well, no. A Dr. Dandrik, of the physics department of the Imperial University here in Asgard announced that a definite limit of accuracy in measuring the velocity of accelerated subnucleonic particles had been established—16.067543333—times light-speed. That seemed to be typical; the frontiers of science, now, were all decimal points. The Ministry of Education had a little to offer; historical scholarship was still active, at least. He was reading about a new trove of source-material that had come to light on Uller, from the Sixth Century Atomic Era, when the door screen buzzed and flashed.

He lit it, and his son Rodrik appeared in it, with Snooks, the little red hound, squirming excitedly in the Crown Prince's arms. The dog began barking at once, and the boy called through the phone:

"Good morning, father; are you busy?"

"Oh, not at all." He pressed the release button. "Come on in."

Immediately, the little hound leaped out of the princely arms and came dashing into the study and around the desk, jumping onto his lap. The boy followed more slowly, sitting down in the deskside chair and drawing his foot up under him. Paul greeted Snooks first—people can wait, but for little dogs everything has to be right now—and rummaged in a drawer until he found some wafers, holding one for Snooks to nibble. Then he became aware that his son was wearing leather shorts and tall buskins.

"Going out somewhere?" he asked, a trifle enviously.

"Up in the mountains, for a picnic. Olva's going along."

And his tutor, and his esquire, and Olva's companion-lady, and a dozen Thoran riflemen, of course, and they'd be in continuous screen-contact with the Palace.

"That ought to be a lot of fun. Did you get all your lessons done?"

"Physics and math and galactiography," Rodrik told him. "And Professor Guilsan's going to give me and Olva our history after lunch."

They talked about lessons, and about the picnic. Of course, Snooks was going on the picnic, too. It was evident, though, that Rodrik had something else on his mind. After a while, he came out with it.

"Father, you know I've been a little afraid, lately," he said.

"Well, tell me about it, son. It isn't anything about you and Olva, is it?"

Rod was fourteen; the little Princess Olva thirteen. They

would be marriageable in six years. As far as anybody could tell, they were both quite happy about the marriage which had been arranged for them years ago.

"Oh, no; nothing like that. But Olva's sister and a couple others of mother's ladies-in-waiting were to a psi-medium, and the medium told them that there were going to be changes. Great and frightening changes was what she said."

"She didn't specify?"

"No. Just that: great and frightening changes. But the only change of that kind I can think of would be . . . well, something happening to you."

Snooks, having eaten three wafers, was trying to lick his ear. He pushed the little dog back into his lap and pummeled him gently with his left hand.

"You mustn't let mediums' gabble worry you, son. These psi-mediums have real powers, but they can't turn them off and on like a water tap. When they don't get anything, they don't like to admit it, so they invent things. Always generalities like that; never anything specific."

"I know all that." The boy seemed offended, as though somebody were explaining that his mother hadn't really found him out in the rose garden. "But they talked about it to some of their friends, and it seems that other mediums are saying the same thing. Father, do you remember when the Haval Valley generator blew up? All over Odin, the mediums had been talking about a terrible accident, for a month before that happened."

"I remember that." Harv Dorflay believed that somebody had been falsely informed that the emperor would visit the plant that day. "These great and frightening changes will probably turn out to be a new fad in abstract sculpture. Any change frightens most people."

They talked more about mediums, and then about aircars and aircar racing, and about the Emperor's Cup race that was to be flown in a month. The communications screen began flashing and buzzing, and after he had silenced it with the busy-button for the third time, Rodrik said that it was time for him to go, came around to gather up Snooks, and went out, saying that he'd be home in time for the banquet. The screen began to flash again as he went out.

It was Prince Ganzay, the Prime Minister. He looked as though he had a persistent low-level toothache, but that was his ordinary expression.

"Sorry to bother Your Majesty. It's about these chiefs-of-state. Count Gadvan, the Chamberlain, appealed to me, and I feel I should ask your advice. It's the matter of precedence."

"Well, we have a fixed rule on that. Which one arrived first?"

"Why, the Adityan, but it seems King Ranulf insists that he's entitled to precedence, or, rather, his Lord Marshal does. This Lord Koreff insists that his king is not going to yield precedence to a commoner."

"Then he can go home to Durendal!" He felt himself growing angry—all the little angers of the morning were focusing on one spot. He forced the harshness out of his voice. "At a court function, somebody has to go first, and our rule is order of arrival at the Palace. That rule was established to avoid violating the principle of equality to all civilized peoples and all planetary governments. We're not going to set it aside for the King of Durendal, or anybody else."

Prince Ganzay nodded. Some of the toothache expression had gone out of his face, now that he had been relieved of the decision.

"Of course, Your Majesty." He brightened a little. "Do you think we might compromise? Alternate the precedence, I mean?"

"Only if this First Citizen Yaggo consents. If he does, it would be a good idea."

"I'll talk to him, sir." The toothache expression came back. "Another thing, Your Majesty. They've both been invited to attend the Plenary Session, this afternoon."

"Well, no trouble there; they can enter by different doors and sit in visitors' boxes at opposite ends of the hall."

"Well, sir, I wasn't thinking of precedence. But this is to

be an Elective Session—new Ministers to replace Prince Havaly, of Defense, deceased, and Count Frask, of Science and Technology, elevated to the Bench. There seems to be some difference of opinion among some of the Ministers and Counselors. It's very possible that the Session may degenerate into an outright controversy.''

"Horrible," Paul said seriously. "I think, though, that our distinguished guests will see that the Empire can survive difference of opinion, and even outright controversy. But if you think it might have a bad effect, why not postpone the election?''

"Well—It's been postponed three times, already, sir.''

"Postpone it permanently. Advertise for bids on two robot Ministers, Defense, and Science and Tehcnology. If they're a success, we can set up a project to design a robot emperor.''

The Prime Minister's face actually twitched and blanched at the blasphemy. "Your Majesty is joking," he said, as though he wanted to be reassured on the point.

"Unfortunately, I am. If my job could be robotized, maybe I could take my wife and my son and our little dog and go fishing for a while.''

But, of course, he couldn't. There were only two alternatives: the Empire or Galactic anarchy. The galaxy was too big to hold general elections, and there had to be a supreme ruler, and a positive and automatic—which meant hereditary—means of succession.

"Whose opinion seems to differ from whose, and about what?'' he asked.

"Well, Count Duklass and Count Tammsan want to have the Ministry of Science and Technology abolished, and its functions and personnel distributed. Count Duklass means to take over the technological sections under Economics, and Count Tammsan will take over the science part under Education. The proposal is going to be introduced at this Session by Count Guilfred, the Minister of Health and Sanity. He hopes to get some of the bio- and psycho-science sections for his own Ministry.''

"That's right. Duklass gets the hide, Tammsan gets the

head and horns, and everybody who hunts with them gets a cut of the meat. That's good sound law of the chase. I'm not in favor of it, myself. Prince Ganzay at this session, I wish you'd get Captain-General Dorflay nominated for the Bench. I feel that it is about time to honor him with elevation.''

"General Dorflay? But why, Your Majesty?''

"Great galaxy, do you have to ask? Why, because the man's a raving lunatic. He oughtn't even to be trusted with a sidearm, let alone five companies of armed soldiers. Do you know what he told me this morning?''

"That somebody is training a Nidhog swamp-crawler to crawl up the Octagon Tower and bite you at breakfast, I suppose. But hasn't that been going on for quite a while, sir?''

"It was a gimmick in one of the cooking robots, but that's aside from the question. He's finally named the master mind behind all these nightmares of his, and who do you think it is? Yorn Travann!''

The Prime Minister's face grew graver than usual. Well, it was something to look grave about; some of these days—

"Your Majesty, I couldn't possibly agree more about the general's mental condition, but I really should say that, crazy or not, he is not alone in his suspicions of Prince Travann. If sharing them makes me a lunatic, too, so be it, but share them I do.''

Paul felt his eyebrows lift in surprise. "That's quite too much and too little, Prince Ganzay,'' he said.

"With your permission, I'll elaborate. Don't think that I suspect Prince Travann of any childish pranks with elevators or viewscreens or cooking-robots,'' the Prime Minister hastened to disclaim, "but I definitely do suspect him of treasonous ambitions. I suppose Your Majesty knows that he is the first Minister of Security in centuries who has assumed personal control of both the planetary and municipal police, instead of delegating his *ex officio* powers.

"Your Majesty may not know, however, of some of the peculiar uses he has been making of those authorities. Does Your Majesty know that he has recruited the Security Guard

up to at least ten times the strength needed to meet any
conceivable peace-maintenance problem on this planet, and
that he has been piling up huge quantities of heavy combat
equipment—guns up to 200-millimeter, heavy contragravity, even gun-cutters and bomb-and-rocket boats? And does
Your Majesty know that most of this armament is massed
within fifteen minutes' flight-time of this Palace? Or that
Prince Travann has at his disposal from two and a half to
three times, in men and firepower, the combined strength of
the Planetary Militia and the Imperial Army on this planet?''

"I know. It has my approval. He's trying to salvage some
of the young nonworkers through exposing them to military
discipline. A good many of them, I believe, have gone off
planet on their discharge from the SG and hired as mercenaries, which is a far better profession than vote-selling.''

"Quite a plausible explanation; Prince Travann is nothing
if not plausible,'' the Prime Minister agreed. "And does
Your Majesty know that, because of repeated demands for
support from the Ministry of Secuirty, the Imperial Navy has
been scattered all over the Empire, and that there is not a
naval craft bigger than a scout-boat within fifteen hundred
light-years of Odin?''

That was absolutely true. Paul could only nod agreement.
Prince Ganzay continued:

"He has been doing some peculiar things as Police Chief
of Asgard, too. For instance, there are two powerful nonworkers' voting-bloc bosses, Big Moogie Blisko and Zikko
the Nose—I assure' Your Majesty that I am not inventing
these names; that's what the persons are actually called—
who have been enjoying the favor and support of Prince
Travann. On a number of occasions, their smaller rivals,
leaders of less important gangs, have been arrested, often on
trumped-up charges, and held incommunicado until either
Moogie or Zikko could move into their territories and annex
their nonworker followers. These two bloc-bosses are sub-
sidized, respectively, by the Steel and Shipbuilding Cartels
and by the Reaction Products and Chemical Cartels, but
actually, they are controlled by Prince Travann. They, in

turn, control between them about seventy per cent of the nonworkers in Asgard.''

''And you think this adds up to a plot against the Throne?''

''A plot to sieze the Throne, Your Majesty.''

''Oh, come, Prince Ganzay! You're talking like Dorflay!''

''Hear me out, Your Majesty. His Imperial Highness is fourteen years old; it will be eleven years before he will be legally able to assume the powers of emperor. In the dreadful event of your immediate death, it would mean a regency for that long. Of course, your Ministers and Counselors would be the ones to name the Regent, but I know how they would vote with Secuirty Guard bayonets at their throats. And regency might not be the limit of Prince Travann's ambitions.''

''In your own words, quite plausible, Prince Ganzay. It rests, however, on a very questionable foundation. The assumption that Prince Travann is stupid enough to want the Throne.''

He had to terminate the conversation himself and blank the screen. Viktor Ganzay was still staring at him in shocked incredulity when his image vanished. Viktor Ganzay could not imagine anybody not wanting the Throne, not even the man who had to sit on it.

He sat, for a while, looking at the darkened screen, a little worried. Viktor Ganzay had a much better intelligence service than he had believed. He wondered how much Ganzay had found out that he hadn't mentioned. Then he went back to the reports. He had gotten down to the Ministry of Fine Arts when the communications screen began calling attention to itself again.

When he flipped the switch, a woman smiled out of it at him. Her blond hair was rumpled, and she wore a dressing gown; her smile brightened as his face appeared in her screen.

''Hi!'' she greeted him.

''Hi, yourself. You just get up?''

She raised a hand to cover a yawn. ''I'll bet you've been up reigning for hours. Were Rod and Snooks in to see you yet?''

He nodded. ''They just left. Rod's going on a picnic with Olva in the mountains.'' How long had it been since he and Marris had been on a picnic—a real picnic, with less than fifty guards and as many courtiers along? ''Do you have much reigning to do, this afternoon?''

She grimaced. ''Flower Festivals. I have to make personal tri-di appearances, live, with messages for the loving subjects. Three minutes on, and a two-minute break between. I have forty for this afternoon.''

''Ugh! Well, have a good time, sweetheart. All I have is lunch with the Bench, and then this Plenary Session.'' He told her about Ganzay's fear of outright controversy.

''Oh, fun! Maybe somebody'll pull somebody's whiskers, or something. I'm in on that, too.''

The call-indicator in front of him began glowing with the code-symbol of the Minister of Security.

''We can always hope, can't we? Well, Yorn Travann's trying to get me, now.''

''Don't keep him waiting. Maybe I can see you before the Session. She made a kissing motion with her lips at him, and blanked the screen.

He flipped the switch again, and Prince Travann was on the screen. The Security Minister didn't waste time being sorry to bother him.

''Your Majesty, a report's just come in that there's a serious riot at the University; between five and ten thousand students are attacking the Administration Center, lobbing stench bombs into it, and threatening to hang Chancellor Khane. They have already overwhelmed and disarmed the campus police, and I've sent two companies of the Gendarme riot brigade, under an officer I can trust to handle things firmly but intelligently. We don't want any indiscriminate stunning or tear-gassing or shooting; all sorts of people can have sons and daughters mixed up in a student riot.''

''Yes. I seem to recall student riots in which the sons of his late Highness Prince Travann and his late Majesty Rodrik XXI were involved.'' He deliberated the point for a moment, and added: ''This scarcely sounds like a frat-fight or a panty-raid, though. What seems to have triggered it?''

''The story I got—a rather hysterical call for help from Khane himself—is that they're protesting an action of his in dismissing a faculty member. I have a couple of undercovers at the University, and I'm trying to contact them. I sent more undercovers, who could pass for students, ahead of the Gendarmes to get the student side of it and the names of the ringleaders.'' He glanced down at the indicator in front of him, which had begun to glow. ''If you'll pardon me, sir, Count Tammsan's trying to get me. He may have particulars. I'll call Your Majesty back when I learn anything more.''

There hadn't been anything like that at the University within the memory of the oldest old grad. Chancellor Khane, he knew, was a stupid and arrogant old windbag with a swollen sense of his own importance. He made a small bet with himself that the whole thing was Khane's fault, but he wondered what lay behind it, and what would come out of it. Great plagues from little microbes start. Great and frightening changes—

The screen got itself into an uproar, and he flipped the switch. It was Viktor Ganzay again. He looked as though his permanent toothache had deserted him for the moment.

''Sorry to bother Your Majesty, but it's all fixed up,'' he reported. ''First Citizen Yaggo agreed to alternate in precedence with King Ranulf, and Lord Koreff has withdrawn all his objections. As far as I can see, at present, there should be no trouble.''

''Fine. I suppose you heard about the excitement at the University?''

''Oh, yes, Your Majesty. Disgraceful affair!''

''Simply shocking. What seems to have started it, have you heard?'' he asked. ''All I know is that the students were protesting the dismissal of a faculty member. He must have been exceptionally popular, or else he got a more than ordinary raw deal from Khane.''

''Well, as to that, sir, I can't say. All I learned was that it was the result of some faculty squabble in one of the science departments; the grounds for the dismissal were insubordination and contempt for authority."

"I always thought that when authority began inspiring contempt, it had stopped being authority. Did you say science? This isn't going to help Duklass and Tammsan any."

"I'm afraid not, Your Majesty." Ganzay didn't look particularly regretful. "The News Cartel's gotten hold of it and are using it; it'll be all over the Empire."

He said that as though it meant something. Well, maybe it did; a lot of Ministers and almost all the Counselors spent most of their time worrying about what people on planets like Chermosh and Zarathustra and Deirdre and Quetzalcoatl might think, in ignorance of the fact that interest in Empire politics varied inversely as the square of the distance to Odin and the level of corruption and inefficiency of the local government.

"I notice you'll be at the Bench luncheon. Do you think you could invite our guests, too? We could have an informal presentation before it starts. Can do? Good. I'll be seeing you there."

When the screen was blanked, he returned to the reports, ran them off hastily to make sure that nothing had been red-starred, and called a robot to clear the projector. After a while, Prince Travann called again.

"Sorry to bother Your Majesty, but I have most of the facts on the riot, now. What happened was that Chancellor Khane sacked a professor, physics department, under circumstances which aroused resentment among the science students. Some of them walked out of class and went to the stadium to hold a protest meeting, and the thing snowballed until half the students were in it. Khane lost his head and ordered the campus police to clear the stadium; the students rushed them and swamped them. I hope, for their sakes, that none of my men ever let anything like that happen. The man I sent, a Colonel Handrosan, managed to talk the students into going back to the stadium and continuing the meeting under Gendarme protection."

"Sounds like a good man."

"Very good, Your Majesty. Especially in handling distur-
bances. I have complete confidence in him. He's also inves-
tigating the background of the affair. I'll give Your Majesty
what he's learned, to date. It seems that the head of the
physics department, a Professor Nelse Dandrik, had been
conducting an experiment, assisted by a Professor Klenn
Faress, to establish more accurately the velocity of subnucleonic particles, beta micropositos, I believe. Dandrik's
sorty, as relayed to Handrosan by Khane, is that he reached a
limit and the apparatus began giving erratic results."

Prince Travann stopped to light a cigarette. "At this point,
Professor Dandrik ordered the experiment stopped, and Professor Faress insisted on continuing. When Dandrik ordered
the apparatus dismantled, Faress became rather emotional
about it—obscenely abusive and threatening, according to
Dandrik. Dandrik complained to Khane, Khane ordered
Faress to apologize, Faress refused, and Khane dismissed
Faress. Immediately, the students went on strike. Faress
confirmed the whole story, and he added one small detail that
Dandrik hadn't seen fit to mention. According to him, when
these micropositos were accelerated beyond sixteen and a
fraction times light-speed, they began registering at the target
before the source registered the emission."

"Yes, I—*What did you say?*"

Prince Travann repeated it slowly, distinctly and tone-
lessly.

"That was what I thought you said. Well, I'm going to
insist on a complete investigation, including a repetition of
the experiment. Under direction of Professor Faress."

"Yes, Your Majesty. And when that happens, I mean to
be on hand personally. If somebody is just before discovering
time-travel, I think Security has a very substantial interest in
it."

The Prime Minister called back to confirm that First Citizen Yaggo and King Ranulf would be at the luncheon. The
Chamberlain, Count Gadvan, called with a long and dreary
problem about the protocol for the banquet. Finally, at noon,

he flashed a signal for General Dorflay, waited five minutes, and then left his desk and went out, to find the mad general and his wirehaired soldiers drawn up in the hall.

There were more Thorans on the South Upper Terrace, and after a flurry of porting and presenting and ordering arms and hand-saluting, the Prime Minister advanced and escorted him to where the Bench of Counselors, all thirty of them, total age close to twenty-eight hundred years, were drawn up in a rough crescent behind the three distinguished guests. The King of Durendal wore a cloth-of-silver leotard and pink tights, and a belt of gold links on which he carried a jeweled dagger only slightly thicker than a knitting needle. He was slender and willowy, and he had large and soulful eyes, and the royal beautician must have worked on him for a couple of hours. Wait till Marris sees this; oh, brother!

Koreff, the Lord Marshal, wore what was probably the standard costume of Durendal, a fairly long jerkin with short sleeves, and knee-boots, and his dress dagger looked as though it had been designed for use. Lord Koreff looked as though he would be quite willing and able to use it; he was fleshy and full-faced, with hard muscles under the flesh.

First Citizen Yaggo, People's Manager-in-Chief of and for the Planetary Commonwealth of Aditya, wore a one-piece white garment like a mechanic's coveralls' with the emblem of his government and the numeral 1 on his breast. He carried no dagger; if he had worn a dress weapon, it would probably have been a slide rule. His head was completely shaven, and he had small, pale eyes and a rat-trap mouth. He was regarding the Durendalians with a distaste that was all too evidently reciprocated.

King Ranulf appeared to have won the toss for first presentation. He squeezed the Imperial hand in both of his and looked up adoringly as he professed his deep honor and pleasure. Yaggo merely clasped both his hands in front of the emblem on his chest and raised them quickly to the level of his chin, saying: "At the service of the Imperial State," and adding, as though it hurt him, "Your Imperial Majesty."

Not being a chief of state, Lord Koreff came third; he merely shook hands and said, "A great honor, Your Imperial Majesty, and the thanks, both of myself and my royal master, for a most gracious reception." The attempt to grab first place having failed, he was more than willing to forget the whole subject. There was a chance that finding a way to dispose of the grain surplus might make the difference between his staying in power at home or not.

Fortunately, the three guests had already met the Bench of Counselors. Immediately after the presentation of Lord Koreff, they all started the two hundred yards' march to the luncheon pavilion, the King of Durendal clinging to his left arm and First Citizen Yaggo stumping dourly on his right, with Prince Ganzay beyond him and Lord Koreff on Ranulf's left.

"Do you plan to stay long on Odin?" he asked the king.

"Oh, I'd *love* to stay for simply *months!* Everything is so *wonderful*, here in Asgard; it makes our little capital of Roncevaux seem so *utterly* provincial. I'm going to tell Your Imperial Majesty a secret. I'm going to see if I can lure some of your *wonderful* ballet dancers back to Durendal with me. Aren't I *naughty,* raiding Your Imperial Majesty's theaters?"

"In keeping with the traditions of your people," he replied gravely. "You Sword-Worlders used to raid everywhere you went."

"I'm afraid those bad old days are long past, Your Imperial Majesty," Lord Koreff said. "But we Sword-Worlders got around the galaxy, for a while. In fact, I seem to remember reading that some of our brethren from Morglay or Flamberge even occupied Aditya for a couple of centuries. Not that you'd guess it to look at Aditya now."

It was First Citizen Yaggo's turn to take precedence—the seat on the right of the throne chair. Lord Koreff sat on Ranulf's left, and, to balance him, Prince Ganzay sat beyond Yaggo and dutifully began inquiring of the People's Manager-in-Chief about the structure of his government, launching him on a monologue that promised to last at least half the luncheon. That left the King of Durendal to Paul; for a start, he dropped a compliment on the cloth-of-silver leotard.

King Ranulf laughed dulcetly, brushed the garment with his fingertips, and said that it was just a simple thing patterned after the Durendalian peasant costume.

"You have peasants on Durendal?"

"Oh, *dear*, yes! Such quaint, *charming* people. Of course, they're all poor, and they wear such *funny* ragged clothes, and travel about in rackety old aircars, it's a wonder they don't fall apart in the air. But they're so *wonderfully* happy and carefree. I often wish I were one of them, instead of king."

"Nonworking class, Your Imperial Majesty," Lord Koreff explained.

"On Aditya," First Citizen Yaggo declared, "there are no classes, and on Aditya everybody works. 'From each according to his ability; to each according to his need.' "

"On Aditya," an elderly Counselor four places to the right of him said loudly to his neighbor, "they don't call them classes, they call them sociological categories, and they have nineteen of them. And on Aditya, they don't call them nonworkers, they call them occupational reservists, and they have more of them than we do."

"But of course, I was born a king," Ranulf said sadly and nobly. "I have a duty to my people."

"No, they don't vote at all," Lord Koreff was telling the Counselor on his left. "On Durendal, you have to pay taxes before you can vote."

"On Aditya the crime of taxation does not exist," the First Citizen told the Prime Minister.

"On Aditya," the Counselor four places down said to his neighbor, "there's nothing to tax. The state owns all the property, and if the Imperial Constitution and the Space Navy let them, the State would own all the people, too. Don't tell me about Aditya. First big-ship command I had was the old *Invictus*, 374, and she was based on Aditya for four years, and I'd sooner have spent that time in orbit around Nifflheim.''

Now Paul remembered who he was; old Admiral—now Prince-Counselor—Geklar. He and Prince-Counselor Dorflay would get along famously. The Lord Marshal of Durendal was replying to some objection somebody had made:

"No, nothing of the sort. We hold the view that every civil or political right implies a civil or political obligation. The citizen has a right to protection from the Realm, for instance; he therefore has the obligation to defend the Realm. And his right to participate in the government of the Realm includes his obligation to support the Realm financially. Well, we tax only property; if a nonworker acquires taxable property, he has to go to work to earn the taxes. I might add that our nonworkers are very careful to avoid acquiring taxable property.''

"But if they don't have votes to sell, what do they live on?'' a Counselor asked in bewilderment.

"The nobility supports them; the landowners, the trading barons, the industrial lords. The more nonworking adherents they have, the greater their prestige.'' And the more rifles they could muster when they quarreled with their fellow nobles, of course. "Besides, if we didn't do that, they'd turn brigand, and it costs less to support them than to have to hunt them out of the brush and hang them.''

"On Aditya, brigandage does not exist.''

"On Aditya, all the brigands belong to the Secret Police, only on Aditya they don't call them Secret Police, they call them Servants of the People, Ninth Category.''

A shadow passed quickly over the pavilion, and then another. He glanced up quickly, to see two long black troop carriers, emblazoned with the Sun and Cogwheel and armored fist of Security, pass back of the Octagon Tower and let down on the north landing stage. A third followed. He rose quickly.

"Please remain seated, gentlemen, and continue with the luncheon. If you will excuse me for a moment, I'll be back directly." I hope, he added mentally.

Captain-General Dorflay, surrounded by a dozen officers, Thoran and human, had arrived on the lower terrace at the base of the Octagon Tower. They had a full Thoran rifle company with them. As he went down to them, Dorflay hurried forward.

"It has come, Your Majesty!" he said, as soon as he could make himself heard without raising his voice. "We are all ready to die with Your Majesty!"

"Oh, I doubt it'll come quite to that, Harv," he said. "But just to be on the safe side, take that company and the gentlemen who are with you and get up to the mountains and join the Crown Prince and his party. Here." He took a notepad from his belt pouch and wrote rapidly, sealing the note and giving it to Dorflay. "Give this to His Highness, and place yourself under his orders. I know; he's just a boy, but he has a good head. Obey him exactly in everything, but under no circumstances return to the Palace or allow him to return until I call you."

"Your Majesty is ordering me away?" The old soldier was aghast.

"An emperor who has a son can be spared. An emperor's son who is too young to marry can't. You know that."

Harv Dorflay was only mad on one subject, and even within the frame of his madness he was intensely logical. He nodded. "Yes, Your Imperial Majesty. We both serve the Empire as best we can. And I will guard the little Princess Olva, too." He grapsed Paul's hand, said, "Farewell, Your Majesty!" and dashed away, gathering his staff and the company of Thorans as he went. In an instant, they had vanished down the nearest rampway.

The emperor watched their departure, and, at the same time, saw a big black aircar, bearing the three-mooned planet, argent on sable, of Travann, let down onto the south landing stage, and another troop carrier let down after it.

Four men left the aircar—Yorn, Prince Travann, and three officers in the black of the Security Guard. Prince Ganzay had also left the table; he came from one direction as Prince Travann advanced from the other. They converged on the emperor.

"What's happening here, Prince Travann?" Prince Ganzay demanded. "Why are you bringing all these troops to the Palace?"

"Your Majesty," Prince Travann said smoothly, "I trust that you will pardon this disturbance. I'm sure nothing serious will happen, but I didn't dare take chances. The students from the University are marching on the Palace—perfectly peaceful and loyal procession; they're bringing a petition for Your Majesty—but on the way, while passing through a nonworkers' district, they were attacked by a gang of hooligans connected with a voting-bloc boss called Nutchy the Knife. None of the students were hurt, and Colonel Handrosan got the procession out of the district promptly, and then dropped some of his men, who have since been re-enforced, to deal with the hooligans. That's still going on, and these riots are like forest fires; you never know when they'll shift and get out of control. I hope the men I brought won't be needed here. Really, they're a reserve for the riot work; I won't commit them, though, until I'm sure the Palace is safe."

He nodded. "Prince Travann, how soon do you estimate that the student procession will arrive here?" he asked.

"They're coming on foot, Your Majesty. I'd give them an hour, at least."

"Well, Prince Travann, will you have one of your officers see that the public-address screen in front is ready; I'll want to talk to them when they arrive. And meanwhile, I'll want to talk to Chancellor Khane, Professor Dandrik, Professor Faress and Colonel Handrosan, together. And Count Tammsan, too; Prince Ganzay, will you please screen him and invite him here immediately?"

"Now, Your Majesty?" At first, the Prime Minister was trying to suppress a look of incredulity; then he was trying to keep from showing comprehension. "Yes, Your Majesty; at once." He frowned slightly when he saw two of the Security Guard officers salute Prince Travann instead of the emperor before going away. Then he turned and hurried toward the Octagon Tower.

The officer who had gone to the aircar to use the radio returned and reported that Colonel Handrosan was bringing the Chancellor and both professors from the University in his command-car, having anticipated that they would be wanted. Paul nodded in pleasure.

"You have a good man there, Prince," he said. "Keep an eye on him."

"I know it, Your Majesty. To tell the truth, it was he who organized this march. Thought they'd be better employed coming here to petition you than milling around the University getting into further mischief."

The other officer also returned, bringing a portable viewscreen with him on a contragravity-lifter. By this time, the Bench of Counselors and the three off-planet guests had become anxious and left the luncheon pavilion in a body. The Counselors were looking about uneasily, noticing the black uniformed Security Guards who had left the troop carrier and were taking position by squads all around the emperor. First Citizen Yaggo, and King Ranulf and Lord Koreff, also seemed uneasy. They were avoiding the proximity of Paul as though he had the green death.

The viewscreen came on, and in it the city, as seen from an aircar at two thousand feet, spread out with the Palace visible in the distance, the golden pile of the Octagon Tower jutting up from it. The car carrying the pickup was behind the procession, which was moving toward the Palace along one of the broad skyways, with Gendarmes and Security Guards leading, following and flanking. There were a few Imperial and planetary and school flags, but none of the quantity-made banners and placards which always betray a planned demonstration.

Prince Ganzay had been gone for some time, now. When he returned, he drew Paul aside.

"Your Majesty," he whispered softly, "I tried to summon Army troops, but it'll be hours before any can get here. And the Militia can't be mobilized in anything less than a day. There are only five thousand Army Regulars on Odin, now, anyhow."

And half of them officers and noncoms of skeleton regiments. Like the Navy, the Army had been scattered all over the Empire—on Behemoth and Amida and Xipetotec and Astarte and Jotunnheim—in response to calls for support from Security.

"Let's have a look at this rioting, Prince Travann," one of the less decrepit Counselors, a retired general, said. "I want to see how your people are handling it."

The officers who had come with Prince Travann consulted briefly, and then got another pickup on the screen. This must have been a regular public pickup, on the front of a tall building. It was a couple of miles farther away; the Palace was visible only as a tiny glint from the Octagon Tower, on the skyline. Half a dozen Security aircars were darting about, two of them chasing a battered civilian vehicle and firing at it. On rooftops and terraces and skyways, little clumps of Security Guards were skirmishing, dodging from cover to cover, and sometimes individuals or groups in civilian clothes fired back at them. There was s surprising absence of casualties.

"Your Majesty!" the old general hissed in a scandalized whisper. "That's nothing but a big fake! Look, they're all firing blanks! The rifles hardly kick at all, and there's too much smoke for propellant-powder."

"I noticed that." This riot must have been carefully prepared, long in advance. Yet the student riot seemed to have been entirely spontaneous. That puzzled him; he wished he knew just what Yorn Travann was up to. "Just keep quiet about it," he advised.

More aircars were arriving, big and luxurious, emblazoned with the arms of some of the most distinguished families in Asgard. One of the first to let down bore the device of Duklass, and from it the Minister of Economics, the Minister of Education, and a couple of other Ministers, alighted. Count Duklass went at once to Prince Travann, drawing him away from King Ranulf and Lord Koreff and talking to him rapidly and earnestly. Count Tammsan approached at a swift half-run.

"Save Your Majesty!" he greeted, breathlessly. "What's going on, sir? We heard something about some petty brawl at the University, that Prince Ganzay had become alarmed about, but now there seems to be fighting all over the city. I never saw anything like it; on the way here we had to go up to ten thousand feet to get over a battle, and there's a vast crowd on the Avenue of the Arts, and—" He took in the Security Guards. "Your Majesty, just what *is* going on?"

"Great and frightening changes." Count Tammsan started; he must have been to a psi-medium, too. "But I think the Empire is going to survive them. There may even be a few improvements, before things are done."

A blue-uniformed Gendarme officer approached Prince Travann, drawing him away from Count Duklass and speaking briefly to him. The Minister of Security nodded, then turned back to the Minister of Economics. They talked for a few moments longer, then clasped hands, and Travann left Duklass with his face wreathed in smiles. The Gendarme officer accompanied him as he approached.

"Your Majesty, this is Colonel Handrosan, the officer who handled the affair at the University."

"And a very good piece of work, colonel." He shook hands with him. "Don't be surprised if it's remembered next Honors Day. Did you bring Khane and the two professors?"

"They're down on the lower landing-stage, Your Majesty. We're delaying the students, to give Your Majesty time to talk to them."

"We'll see them now. My study will do." The officer saluted and went away. He turned to Count Tammsan. "That's why I asked Prince Ganzay to invite you here. This thing's become too public to be ignored; some sort of action will have to be taken. I'm going to talk to the students; I want to find out just what happened before I commit myself to anything. Well, gentlemen, let's go to my study.''

Count Tammsan looked around, bewildered. ''But I don't understand—'' He fell into step with Paul and the Minister of Security; a squad of Security Guards fell in behind them. ''I don't understand what's happening,'' he complained.

An emperor about to have his throne yanked out from under him, and a minister about to stage a *coup d'etat*, taking time out to settle a trifling academic squabble. One thing he did understand, though, was that the Ministry of Education was getting some very bad publicity at a time when it could be least afforded. Prince Travann was telling him about the hooligans' attack on the marching students, and that worried him even more. Nonworking hooligans acted as voting-bloc bosses ordered; voting-bloc bosses acted on orders from the political manipulators of Cartels and pressure-groups, and action downward through the nonworkers was usually accompanied by action upward through influences to which ministers were sensitive.

There were a dozen Security Guards in black tunics, and as many Household Thorans in red kilts, in the hall outside the study, fraternizing amicably. They hurried apart and formed two ranks, and the Thoran officer with them saluted.

Going into the study, he went to his desk; Count Tammsan lit a cigarette and puffed nervously, and sat down as though he were afraid the chair would collapse under him. Prince Travann sank into another chair and relaxed, closing his eyes. There was a bit of wafer on the floor by Paul's chair, dropped by the little dog that morning. He stooped and picked it up, laying it on his desk, and sat looking at it until the door screen flashed and buzzed. Then he pressed the release button.

Colonel Handrosan ushered the three University men in ahead of him—Khane, with a florid, arrogant face that showed worry under the arrogance; Dandrik, gray-haired and stoop-shouldered, looking irritated; Faress, young, with a scrubby red mustache, looking bellicose. He greeted them collectively and invited them to sit, and there was a brief uncomfortable silence which everybody expected him to break.

"Well, gentlemen," he said, "we want to get the facts about this affair in some kind of order. I wish you'd tell me, as briefly and as completely as possible, what you know about it."

"There's the man who started it!" Khane declared, pointing at Faress.

"Professor Faress had nothing to do with it," Colonel Handrosan stated flatly. "He and his wife were in their apartment, packing to move out, when it started. Somebody called him and told him about the fighting at the stadium, and he went there at once to talk his students into dispersing. By that time, the situation was completely out of hand; he could do nothing with the students."

"Well, I think we ought to find out, first of all, why Professor Faress was dismissed," Prince Travann said. "It will take a good deal to convince me that any teacher able to inspire such loyalty in his students is a bad teacher, or deserves dismissal."

"As I understand," Paul said, "the dismissal was the result of a disagreement between Professor Faress and Professor Dandrik about an experiment on which they were working. I believe, an experiment to fix more exactly the velocity of accelerated subnucleonic particles. Beta micropositos, wasn't it, Chancellor Khane?"

Khane looked at him in surprise. "Your Majesty, I know nothing about that. Professor Dandrik is head of the physics department; he came to me, about six months ago, and told me that in his opinion this experiment was desirable. I simply deferred to his judgment and authorized it."

"Your Majesty has just stated the prupose of the experiment," Dandrik said. "For centuries, there have been inaccuracies in mathematical descriptions of subnucleonic events, and this experiment was undertaken in the hope of eliminating these inaccuracies." Before he could get into a lenghty mathematical explanation, Paul interrupted. "Yes, I understand that, professor. But just what was the actual experiment, in terms of physical operations?''

Dandrik looked helpless for a moment. Faress, who had been choking back a laugh, interrupted:

"Your Majesty, we were using the big turbo-linear accelerator to project fast micropositos down an evacuated tube one kilometer in length, and clocking them with light, the velocity of which has been established almost absolutely. I will say that with respect to the light, there were no observable inaccuracies at any time, and until the micropositos were accelerated to 16.067543333⅓ times light-speed, they registered much as expected. Beyond that velocity, however, the target for the micropositos began registering impacts before the source registered emission, although the light target was still registering normally. I notified Professor Dandrik about this, and—''

"You notified him. Wasn't he present at the time?''

"No, Your Majesty.''

"Your Majesty, I am head of the physics department of the University. I have too much administrative work to waste time on the technical aspects of experiments like this,'' Dandrik interjected.

"I understand. Professor Faress was actually performing the experiment. You told Professor Dandrik what had happened. What then?''

"Why, Your Majesty, he simply declared that the limit of accuracy had been reached, and ordered the experiment dropped. He then reported the highest reading before this anticipation effect was observed as the newly established limit of accuracy in measuring the velocity of accelerated micropositos, and said nothing whatever in his report about the anticipation effect.''

"I read a summary of the report. Why, Professor Dandrik, did you omit mentioning this slightly unusual effect?''

"Why, because the whole thing was utterly preposterous, that's why!'' Dandrik barked, and then hastily added, "Your Imperial Majesty.'' He turned and glared at Faress; professors do not glare at galactic emperors. "Your Majesty, the limit of accuracy had been reached. After that, it was only to be expected that the apparatus would give erratic reports.''

"It might have been expected that the apparatus would stop registering increased velocity relative to the light-speed standard, or that it would begin registering disproportionately," Faress said. "But, Your Majesty, I'll submit that it was not to be expected that it would register impacts before emissions. And I'll add this. After registering this slight apparent jump into the future, there was no proportionate increase in anticipation with further increase of acceleration. I wanted to find out why. But when Professor Dandrik saw what was happening, he became almost hysterical, and ordered the accelerator shut down as though he were afraid it would blow up in his face.''

"I think it has blown up in his face," Prince Travann said quietly. "Professor, have you any theory, or supposition, or even any wild guess, as to how this anticipation effect occurs?''

"Yes, Your Highness. I suspect that the apparent anticipation is simply an observational illusion, similar to the illusion of time-reversal experienced when it was first observed, though not realized, that positrons sometimes exceeded light-speed.''

"Why, that's what I've been saying, all along!" Dandrik broke in. "The whole thing is an illusion, due—''

"To having reached the limit of observational accuracy; I understand, Professor Dandrik. Go on, Professor Faress.''

"I think that beyond $16.067543333\frac{1}{3}$ times light-speed, the micropositos ceased to have any velocity at all, velocity being defined as rate of motion in four-dimensional spacetime. I believe they moved through the three spatial dimensions without moving at all in the fourth, temporal, dimension. They made that kilometer from source to target, literally, in nothing flat. Instantaneity.''

That must have been the first time he had actually come out and said it. Dandrik jumped to his feet with a cry that was just short of being a shriek.

"He's crazy! Your Majesty, you mustn't . . . that is,

well, I mean—Please, Your Majesty, don't listen to him. He doesn't know what he's saying. He's raving!''

"He knows perfectly well what he's saying, and it probably scares him more than it does you. The difference is that he's willing to face it and you aren't.''

The difference was that Faress was a scientist and Dandrik was a science teacher. To Faress, a new door had opened, the first new door in eight hundred years. To Dandrik, it threatened invalidation of everything he had taught since the morning he had opened his first class. He could no longer say to his pupils, "You are here to learn from me." He would have to say, more humbly, "*We* are here to learn from the Universe.''

It had happened so many times before, too. The comfortable and established Universe had fitted all the known facts—and then new facts had been learned that wouldn't fit it. The third planet of the Sol system had once been the center of the Universe, and then Terra, and Sol, and even the galaxy, had been forced to abdicate centricity. The atom had been indivisible—until somebody divided it. There had been intangible substance that had permeated the Universe, because it had been necessary for the transmission of light—until it was demonstrated to be unnecessary and nonexistent. And the speed of light had been the ultimate velocity, once, and could be exceeded no more than the atom could be divided. And light-speed had been constant, regardless of distance from source, and the Universe, to explain certain observed phenomena, had been believed to be expanding simultaneously in all directions. And the things that had happened in psychology, when psi-phenomena had become too obvious to be shrugged away.

"And then, when Dr. Dandrik ordered you to drop this experiment, just when it was becoming interesting, you refused?''

"Your Majesty, I couldn't stop, not then. But Dr. Dandrik ordered the apparatus dismantled and scrapped, and I'm afraid I lost my head. Told him I'd punch his silly old face in, for one thing.''

"You admit that?" Chancellor Khane cried.

"I think you showed admirable self-restraint in not doing it. Did you explain to Chancellor Khane the importance of this experiment?"

"I tried to, Your Majesty, but he simply wouldn't listen."

"But, Your Majesty!" Khane expostulated. "Professor Dandrik is head of the department, and one of the foremost physicists of the Empire, and this young man is only one of the junior assistant-professors. Isn't even a full professor, and he got his degree from some school away off-planet. University of Brannerton, on Gimli."

"Professor Faress, were you a pupil of Professor Vann Evaratt?" Prince Travann asked sharply.

"Why, yes, sir. I—"

"Ha, no wonder!" Dandrik crowed. "Your Majesty, that man's an out-and-out charlatan! He was kicked out of the University here ten years ago, and I'm surprised he could even get on the faculty of a school like Brannerton, on a planet like Gimli."

"Why, you stupid old fool!" Faress yelled at him. "You aren't enough of a physicist to oil robots in Vann Evaratt's lab!"

"There, Your Majesty," Khane said. "You see how much respect for authority this hooligan has!"

On Aditya, such would be unthinkable; on Aditya, everybody respects authority. Whether it's respectable or not.

Count Tammsan laughed, and he realized that he must have spoken aloud. Nobody else seemed to have gotten the joke.

"Well, how about the riot, now?" he asked. "Who started that?"

"Colonel Handrosan made an investigation on the spot," Prince Travann said. "May I suggest that we hear his report?"

"Yes indeed. Colonel?"

Handrosan rose and stood with his hands behind his back, looking fixedly at the wall behind the desk.

"Your Majesty, the students of Professor Faress' advanced subnucleonic physics class, postgraduate students, all of them, were told of Professor Faress' dismissal by a faculty member who had taken over the class this morning. They all got up and walked out in a body, and gathered outdoors on the campus to discuss the matter. At the next class break, they were joined by other science students, and they went into the stadium, where they were joined, half an hour later, by more students who had learned of the dismissal in the meantime. At no time was the gathering disorderly. The stadium is covered by a viewscreen pickup which is fitted with a recording device; there is a complete audio-visual of the whole thing, including the attack on them by the campus police.

"This attack was ordered by Chancellor Khane, at about 1100, the chief of the campus police was told to clear the stadium, and when he asked if he was to use force, Chancellor Khane told him to use anything he wanted to."

"I did not! I told him to get the students out of the stadium, but—"

"The chief of campus police carries a personal wire recorder," Handrosan said, in his flat monotone. "He has a recording of the order, in Chancellor Khane's own voice. I heard it myself. The police," he continued, "first tried to use gas, but the wind was against them. They then tried to use sono-stunners, but the students rushed them and overwhelmed them. If Your Majesty will permit a personal opinion, while I do not sympathize with their subsequent attack on the Administration Center, they were entirely within their rights in defending themselves in the stadium, and it's hard enough to stop trained and disciplined troops when they are winning. After defeating the police, they simply went on by what might be called the momentum of victory."

"Then you'd say that it's positively established that the students were behaving in a peaceable and orderly manner the stadium when they were attacked, and that Chancellor Khane ordered the attack personally?"

"I would, emphatically, Your Majesty."

"I think we've done enough here, gentlemen." He turned

to Count Tammsan. "This is, jointly, the affair of Education and Security. I would suggest that you and Prince Travann join in a formal and public inquiry, and until all the facts have been established and recorded and action decided upon, the dismissal of Professor Faress be reversed and he be restored to his position on the faculty."

"Yes, Your Majesty," Tammsan agreed. "And I think it would be a good idea for Chancellor Khane to take a vacation till then, too."

"I would further suggest that, as this microposito experiment is crucial to the whole question, it should be repeated. Under the personal direction of Professor Faress."

"I agree with that, Your Majesty," Prince Travann said. "If it's as important as I think it is, Professor Dandrik is greatly to be censured for ordering it stopped and for failing to report this anticipation effect."

"We'll consult about the inquiry, including the experiment, tomorrow, Your Highness," Tammsan told Travann.

Paul rose, and everybody rose with him. "That being the case, you gentlemen are all excused. The students' procession ought to be arriving, now, and I want to tell them what's going to be done. Prince Travann, Count Tammsan; do you care to accompany me?"

Going up to the central terrace in front of the Octagon Tower, he turned to Count Tammsan.

"I notice you laughed at that remark of mine about Aditya," he said. "Have you met the First Citizen?"

"Only on screen, sir. He was at me for about an hour, this morning. It seems that they are reforming the educational system on Aditya. On Aditya, everything gets reformed every ten years, whether it needs it or not. He came here to find somebody to take charge of the reformation."

He stopped short, bringing the others to a halt beside him, and laughed heartily.

"Well, we'll send First Citizen Yaggo away happy; we'll make him a present of the most distinguished educator on Odin."

"Khane?" Tammsan asked.

"Khane. Isn't it wonderful; if you have a few problems, you have trouble, but if you have a whole lot of problems, they start solving each other. We get a chance to get rid of Khane, and create a vacancy that can be filled by somebody big enough to fill it; the Ministry of Education gets out from under a nasty situation; First Citizen Yaggo gets what he thinks he wants—"

"And if I know Khane, and if I know the People's Commonwealth of Aditya, it won't be a year before Yaggo has Khane shot or stuffs him into jail, and then the Space Navy will have an excuse to visit Aditya, and Aditya'll never be the same afterward," Prince Travann added.

The students massed on the front lawns were still cheering as they went down after addressing them. The Security Guards were conspicuously absent and it was a detail of red-kilted Thoran riflemen who met them as they entered the hall to the Session Chamber. Prince Ganzay approached, attended by two Household Guard officers, a human and a Thoran. Count Tammsan looked from one to the other of his companions, bewildered. The bewildering thing was that everything was as it should be.

"Well, gentlemen," Paul said, "I'm sure that both of you will want to confer for a moment with your colleagues in the Rotunda before the Session. Please don't feel obliged to attend me further."

Prince Ganzay approached as they went down the hall. "Your Majesty, what *is* going on here?" he demanded querulously. "Just who is in control of the Palace—you or Prince Travann? And where is His Imperial Highness, and where is General Dorflay?"

"I sent Dorflay to join Prince Rodrik's picnic party. If you're upset about this, you can imagine what he might have done here."

Prince Ganzay looked at him curiously for a moment. "I thought I understood what was happening," he said. "Now I—This business about the students, sir; how did it come out?"

Paul told him. They talked for a while, and then the Prime Minister looked at his watch, and suggested that the Session ought to be getting started. Paul nodded, and they went down the hall and into the Rotunda.

The big semicircular lobby was empty, now, except for a platoon of Household Guards, and the Empress Marris and her ladies-in-waiting. She advanced as quickly as her sheath gown would permit, and took his arm; the ladies-in-waiting fell in behind her, and Prince Ganzay went ahead, crying: "My Lords, Your Venerable Highnesses, gentlemen; His Imperial Majesty!"

Marris tightened her grip on his arm as they started forward. "Paul!" she hissed into his ear. "What is this silly story about Yorn Travann trying to seize the Throne?"

"Isn't it? Yorn's been too close to the Throne for too long not to know what sort of a seat it is. He'd commit any crime up to and including genocide to keep off it."

She gave a quick skip to get into step with him. "Then why's he filled the Palace with these blackcoats? Is Rod all right?"

"Perfectly all right; he's somewhere out in the mountains, keeping Harv Dorflay out of mischief."

They crossed the Session Hall and took their seats on the double throne; everybody sat down, and the Prime Minister, after some formalities, declared the Plenary Session in being. Almost at once, one of the Prince-Counselors was on his feet begging His Majesty's leave to interrogate the Government.

"I wish to ask His Highness the Minister of Security the meaning of all this unprecedented disturbance, both here in the Palace and in the city," he said.

Prince Travann rose at once. "Your Majesty, in reply to the question of His Venerable Highness," he began, and then launched himself into an account of the student riot, the march to petition the emperor, and the clash with the non-working class hooligans. "As to the affair at the University, I hesitate to speak on what is really the concern of His Lordship the Minister of Education, but as to the fighting in the city, if it is still going on, I can assure His Venerable Highness that the Gendarmes and Security Guards have it well in hand; the persons responsible are being rounded up, and, if the Minister of Justice concurs, an inquiry will be started tomorrow.''

The Minister of Justice assured the Minister of Security that his Ministry would be quite ready to co-operate in the inquiry. Count Tammsan then got up and began talking about the riot at the University.

"What did happen, Paul?'' Marris whispered.

"Chancellor Khane sacked a science professor for being too interested in science. The student's didn't like it. I think Khane's successor will rectify that. Have a good time at the Flower Festivals?''

She raised her fan to hide a grimmace. "I made my schedule,'' she said. "Tomorrow, I have fifty more booked.''

"Your Imperial Majesty!'' The Counselor who had risen paused, to make sure that he had the Imperial attention, before continuing: "Inasmuch as this question also seems to involve a scientific experiment, I would suggest that the Ministry of Science and Technology is also interested, and since there is at present no Minister holding that portfolio, I would suggest that the discussion be continued after a Minister has been elected.''

The Minister of Health and Sanity jumped to his feet.

"Your Imperial Majesty; permit me to concur with the proposal of His Venerable Highness, and to extend it with the subproposal that the Ministry of Science and Technology be abolished, and its functions and personnel divided among the other Ministries, specifically those of Education and of Economics.''

The Minister of Fine Arts was up before he was fully seated.

"Your Imperial Majesty; permit me to concur with the proposal of Count Guilfred, and to extend it further with the proposal that the Ministry of Defense, now also vacant, be likewise abolished, and its functions and personnel added to the Ministry of Security under His Highness Prince Travann.''

So that was it! Marris, beside him, said, ''Well!'' He had long ago discovered that she could pack more meaning into that monosyllable than the average couselor could into a half-hour's speech. Prince Ganzay was thunderstruck, and from the Bench of Counselors six or eight voices were babbling loudly at once. Four Ministers were on their feet clamoring for recognition; Count Duklass of Economics was yelling the loudest, so he got it.

''Your Imperial Majesty; it would have been most unseemly in me to have spoken in favor of the proposal of Count Guilfred, being an interested party, but I feel no such hesitation in concurring with the proposal of Baron Garatt, the Minister of Fine Arts. Indeed, I consider it a most excellent proposal—''

''And I consider it the most diabolically dangerous proposal to be made in this Hall in the last six centuries!'' old Admiral Geklar shouted. ''This is a propsal to concentrate all the armed force of the Empire in the hands of one man. Who can say what unscrupulous use might be made of such power?''

''Are you intimating, Prince-Counselor, that Prince Travann is contemplating some tyranical or subversive use of such power?'' Count Tammsan, of all people, demanded.

There was a concerted gasp at that; about half the Plenary Session were absolutely sure that he was. Admiral Geklar backed quickly away from the question.

''Prince Travann will not be the last Minister of Security,'' he said.

''What I was about to say, Your Majesty, is that as matters stand, Security has a virtual monopoly on armed power on this planet. When these disorders in the city—which Prince Travann's men are now bringing under control—broke out, there was, I am informed, an order sent out to bring Regular Army and Planetary Militia into Asgard. It will be hours before any of the former can arrive, and at least a day before the latter can even be mobilized. By the time any of them get here, there will be nothing for them to do. Is that not correct, Prince Ganzay?"

The Prime Minister looked at him angrily, stung by the realization that somebody else had a personal intelligence service as good as his own, then swallowed his anger and assented.

"Furthermore," Count Duklass continued, "the Ministry of Defense, itself, is an anachronism, which no doubt accounts for the condition in which we now find it. The Empire has no external enemies whatever; all our defense problems are problems of internal security. Let us therefore turn the facilities over to the Ministry responsible for the tasks."

The debate went on and on; he paid less and less attention to it, and it became increasingly obvious that opposition to the proposition was dwindling. Cries of, "Vote! Vote!" began to be heard from its supporters. Prince Ganzay rose from his desk and came to the throne.

"Your Imperial Majesty," he said softly. "I am opposed to this proposition, but I am convinced that enough favor it to pass it, even over Your Majesty's veto. Before the vote is called, does Your Majesty wish my resignation?"

He rose and stepped down beside the Prime Minister, putting an arm over Prince Ganzay's shoulder.

"Far from it, old friend," he said, in a distinctly audible voice. "I will have too much need for you. But, as for the proposal, I don't oppose it. I think it an excellent one; it has my approval." He lowered his voice. "As soon as it's passed, place General Dorflay's name in nomination."

The Prime Minister looked at him sadly for a moment, then nodded, returning to his desk, where he rapped for order and called for the vote.

"Well, if you can't lick them, join them," Marris said as he sat down beside her. "And if they start chasing you, just yell, 'There he goes; follow me!' "

The proposal carried, almost unanimously. Prince Ganzay then presented the name of Captain-General Dorflay for elevation to the Bench of Counselors, and the emperor decreed it. As soon as the Session was adjourned and he could do so, he slipped out the little door behind the throne, into an elevator.

In the room at the top of the Octagon Tower, he laid aside his belt and dress dagger and unfastened his tunic, then sat down in his deep chair and called a serving robot. It was the one which had brought him his breakfast, and he greeted it as a friend; it lit a cigarette for him, and poured a drink of brandy. For a long time he sat, smoking and sipping and looking out the wide window to the west, where the orange sun was firing the clouds behind the mountains, and he realized that he was abominably tired. Well, no wonder; more Empire history had been made today than in the years since he had come to the Throne.

Then something behind him clicked. He turned his head, to see Yorn Travann emerge from the concealed elevator. He grinned and lifted his drink in greeting.

"I thought you'd be a little late," he said. "Everybody trying to climb onto the bandwagon?"

Yorn Travann came forward, unbuckling his belt and laying it with Paul's; he sank into the chair opposite, and the robot poured him a drink.

"Well, do you blame them? What would it have looked like to you, in their place?"

"A *coup d'etat*. For that matter, wasn't that what it was? Why didn't you tell me you were springing it?"

"I didn't spring it; it was sprung on me. I didn't know a thing about it till Max Duklass buttonholed me down by the landing stage. I'd intended fighting this proposal to partition Science and Technology, but this riot blew up and scared Duklass and Tammsan and Guilfred and the rest of them. They weren't too sure of their majority—that's why they had the election postponed a couple of times—but they were sure that the riot would turn some of the undecided Counselors against them. So they offered to back me to take over Defense in exchange for my supporting their proposal. It looked too good to pass up."

"Even at the price of wrecking Science and Technology?"

"It was wrecked, or left to rust into uselessness, long ago. The main function of Technology has been to suppress anything that might threaten this state of economic *rigor mortis* that Duklas calls stability, and the function of Science has been to let muttonheads like Khane and Dandrik dominate the teaching of science. Well, Defense has its own scientific and technical sections, and when we come to carving the bird, Duklass and Tammsan are going to see a lot of slices going onto my plate."

"And when it's all cut up, it will be discovered that there is no provision for original research. So, it will please My Majesty to institute an Imperial Office of Scientific Research, independent of any Ministry, and guess who'll be named to head it."

"Faress. And, by the way, we're all set on Khane, too. First Citizen Yaggo is as delighted to have him as we are to get rid of him. Why don't we get Vann Evaratt back, and give him the job?"

"Good. If he takes charge there at the opening of the next academic year, in ten years we'll have a thousand young men, maybe ten times that many, who won't be afraid of new things and new ideas. But the main thing is that now you have Defense, and now the plan can really start firing all jets."

"Yes." Yorn Travann got out his cigarettes and lit one. Paul glanced at the robot, hoping that its feelings hadn't been hurt. "All these native uprisings I've been blowing up out of inter-tribal knife fights, and all these civil wars my people have been manufacturing; there'll be more of them, and I'll start yelling my head off for an adequate Space Navy, and after we get it, these local troubles will all stop, and then what'll we be expected to do? Scrap the ships?"

They both knew what would be done with some of them. It would have to be done stealthily, while nobody was looking, but some of those ships would go far beyond the boundaries of the Empire, and new things would happen. New worlds, new problems. Great and frightening changes.

"Paul, we agreed upon this long ago, when we were still boys at the University. The Empire stopped growing, and when things stop growing, they start dying, the death of petrifaction. And when petrifaction is complete, the cracking and the crumbling starts, and there's no way of stopping it. But if we can get people out onto new planets, the Empire won't die; it'll start growing again.''

"You didn't start that thing at the University, this morning, yourself, did you?''

"Not the student riot, no. But the hooligan attack, yes. That was some of my own men. The real hooligans began looting after Handrosan had gotten the students out of the district. We collared all of them, including their boss, Nutchy the Knife, right away, and as soon as we did that, Big Moogie and Zikko the Nose tried to move in. We're cleaning them up now. By tomorrow morning there won't be one of these nonworkers' voting blocks left in Asgard, and by the end of the week they'll be cleaned up all over Odin. I have discovered a plot, and they're all involved in it.''

"Wait a moment.'' Paul got to his feet. "That reminds me; Harv Dorflay's hiding Rod and Olva out in the mountains. I wanted him out of here while things were happening. I'll have to call him and tell him it's safe to come in, now.''

"Well, zip up your tunic and put your dagger on; you look as though you'd been arrested, disarmed and searched.''

"That's right.'' He hastily repaired his appearance and went to the screen across the room, punching out the combination of the screen with Rodrik's picnic party.

A young lieutenant of the Household Troops appeared in it, and had to be reassured. He got General Dorflay.

"Your Majesty! You are all right?''

"Perfectly all right, general, and it's quite safe to bring His Imperial Highness in. The conspiracy against the Throne has been crushed.''

"Oh, thank the gods! Is Prince Travann a prisoner?''

"Quite the contrary, general. It was our loyal and devoted subject, Prince Travann, who crushed the conspiracy.''

"But—But, Your Majesty—!''

"You aren't to be blamed for suspecting him, general. His agents were working in the very innermost councils of the conspirators. Every one of the people whom you suspected—with excellent reason—was actually working to defeat the plot. Think back, general; the scheme to put the gun in the viewscreen, the scheme to sabotage the elevator, the scheme to introduce assassins into the orchestra with guns built into their trumpets—every one came to your notice because of what seemed to be some indiscretion of the plotters, didn't it?''

''Why . . . why, yes, Your Majesty!'' By this time tomorrow, he would have a complete set of memories for each one of them. ''You mean, the indiscretions were deliberate?''

''Your vigilance and loyalty made it necessary for them to resort to these fantastic expedients, and your vigilance defeated them as fast as they came to your notice. Well, today, Prince Travann and I struck back. I may tell you, in confidence, that every one of the conspirators is dead. Killed in this afternoon's rioting—which was incited for that purpose by Prince Travann.''

''Then— Then there will be no more plots against your life?'' There was a note of regret in the old man's voice.

''No more, Your Venerable Highness.''

''But— What did Your Majesty call me?'' he asked incredulously.

''I took the honor of being the first to address you by your new title, Prince-Counselor Dorflay.''

He left the old man overcome, and blubbering happily on the shoulder of the Crown Prince, who winked at his father out of the screen. Prince Travann had gotten a couple of fresh drinks from the robot and handed one to him when he returned to his chair.

''He'll be finding the Bench of Counselors riddled with treason inside a week,'' Travann said. ''You handled that just right, though. Another case of making problems solve each other.''

''You were telling me about a plot you'd discovered.''

''Oh, yes; this is one to top Dorflay's best efforts. All the voting-bloc bosses on Odin are in a conspiracy to start a civil war to give them a chance to loot the planet. There isn't a word of truth in it, of course, but it'll do to arrest and hold them for a few days, and by that time some of my undercovers will be in control of every nonworker vote on the planet. After all, the Cartels put an end to competition in every other business; why not a Voting Cartel, too? Then, whenever there's an election, we just advertise for bids.''

"Why, that would mean absolute control—''

"Of the nonworking vote, yes. And I'll guarantee, personally, that in five years the politics of Odin will have become so unbearably corrupt and abusive that the intellectuals, the technicians, the business people, even the nobility, will be flocking to the polls to vote, and if only half of them turn out, they'll snow the nonworkers under. And that'll mean, eventually, an end to vote-selling, and the nonworkers'll have to find work. We'll find it for them.''

"Great and frightening changes.'' Yorn Travann laughed; he recognized the phrase. Probably started it himself. Paul lifted his glass. "To the Minister of Disturbance!''

"Your Majesty!'' They drank to each other, and then Yorn Travann said, "We had a lot of wild dreams, when we were boys; it looks as though we're starting to make some of them come true. You know, when we were in the University, the students would never have done what they did today. They didn't even do it ten years ago, when Vann Evaratt was dismissed.''

"And Van Evaratt's pupil came back to Odin and touched this whole thing off.'' He thought for a moment. "I wonder what Faress has, in that anticipation effect.''

"I think I can see what can come out of it. If he can propagate a wave that behaves like those micropositos, we may not have to depend on ships for communication. We may be able, some day, to screen Baldur or Vishnu or Aton or Thor as easily as you screened Dorflay, up in the mountains.'' He thought silently for a moment. "I don't know whether that would be good or bad. But it would be new, and that's what matters. That's the only thing that matters.''

"Flower Festivals,'' Paul said, and, when Yorn Travann

wanted to know what he meant, he told him. "When Princess Olva's Empress, she's going to curse the name of Klenn Faress. Flower Festivals, all around the galaxy, without end."

Introduction to "The Return"

One of the many mysteries of the Terro-Human Future History is what happened to Terra after the fall of the Federation. There is no mention of Terra in Space Viking, "A Slave is a Slave," or "Ministry of Disturbance." Jerry Pournelle remembers Beam mentioning that Terra was bombed back to the Stone Age in one of the many wars that followed the Federation breakup. It is not until "The Keeper" that we hear of Terra again and then she is a backward world suffering badly under the harsh clime of a new Ice Age.

Like many other writers of the fifties and early sixties, Piper wrote a great deal about nuclear war and its possible effects. It is in the midst of a nuclear hellfire that the Terran Federation is born. But the peoples of the new Federation recover quite quickly, although the center of civilization has changed from the Northern to the Southern Hemisphere. In "The Return," the best of Beam's nuclear war stories, we learn of a time when the peoples of earth did not recover so quickly from the first atomic war. While this is not a Terro-Human Future History story, it does give us a good look at what life might have been like on Terra after the Interstellar Wars.

THE RETURN

ALTAMONT cast a quick, routine, glance at the instrument panels and then looked down through the transparent nose of the helicopter at the yellow-brown river five hundred feet below. Next he scraped the last morsel from his plate and ate it.

"What did you make this out of, Jim?" he asked. "I hope you kept notes, while you were concocting it. It's good."

"The two smoked pork chops left over from yesterday evening," Loudons said, "and that bowl of rice that's been taking up space in the refrigerator the last couple of days together with a little egg powder, and some milk. I ground the chops up and mixed them with the rice and other stuff. Then added some bacon, to make grease to fry it in."

Altamont chuckled. That was Loudons, all right; he could take a few left-overs, mess them together, pop them in a skillet, and have a meal that would turn the chef back at the fort green with envy. He filled his cup and offered the pot.

"Caffchoc?" he asked.

Loudons held his cup out to be filled, blew on it, sipped,

and then hunted on the ledge under the desk for the butt of the cigar he had half-smoked the evening before.

"Did you ever drink coffee, Monty?" the socio-psychologist asked, getting the cigar drawing to his taste.

"Coffee? No. I've read about it, of course. We'll have to organize an expedition to Brazil, some time, to get seeds, and try raising some."

Loudons blew a smoke ring toward the rear of the cabin.

"A much overrated beverage," he replied. "We found some, once, when I was on that expedition into Idaho, in what must have been the stockroom of a hotel. Vacuum-packed in moisture-proof containers, and free from radioactivity. It wasn't nearly as good as caffchoc. But then, I suppose, a pre-bustup coffee drinker couldn't stomach this stuff we're drinking." He looked forward, up the river they were following. "Get anything on the radio?" he asked. "I noticed you took us up to about ten thousand, while I was shaving."

Altamont got out his pipe and tobacco pouch, filling the former slowly and carefully. "Not a whisper. I tried Colony Three, in the Ozarks, and I tried to call in that tribe of workers in Louisiana; I couldn't get either."

"Maybe if we tried to get a little more power on the set—"

That was Loudons, too, Altamont thought. There wasn't a better man at the Fort, when it came to dealing with people, but confront him with a technological problem, and he was lost. That was one of the reasons why he and the stocky, phlegmatic social scientist made such a good team, he thought. As far as he, himself, was concerned, people were just a mysterious, exasperatingly unpredictable, order of things which were subject to no known natural laws. That was about the way Loudons thought of things; he couldn't psychoanalyze them.

He gestured with his pipe toward the nuclear-electric conversion unit, between the control cabin and the living quarters in the rear of the box-car-sized helicopter.

"We have enough power back there to keep this windmill in the air twenty-four hours a day, three hundred and sixty-five days a year, for the next fifteen years," he said. "We just don't have enough radio. If I'd step up the power on this set any more, it'd burn out before I could say, 'Altamont calling Fort Ridgeway.' "

"How far are we from Pittsburgh, now?" Loudons wanted to know.

Altamont looked across the cabin at the big map of the United States, with its red and green and blue and yellow patchwork of vanished political divisions, and the transparent overlay on which they had plotted their course. The red line started at Fort Ridgeway, in what had once been Arizona. It angled east by a little north, to Colony Three, in Northern Arkansas; then sharply northeast to St. Louis and its lifeless ruins; then Chicago and Gary, where little bands of Stone Age reversions stalked and fought and ate each other; Detroit, where things that had completely forgotten that they were human emerged from their burrows only at night; Cleveland, where a couple of cobalt bombs must have landed in the lake and drenched everything with radioactivity that still lingered after two centuries; Akron, where vegetation was only beginning to break through the glassy slag; Cincinnati, where they had last stopped—

"How's the leg, this morning, Jim?" he asked.

"Little stiff. Doesn't hurt much, though."

"Why, we're about fifty miles, as we follow the river, and that's relatively straight." He looked down through the transparent nose of the 'copter at a town, now choked with trees that grew through tumbled walls. "I think that's Aliquippa."

Loudons looked and shrugged, then looked again and pointed.

"There's a bear. Just ducked into that church or movie theater or whatever. I wonder what he thinks we are."

Altamont puffed slowly at his pipe. "I wonder if we're going to find anything at all in Pittsburgh."

"You mean people, as distinct from those biped beasts we've found so far? I doubt it," Loudons replied, finishing his caffchoc and wiping his mustache on the back of his hand.

"I think the whole eastern half of the country is nothing but forest like this, and the highest type of life is just about three cuts below *Homo Neanderthalensis,* almost impossible to contact, and even more impossible to educate."

"I wasn't thinking about that; I've just about given up hope of finding anybody or even a reasonably high level of barbarism," Altamont said. "I was thinking about that cache of microfilmed books that was buried at the Carnegie library."

"If it was buried," Loudon qualified. "All we have is that article in that two-century-old copy of *Time* about how the people at the library had constructed the crypt and were beginning the microfilming. We don't know if they ever had a chance to get it finished, before the rockets started landing." They passed over a dam of flotsam that had banked up at a wrecked bridge and accumulated enough mass to resist the periodic floods that had kept the river usually clear. Three human figures fled across a sand-flat at one end of it and disappeared into the woods; two of them carried spears tipped with something that sparkled in the sunlight, probably shards of glass.

"You know, Monty, I get nightmares, sometimes, about what things must be like in Europe," Loudons said.

Five or six wild cows went crashing through the brush below. Altamont nodded when he saw them.

"Maybe tomorrow, we'll let down and shoot a cow," he said. "I was looking in the freezer-locker; the fresh meat's getting a little low. Or a wild pig, if we find a good stand of oak trees. I could enjoy what you'd do with some acorn-fed pork. Finished?" He asked Loudons. "Take over, then; I'll go back and wash the dishes."

They rose and Loudons, favoring his left leg, moved over to the seat at the controls. Altamont gathered up the two cups, the stainless-steel dishes, and the knives and forks and spoons, going up the steps over the shielded converter and ducking his head to avoid the seat in the forward top machinegun turret. He washed and dried the dishes, noticing with satisfaction that the gauge of the water tank was still reasonably high, and glanced out one of the windows. Loudons was taking the helicopter upstairs, for a better view.

Now and then, among the trees, there would be a glint of glassy slag, usually in a fairly small circle. That was to be expected; beside the three or four H-bombs that had fallen on the Pittsburgh area, mentioned in the transcripts of the last news to reach the fort from outside, the whole district had been pelted, more or less at random, with fission bombs. West of the confluence of the Allegheny and Monongahela, it would probably be worse than this.

"Can you see Pittsburgh yet, Jim?" he called out.

"Yes; it's a mess! Worse than Gary; worse than Akron, even. *Monty!* Come here! I think I have something!"

Picking up the pipe he had laid down, Altamont hurried forward, dodging his six-foot length under the gun turret and swinging down from the walkway over the converter.

"What is it?" he asked.

"Smoke. A lot of smoke, twenty or thirty fires, at the very least." Loudons had shifted from *Forward* to *Hover*, and was peering through a pair of binoculars. "See that island, the long one? Across the river from it, on the north side, toward this end. Yes, by Einstein! And I can see cleared ground, and what I think are houses, inside the stockade—"

Murray Hughes walked around the corner of the cabin, into the morning sunlight, lacing his trousers, with his hunting shirt thrown over his shoulders, and found, without much surprise, that his father had also slept late. Verner Hughes was just beginning to shave. Inside the kitchen, his mother and the girls were clattering pots and skillets; his younger brother, Hector, was noisily chopping wood. Going through the door, he filled another of the light-metal basins with hot water, found his razor, and went outside again, setting the basin on the bench. Most of the ware in the Hughes cabin was of light-metal; Murray and his father had mined it in the dead city up the river, from the place where it had floated to the top of a puddle of slag, back when the city had been blasted, at the end of the Old Times. It had been hard work, but the stuff had been easy to carry down to where they had hidden their boat, and, for once, they'd had no trouble with the Scowrers. Too bad they couldn't say as much for yesterday's hunting trip!

As he rubbed lather into the stubble on his face, he cursed with irritation. That had been a bad-luck hunt, all around. They'd gone out before dawn, hunting into the hills to the north, they'd spent all day at it, and shot one small wild pig. Lucky it was small, at that. They'd have had to abandon a full-grown one, after the Scowrers began hunting them. Six of them, as big a band as he'd ever seen together at one time, and they'd gotten between them and the stockade and forced them to circle miles out of their way. His father had shot one, and he'd had to leave his hatchet sticking in skull of another, when his rifle had misfired. That meant another trip to the gunsmith's, for a new hatchet and to have the mainspring of the rifle replaced. Nobody could afford to have a rifle that couldn't be trusted, least of all a hunter and prospector. And he'd had words with Alex Barrett, the gunsmith, just the other day. Not that Barrett wouldn't be more than glad to do business with him, once he saw that hard tool-steel he'd dug out of that place down the river. Hardest steel he'd ever found, and hadn't been atom-spoiled, either.

He cleaned, wiped and stropped his razor and put it back in the case; he threw out the wash-water on the compost pile, and went into the cabin, putting on his shirt and his belt, and passed on through to the front porch, where his father was already eating at the table. The people of the Toon liked to eat in the open; it was something they'd always done, just as they'd always liked to eat together in the evenings.

He sweetened his mug of chicory with a lump of maple sugar and began to sip it before he sat down, standing with one foot on the bench and looking down across the parade ground, past the Aitch-Cue house, toward the river and the wall.

"If you're coming around to Alex's way of thinking—and mine—it won't hurt you to admit it, son," his father said.

He turned, looking at his father with the beginning of

anger, and then grinned. The elders were constantly keeping
the young men alert with these tests. He checked back over
his actions since he had come out onto the porch.

To the table, sugar in his chicory, one foot on the bench,
which had reminded him again of the absence of the hatchet
from his belt and brought an automatic frown. Then the
glance toward the gunsmith's shop, and across the parade
ground, at the houses into which so much labor had gone; the
wall that had been built from rubble and topped with pointed
stakes; the white slabs of marble from the ruined building that
marked the graves of the First Tenant and the men of the Old
Toon. He *had* thought, in that moment, that maybe his father
and Alex Barrett and Reader Rawson and Tenant Mycroft
Jones and the others were right—there were too many things
here that could not be moved along with them, if they decided
to move.

It would be false modesty, refusal to see things as they
were, not to admit that he was the leader of the younger men,
and the boys of the Irregulars. And last winter, the usual
theological arguments about the proper chronological order
of the Sacred Books and the true nature of the Risen One had
been replaced by a violent controversy when Sholto Jimenez
and Birdy Edwards had reopened the old question of the
advisability of moving the Toon and settling elsewhere. He'd
been in favor of the idea, himself, but for the last month or so
he had begun to doubt the wisdom of it. It was probably
reluctance to admit this to himself that had brought on the
strained feelings betwen himself and his old friend the
gunsmith.

''I'll have to drill the Irregulars, today,'' he said. ''Birdy
Edwards has been drilling them while we've been hunting.
But I'll go up and see Alex about a new hatchet and fixing my
rifle. I'll have a talk with him.''

He stepped forward to the edge of the porch. Still munching on a honey-dipped piece of cornbread, and glanced up in
the sky. That was a queer bird; he'd never seen a bird with
wing action like that. Then he realized that the object was not
a bird at all.

His father was staring at it, too.

"Murray! That's . . . that's like the old stories from the time of the wars!"

But Murray was already racing across the parade ground toward the Aitch-Cue House, where the big iron ring hung by its chain from a gallows-like post, with the hammer beside it.

The stockaded village grew larger, details became plainer, as the helicopter came slanting down and began spiraling around it. It was a fairly big place, some forty or fifty acres in a rough parallelogram, surrounded by a wall of varicolored stone and brick and concrete rubble from old ruins, topped with a palisade of pointed poles. There was a small jetty projecting out into the river, to which six or eight boats of different sorts were tied; a gate opened onto this from the wall. Inside the stockade, there were close to a hundred buildings, ranging from small cabins to a structure with a belfry, which seemed to have been a church, partly ruined in the war of two centuries ago and later rebuilt. A stream came down from the woods, across the cultivated land around the fortified village; there was a rough flume which carried the water from a dam close to the edge of the forest and provided a fall to turn a mill wheel.

"Look; strip-farming," Loudons pointed. "See the alternate strips of grass and plowed ground. Those people understand soil conservation. They have horses, too."

As he spoke, three riders left the village at a gallop, through a gate on the far side. They separated, and the people in the fields, who had all started for the village, turned and began hurrying toward the woods. Two of the riders headed for a pasture in which cattle had been grazing, and started herding them, also, into the woods. For a while, there was a scurrying of little figures in the village below, and then not a moving thing was in sight.

"There's good organization," Loudons said. "Everybody seems to know what to do, and how to get it done promptly. And look how neat the whole place is. I'll be anything we'll find that they have a military organization, or a military tradition, at least. We'll have to find out; you can't understand a people till you understand their background and their social organization.''

"Humph. Let me have a look at their artifacts; that'll tell me what kind of people they are,'' Altamont said, swinging his glasses back and forth over the enclosure. "Water-power mill, water-power sawmill—building on the left side of the water wheel; see the pile of fresh lumber beside it. Blacksmith shop, and from that chimney I'd say a small foundry, too. Wonder what that little building out on the tip of the island is; it has a water wheel. Undershot wheel, and it looks as though it could be raised or lowered. But the building's too small for a grist mill. Now, I wonder—''

"Monty, I think we ought to land right in the middle of the enclosure, on that open plaza thing, in front of that building that looks like a reconditioned church. That's probably the Royal Palace, or the Pentagon, or the Kremlin, or whatever.''

Altamont started to object, paused, and then nodded. "I think you're right, Jim. From the way they scattered, and got their livestock into the woods, they probably expect us to bomb them. We have to get inside; that's the quickest way to do it.'' He thought for a moment. "We'd better be armed, when we go out. Pistols, auto-carbines, and a few of those concussion-grenades in case we have to break up a concerted attack. I'll get them.''

The plaza and the houses and cabins around it, and the two-hundred-year-old church, were silent and, apparently, lifeless as they set the helicopter down. Once Loudons caught a movement inside the door of a house, and saw a metallic glint. Altamont pointed up at the belfry.

"There's a gun up there,'' he said. "Looks like about a four-pounder. Brass. I knew that smith-shop was also a foundry. See that little curl of smoke? That's the gunner's slow-match. I'd thought maybe that thing on the island was a powder mill. That would be where they'd put it. Probably extract their niter from the dung of their horses and cows. Sulfur probably from coal-mine drainage. Jim, this is really something!''

"I hope they don't cut loose on us with that thing," Loudons said, looking apprehensively at the brass-rimmed black muzzle that was covering them from the belfry. "I wonder if we ought to—Oh-oh, here they come!"

Three or four young men stepped out of the wide door of the old church. They wore fringed buckskin trousers and buckskin shirts and odd caps with visors to shade their eyes and similar beaks behind to protect the neck. They had powder horns and bullet pouches slung over their shoulders, and long rifles in their hands. They stepped aside as soon as they were out; carefully avoiding any gesture of menace, they stood watching the helicopter which had landed among them.

Three other men followed them out; they, too, wore buckskins, and the odd double-visored caps. One had a close-cropped white beard, and on the shoulders of his buckskin shirt he wore the single silver bars of a first lieutenant of the vanished United States Army. He had a pistol on his belt; it had the saw-handle grip of an automatic, but it was a flintlock, as were the rifles of the young men who stood watchfully on either side of the two middle-aged men who accompanied him. The whole party advanced toward the helicopter.

"All right; come on, Monty," Loudons opened the door and let down the steps. Picking up an auto-carbine, he slung it and stepped out of the helicopter, Altamont behind him. They advanced to meet the party from the old church, halting when they were about twenty feet apart.

"I must apologize, lieutenant, for dropping in on you so unceremoniously." He stopped, wondering if the man with the white beard understood a word of what he was saying.

"The natural way to come in, when you travel in the air," the old man replied. "At least you came in openly. I can promise you a better reception than you got at that city to the west of us a couple of days ago.''

"Now how did you know we'd had trouble at Cincinnati day-before-yesterday?'' Loudons demanded.

The old man's eyes sparkled with childlike pleasure. "That surprises you, my dear sir? In a moment, I daresay, you'll be amazed at the simplicity of it. You have a nasty rip in the left leg of your trousers, and the cloth around it is stained with blood. Through the rip, I perceive a bandage. Obviously, you have suffered a recent wound. I further observe that the side of your flying machine bears recent scratches, as though from the spears or throwing-hatchets of the Scowrers. Evidently they attacked you as you were leaving it; it is fortunate that these cannibal devils are too stupid and too anxious for human flesh to exercise patience.''

"Well, that explains how you knew we'd been recently attacked,'' Loudons told him. "But how did you guess that it had been to the west of here, in a ruined city?''

"I never guess,'' the oldster with the silver bar and the keystone-shaped patch on his left shoulder replied. "It is a shocking habit—destructive to the logical faculty. What seems strange to you is only so because you do not follow my train of thought. For example, the wheels and their frame work under your flying machine are splashed with mud which seems to be predominantly brick-dust, mixed with plaster. Obviously you landed recently in a dead city, either during or after a rain. There was a rain here yesterday evening, the wind being from the west. Obviously, you followed behind the rain as it came up the river. And now that I look at your boots, I see traces of the same sort of mud, around the soles and in front of the heels. But this is heartless of us, keeping you standing here on a wounded leg, sir. Come in, and let our medic look at it.''

"Well, thank you, Lieutenant,'' Loudons replied. "But don't bother your medic; I've attended to the wound myself, and it wasn't serious to begin with.''

"You are a doctor?'' the white-bearded man asked.

"Of sorts. A sort of general scientist. My name is
Loudons. My friend, Mr. Altamont, here, is a scientist,
also."

There was an immediate reaction; all three of the elders of
the village, and the young riflemen who had accompanied
them, exchanged glances of surprise. Loudons dropped his
hand to the grip of his slung auto-carbine, and Altamont
sidled unobtrusively away from him, his hand moving as if
by accident toward the butt of his pistol. The same thought
was in both men's minds, that these people might feel, as a
heritage of the war of two centuries ago, a hostility to science
and scientists. There was no hostility, however, in their
manner as the old man advanced and held out his hand.

I am Tenant Mycroft Jones, the Toon Leader here," he
said. "This is Stanford Rawson, our Reader, and Verner
Hughes, our Toon Sarge. This is his son, Murray Hughes,
the Toon Sarge of the Irregulars. But come into the Aitch-
Cue House, gentlemen. We have much to talk about."

By this time the villagers had begun to emerge from the log
cabins and rubble-walled houses around the plaza and the old
church. Some of them, mostly young men, were carrying
rifles, but the majority were unarmed. About half of them
were women, in short deerskin or homespun dresses; there
were a number of children, the younger ones almost completely naked.

"Sarge," the old man told one of the youths, "post a
guard over this flying machine; don't let anybody meddle
with it. And have all the noncoms and techs report here, on
the double." He turned and shouted up at the truncated
steeple: "Atherton, sound 'All Clear!' "

A horn, up in the belfry, began blowing, to advise the
people who had run from the fields into the woods that there
was no danger.

They went through the open doorway of the old stone
church, and entered the big room inside. The building had
evidently been gutted by fire, two centuries before, and

portions of the wall had been restored. Now there was a rough plank floor, and a plank ceiling at about twelve feet; the room was apparently used as a community center. There were a number of benches and chairs, all very neatly made, and along one wall, out of the way, ten or fifteen long tables had been stacked, the tops in a pile and the trestles on them. The walls were decorated with trophies of weapons—a number of old M-14 rifles and M-16 submachine guns, all in good clean condition, a light machine rifle, two bazookas. Among them were stone- and metal-tipped spears and crude hatchets and knives and clubs, the work of the wild men of the woods. A stairway led up to the second floor, and it was up this that the man who bore the title of Toon Leader conducted them, to a small room furnished with a long table, a number of chairs, and several big wooden chests bound with iron.

"Sit down, gentlemen," the Toon Leader invited, going to a cupboard and producing a large bottle stopped with a corncob and a number of small cups. "It's a little early in the day," he said, "but this is a very special occasion. You smoke a pipe, I take it?" he asked Altamont. "Then try some of this; of our own growth and curing." He extended a doeskin moccasin, which seemed to be the tobacco container.

Altamont looked at the thing dubiously, then filled his pipe from it. The oldster drew his pistol, pushed a little wooden plug into the vent, added some tow to the priming, and, aiming at the wall, snapped it. Evidently, at times, the formality of plugging the vent had been overlooked; there were a number of holes in the wall there. This time, however, the pistol didn't go off. He shook out the smoldering tow, blew it into flame, and lit a candle from it, offering the light to Altamont. Loudons got out a cigar and lit it from the candle; the others filled and lighted pipes. The Toon Leader reprimed his pistol, then holstered it, took off his belt and laid it aside, an example the others followed.

They drank ceremoniously, and then seated themselves at

the table. As they did, two more men came into the room;
they were introduced as Alexander Barrett, the gunsmith,
and Stanley Markovitch, the distiller.

"You come, then, from the west?" the Toon Leader
began by asking.

"Are you from Utah?" the gunsmith interrupted, suspiciously.

"Why, no; we're from Arizona. A place called Fort
Montgomery," Loudons said.

The others nodded, in the manner of people who wish to
conceal to ignorance; it was obvious that none of them had
ever heard of Fort Ridgeway, or Arizona either.

"We've been in what used to be Utah," Altamont said.
"There's nobody there but a few Indians, and a few whites
who are even less civilized."

"You say you come from a fort? Then the wars aren't
over, yet?" Sarge Hughes asked.

"The wars have been over for a long time. You know how
terrible they were. You know how few in all the country were
left alive," Loudons said.

"None that we know of, beside ourselves and the Scowrers until you came," the Toon Leader said.

"We have found only a few small groups, in the whole
country, who have managed to save anything of the Old
Times. Most of them lived in little villages and cultivated
land. A few had horses, or cows. None, that we have ever
found before, made guns and powder for themselves. But
they remembered that they were men, and did not eat one
another. Whenever we find a group of people like this, we try
to persuade them to let us help them."

"Why?" the Toon Leader asked. "Why do you do this for
people you've never met before? What do you want from
them—from us—in return for your help?" He was speaking
to Altamont, rather than to Loudons; it seemed obvious that
he believed Altamont to be the leader and Loudons the
subordinate.

"Because we're trying to bring back the best things of the
Old Times," Altamont told him. "Look; you've had trou-

bles, here. So have we, many times. Years when the crops failed; years of storms, or floods; troubles with the beast-men in the woods. And you were alone, as we were, with no one to help. We want to put all men who are still men in touch with one another, so that they can help each other in trouble, and work together. If this isn't done soon, everything which makes men different from beasts will soon be no more."

"He's right. One of us, alone, is helpless," the Reader said. "It is only in the Toon that there is strength. He wants to organize a Toon of all Toons."

"That's about it. We are beginning to make helicopters like the one Loudons and I came here in. We'll furnish your community with one or more of them. We can give you a radio, so that you can communicate with other communities. We can give you rifles and machine guns and ammunition, to fight the . . . the Scowrers, did you call them? And we can give you atomic engines, so that you can build machines for yourselves."

"Some of our people—Alex Barrett, here, the gunsmith, and Stan Markovitch, the distiller, and Harrison Grant, the iron worker—get their living by making things. How'd they make out after your machines come in here?" Verner Hughes asked.

"We've thought of that; we had that problem with other groups we've helped," Loudons said. "In some communities, everyone owns everything, in common; we don't have much of a problem, there. Is that the way you do it, here?"

"Well, no. If a man makes a thing or digs it out of the ruins, or catches it in the woods, it's his."

"Then we'll work out some way. Give the machines to the people who are already in a trade, or something like that. We'll have to talk it over with you and the people who'd be concerned."

"How is it you took so long finding us," Alex Barrett asked. "It's been two hundred years or so since the Wars."

"Alex! You see but you do not observe!" the Toon Leader rebuked. "These people have their flying machines, which are highly complicated mechanisms. They would have to make tools and machines to make them, and tools and machines to make those tools and machines. They would have to find materials, often going far in search of them. The marvel is not that they took so long, but that they did it so quickly.''

"That's right," Altamont said. "Originally, Fort Ridgeway was a military research and development center. As the country became disorganized, the Government set this project up, to develop ways of improvising power and transportation and communication methods and extracting raw materials. If they'd had a little more time, they might have saved the country. As it was, they were able to keep themselves alive and keep something going at the Fort, while the whole country was breaking up around them. Then, when the rockets stopped falling, they started to rebuild. Fortunately, more than half of the technicians at the Fort were women; there was no question of them dying out. But it's only been in the last twenty years that we've been able to make nuclear-electric engines, and this is the first time any of us have gotten east of the Mississippi.''

"How did your group manage to survive?" Loudons said. "You call it the Toon; I suppose that's what the word platoon has become, with time. You were, originally, a military platoon?''

"*Pla*-toon!'' the white-bearded man said. "Of all the unpardonable stupidity! Of course that was what it was. And the title, Tenant, was originally *Lieu*-tenant; I know that, though we have all dropped the first part of the word. That should have led me, if I'd used my wits, to deduce platoon from toon.

"Yes, sir. We were originally a platoon of soldiers, two hundred years ago, at the time when the Wars ended. The Old Toon, and the First Tenant, were guarding pows, whatever they were. The pows were all killed by a big bomb, and the First Tenant, Lieutenant Gilbert Dunbar, took his . . . his platoon and started to march to Deecee, where the Government was. But there was no government, any more. They fought with the people along the way. When they needed food, or ammunition, or animals to pull their wagons, they took them, and killed those who tried to prevent them. Other people joined the Toon, and when they found women whom they wanted, they took them. They did all sorts of things that would have been crimes if there had been any law, but since there was no law any longer, it was obvious that there could be no crime. The first Ten—Lieutenant—kept his men together, because he had the books. Each evening, at the end of each day's march, he read to his men out of them.

"Finally, they came here. There had been a town here, but it had been burned and destroyed, and there were people camping in the ruins. Some of them fought and were killed; others came in and joined the platoon. At first, they built shelters around this building, and made this their fort. Then they cleared away the ruins, and built new houses. When the cartridges for the rifles began to get scarce, they began to make gunpowder, and new rifles, like those we are using now, to shoot without cartridges. Lieutenant Dunbar did this out of his own knowledge, because there is nothing in The Books about making gunpowder; the guns in The Books are rifles and shotguns and revolvers and airguns; except for the airguns, which we haven't been able to make, these all shot cartridges. As with your people, we did not die out, because we had women. Neither did we increase greatly—too many died or were killed young. But several times we've had to tear down the wall and rebuild it, to make room inside it for more houses, and we've been clearing a little more land for fields each year. We still read and follow the teachings of The Books; we have made laws for ourselves out of them."

"And we are waiting here, for the Slain and Risen One," Tenant Jones added, looking at Altamont intently. "It is impossible that He will not, sooner or later, deduce the existence of this community. If he has not done so already.

"Well, sir," the Toon Leader changed the subject abruptly, "enough of this talk about the past. If I understand rightly, it is the future in which you gentlemen are interested." He pushed back the cuff of his hunting shirt and looked at an old and worn wrist watch. "Eleven hundred; we'll have lunch shortly. This afternoon, you will meet the other people of the Toon, and this evening, at eighteen-hundred, we'll have a mess together outdoors. Then, when we have everybody together, we can talk over your offer to help us, and decide what it is that you can give us that we can use."

"You spoke, a while ago, of what you could do for us in return," Altamont said. "There's one thing you can do, no further away than tomorrow, if you're willing."

"And that is—"

"In Pittsburgh, somewhere, there is an underground crypt, full of books. Not bound and printed books; spools of microfilm. You know what that is?"

The others shook their heads. Altamont continued:

"They are spools on which strips are wound, on which pictures have been taken of books, page by page. We can make other, larger pictures from them, big enough to be read—"

"Oh, photographs, which you enlarge. I understand that. You mean, you can make many copies of them?"

"That's right. And you shall have copies, as soon as we can take the originals back to Fort Ridgeway, where we have equipment for enlarging them. But while we have information which will help us to find the crypt where the books are, we will need help in getting it open."

"Of course! This is wonderful. Copies of The Books!" the Reader exclaimed. "We thought we had the only one left in the world!"

"Not just The Books, Stamford; other books," the Toon Leader told him. "The books which are mentioned in The Books. But of course we will help you. You have a map to show us where they are?"

"Not a map; just some information. But we can work out the location of the crypt."

"A ritual," Stamford Rawson said happily. "Of course."

They lunched together at the house of Toon Sarge Hughes

with the Toon Leader and five or six of the leaders of the community. The food was plentiful, but Altamont found himself wishing that the first book they found in the Carnegie library crypt would be a cook book.

In the afternoon, he and Loudons separated. The latter attached himself to the Tenant, the Reader, and an old woman, Irene Klein, who was almost a hundred years old and was the repository and arbiter of most of the company's oral legends. Altamont, on the other hand, started, with Alex Barrett, the gunsmith, and Mordecai Ricci, the miller, to inspect the gunshop and grist mill. Joined by half a dozen more of the village craftsmen, they visited the forge and foundry, the sawmill, the wagon shop. Altamont looked at the flume, a rough structure of logs lined with sheet aluminum, and at the nitriary, a shed-roofed pit in which potassium nitrate was extracted from the community's animal refuse. Then, loading his guides into the helicopter, they took off for a visit to the gunpowder mill on the island and a trip up the river.

They were a badly scared lot, for the first few minutes, as they watched the ground receding under them through the transparent plastic nose. Then, when nothing disastrous seemed to be happening, exhilaration took the place of fear, and by the time they set down on the tip of the island, the eight men were confirmed aviation enthusiasts. The trip up-river was an even bigger success; the high point came when Altamont set his controls for *Hover*, pointed out a snarl of driftwood in the stream, and allowed his passengers to fire one of the machine guns at it. The lead balls of their own black-powder rifles would have plunked into the water-logged wood without visible effect; the copper-jacketed machine-gun bullets ripped it to splinters. They returned for a final visit to the distillery awed by what they had seen.

"Monty, I don't know what the devil to make of this crowd," Loudons said, that evening, after the feast, when they had entered the helicopter and prepared to retire. "We've run into some weird communities—that lot down in

Old Mexico who live in the church and claim they have a divine mission to redeem the world by prayer, fasting and flagellation, or those yogis in Los Angeles—''

"Or the Blackout Boys in Detroit," Altamont added.

"That's understandable," Loudons said, "after what their ancestors went through in the Last War. But this crowd, here! The descendants of an old United States Army infantry platoon, with a fully developed religion centered on a slain and resurrected god—normally, it would take thousands of years for a slain-god religion to develop, and then only from the field-fertility magic of primitive agriculturists. Well, you saw these people's fields from the air. Some of the members of that platoon were men who knew the latest methods of scientific farming; they didn't need naive fairy tales about the planting and germination of seed.''

"Sure this religion isn't just a variant of Christianity?''

"Absolutely not. In the first place, these Sacred Books can't be the Bible—you heard Tenant Jones say that they mentioned firearms that used cartridges. That means that they can't be older than 1860 at the very earliest. And in the second place, this slain god wasn't crucified or put to death by any form of execution; he perished, together with his enemy, in combat, and both god and devil were later resurrected. The Enemy is supposed to be the master mind in back of these cannibal savages in the woods and also in the ruins.''

"Did you get a look at these Sacred Books, or find out what they might be?''

Loudons shook his head disgustedly. "Every time I brought up the question, they evaded. The Tenant sent the Reader out to bring in this old lady, Irene Klein—she was a perfect gold mine about the history and traditions of the Toon, by the way—and then he sent him out on some other errand, undoubtedly to pass the word not to talk to us about their religion.''

"I don't get that," Altamont said. "They showed me everything they had—their gunshop, their powder mill, their defenses, everything." He smoked in silence for a moment.

"Say, this slain god couldn't be the original platoon commander, could he?"

"No. They have the greatest respect for his memory—decorate his grave regularly, drink toasts to him—but he hasn't been deified. They got the idea for this deity of theirs out of the sacred books." Loudons gnawed the end of his cigar and frowned. "Monty, this has me worried like the devil, because I believe that they suspect that you are the Slain and Risen One."

"Could be, at that. I know the Tenant came up to me, very respectfully, and said, 'I hope you don't think, sir, that I was presumptuous in trying to display my humble deductive abilities to *you*.' "

"What did you say?" Loudons demanded rather sharply.

"Told him certainly not; that he'd used a good quick method of demonstrating that he and his people weren't like those mindless subhumans in the woods."

"That was all right. I don't know how we're going to handle this. They only suspect that you are their deity. As it stands, now, we're on trial, here. And I get the impression that logic, not faith, seems to be their supreme religious virtue; that skepticism is a religious obligation instead of a sin. That's something else that's practically unheard of. I wish I knew—"

Tenant Mycroft Jones, and Reader Stamford Rawson, and Toon Sarge Verner Hughes, and his son Murray Hughes, sat around the bare-topped table in the room, on the second floor of the Aitch-Cue House. A lighted candle flickered in the cool breeze that came in through the open window, throwing their shadows back and forth on the walls.

"Pass the tantalus, Murray," the Tenant said, and the youngest of the four handed the corncob-corked bottle to the eldest. Tenant Jones filled his cup, and then sat staring at it, while Verner Hughes thrust his pipe into the toe of the moccassin and filled it. Finally, he drank about half of the clear, wild-plum brandy.

"Gentlemen, I am baffled," he confessed. "We have three alternate possibilities here, and we dare not disregard any of them. Either this man who calls himself Altamont is truly He, or he is merely what we are asked to believe, one of a community like ours, with more of the old knowledge than we possess."

"You know my views," Verner Hughes said. "I cannot believe that He was more than a man, as we are. A great, a good, a wise man, but a man and mortal."

"Let's not go into that, now." The Reader emptied his cup and took the bottle, filling it again. "You know my views, too. I hold that he is no longer upon earth in the flesh, but lives in the spirit and is only with us in the spirit. There are three possibilities, too, none of which can be eliminated. But what was your third possibility, Tenant?"

"That they are creatures of the Enemy. Perhaps one or the other of them *is* the Enemy."

Reader Rawson, lifting his cup to his lips, almost strangled. The Hugheses, father and son, stared at Tenant Jones in horror.

"The Enemy—with such weapons and resources!" Murray Hughes gasped. Then he emptied his cup and refilled it. "No! I can't believe that; he'd have struck before this and wiped us all out!"

"Not necessarily, Murray," the Tenant replied. "Until he became convinced that his agents, the Scowrers, could do nothing against us, he would bide his time. He sits motionless, like a spider, at the center of the web; he does little himself; his agents are numerous. Or, perhaps, he wishes to recruit us into his hellish organization."

"It is a possibility," Reader Rawson admitted. "One which we can neither accept nor reject safely. And we must learn the truth as soon as possible. If this man is really He, we must not spurn him on mere suspicion. If he is a man, come to help us, we must accept his help; if he is speaking the truth, the people who sent him could do wonders for us, and the greatest wonder would be to make us, again, a part of a civilized community. And if he is the Enemy—"

"If it is really He," Murray said, "I think we are on trial."

"What do you mean, son? Oh, I see. Of course, I don't believe he is, but that's mere doubt, not negative certainty. But if I'm wrong, if this man is truly He, we are being tested. He has come among us incognito; if we are worthy of him, we will penetrate His disguise."

"A very pretty problem, gentlemen," the Tenant said, smacking his lips over his brandy. "For all that it may be a deadly serious one for us. There is, of course, nothing that we can do tonight. But tomorrow, we have promised to help our visitors, whoever they may be, in searching for this crypt in the city. Murray, you were to be in charge of the detail that was to accompany them. Carry on as arranged, and say nothing of our suspicions, but advise your men to keep a sharp watch on the strangers, that they may learn all they can from them. Stamford, you and Verner and I will go along. We should, if we have any wits at all, observe something."

"Listen to this infernal thing!" Altamont raged. "*Wielding a gold-plated spade handled with oak from an original rafter of the Congressional Library, at three-fifteen one afternoon last week—*' One afternoon last week!" He cursed luridly. "Why couldn't that blasted magazine say *what* afternoon? I've gone over a lot of twentieth-century copies of that magazine; that expression was a regular cliché with them."

Loudons looked over his shoulder at the photostated magazine page.

"Well, we know it was between June thirteen and Nineteen, inclusive," he said. "And there's a picture of the university president, complete with gold-plated spade, breaking ground. Call it Wednesday the sixteenth. Over there's the tip of the shadow of the Cathedral of Learning, about a hundred yards away. There are so many inexactitudes that one'll probably cancel out another."

"That's so, and it's also pretty futile getting angry at somebody who's been dead two hundred years, but why couldn't they say Wednesday, or Monday, or Saturday, or whatever?'' He checked back in the astronomical handbook, and the photostated pages of the old almanac, and looked over his calculations. "All right, here's the angle of the shadow, and the compass-bearing. I had a look, yesterday, when I was taking the local citizenry on that junket. The old baseball diamond at Forbes Field is plainly visible, and I located the ruins of the Cathedral of Learning from that. Here's the above-sea-level altitude of the top of the tower. After you've landed us, go up to this altitude—use the barometric altimeter, not the radar—and hold position.''

Loudons leaned forward from the desk to the contraption Altamont had rigged in the nose of the helicopter—one of the telescope-sighted hunting rifles clamped in a vise, with a compass and spirit-level under it.

''Rifle's pointing downward at the correct angle now?'' he asked. "Good. Then all I have to do is hold the helicopter steady, keep it at the right altitude, level, and pointed in the right direction, and watch through the sight while you move the flag around, and direct you by radio. Why wasn't I born quintuplets?''

"Mr. Altamont! Dr. Loudons!'' A voice outside the helicopter called. "Are you ready for us, now?''

Altamont went to the open door and looked out. The Old Toon Leader, the Reader, Toon Sarge Hughes, his son, and four young men in buckskins with slung rifles, were standing outside.

"I have decided,'' the Tenant said, "that Mr. Rawson and Sarge Hughes and I would be of more help than an equal number of younger men. We may not be as active, but we know the old ruins better, especially the paths and hiding places of the Scowrers. There four young men you probably met last evening; it will do no harm to introduce them again. Birdy Edwards, Sholto Jiminez, Jefferson Burns, Murdo Olsen.''

"Very pleased, Tenant, gentlemen. I met you all last evening, I remember you,'' Altamont said. "Now, if you'll all crowd in here, I'll explain what we're going to try to do.''

He showed them the old picture. "You see where the

shadow of a tall building falls? We know the location and height of this building. Dr. Loudons will hold this helicopter at exactly the position of the top of the building, and aim through the sights of the rifle, there. One of you will have this flag in his hand, and will move it back and forth; Dr. Loudons will tell us when the flag is in the sight of the rifle.''

"He'll need a good pair of lungs to do that," Verner Hughes commented.

"We'll use radio. A portable set on the ground, and the helicopter's radio set." He was met, to his surprise, with looks of incomprehension. He had not supposed that these people would have lost all memory of radio communication.

"Why, that's wonderful!" the Reader exclaimed, when he explained. "You can talk directly; how much better than just sending a telegram!"

"But finding the crypt by the shadow; that's exactly like—" Murray Hughes began, then stopped short. Immediately, he began talking loudly about the rifle that was to be used as a surveying transit, comparing it with the ones in the big first-floor room at the Aitch-Cue House.

Locating the point on which the shadow of the old Cathedral of Learning had fallen proved easier than either Altamont or Loudons had expected. The towering building was now a tumbled mass of slagged rubble, but it was quite possible to determine its original center, and with the old data from the excellent reference library at Fort Ridgeway, its height above sea level was known. After a little jockeying, the helicopter came to a hovering stop, and the slanting barrel of the rifle in the vise pointed downward along the line of shadow that had been cast on that afternoon in June, 1993, the cross-hairs of the scope-sight centered almost exactly on the spot Altamont had estimated on the map. While he peered through the sight, Loudons brought the helicopter slanting down to land on the sheet of fused glass that had once been a grassy campus.

"Well, this is probably it," Altamont said. "We didn't have to bother fussing around with the flag, after all. That

hump, over there, looks as though it had been a small building, and there's nothing corresponding to it on the city map.
That may be the bunker over the stair-head to the crypt.''

They began unloading equipment—a small, portable
nuclear-electric conversion unit, a powerful solenoid-
hammer, crowbars and intrenching tools, tins of blasting-
plastic. They took out the two hunting rifles, and the auto-
carbines, and Altamont showed the young men of Murray
Hughes' detail how to use them.

"If you'll pardon me, sir," the Tenant said to Altamont,
"I think it would be a good idea if your companion went up in
the flying machine and circled around over us, to keep watch
for Scowrers. There are quite a few of them, particularly
farther up the river, to the east, where the damage was not so
great and they can find cellars and shelters and buildings to
live in."

"Good idea; that way, we won't have to put out guards,"
Altamont said. "From the looks of this, we'll need everybody to help dig into that thing. Hand out the portable radios,
Jim, and go up to about a thousand feet. If you see anything
suspicious, give us a yell; then spray it with bullets, and find
out what it is afterward."

They waited until the helicopter had climbed to position
and was circling above, and then turned their attention to the
place where the sheet of stone and fused earth bulged upward. It must have been almost ground-zero of one of the
hydrogen-bombs; the wreckage of the Cathedral of Learning
had fallen predominantly to the north, and the Carnegie
Library was tumbled to the east.

"I think the entrance would be on this side, toward the
Library," Altamont said. "Let's try it, to begin with."

He used the solenoid hammer, slowly pounding a hole into
the glaze, and placed a small charge of plastic explosive.
Chunks of the lavalike stuff pelted down between the little
mound and the huge one of the old library, blowing a hole six
feet in diameter and two and a half deep, revealing concrete
bonded with crushed steel-mill slag.

"We missed the door," he said. "That means we'll have

to tunnel in through who knows how much concrete. Well—''

He used a second and larger charge, after digging a hole a foot deep. When he and his helpers came up to look, they found a large mass of concrete blown out, and solid steel behind it. Altamont cut two more holes sidewise, one on either side of the blown-out place, and fired a charge in each of them, bringing down more concrete. He found that he hadn't missed the door, after all. It had merely been concreted over.

A few more shots cleared it, and, after some work, they got it open. There was a room inside, concrete floored and entirely empty. With the others crowding behind him, Altamont stood in the doorway and inspected the interior with his flashlight; he heard somebody back of him say something about a most peculiar sort of dark-lantern. Across the room, on the opposite wall, was a bronze plaque.

It carried quite a lengthy inscription, including the names of all the persons and institutions participating in the microfilm project. The History Department at the Fort would be most interested in that, but the only thing that interested Altamont was the statement that the floor had been laid over the trapdoor leading to the vaults where the microfilms were stored.

"Hello, Jim. We're inside, but the films are stored in an underground vault, and we have to tear up a concrete floor,'' he said. "Go back to the village and gather up all the men you can carry, and tools. Hammers and picks and short steel bars. I don't want to use explosives inside. The interior of the crypt oughtn't to be damaged, and I don't know what a blast in here might do to the film. I don't want to take chances.''

"No, of course not. How thick do you think the floor is?''

"Haven't the least idea. Plenty thick, I'd say. Those films would have to be well buried, to shield them from radioactivity. We can expect that it'll take some time.''

"All right. I'll be back as soon as I can.''

The helicopter turned and went windmilling away, over what had been the Golden Triangle, down the Ohio, Altamont went back to the little concrete bunker and sat down, lighting his pipe. Murray Hughes and his four riflemen spread out, one circling around the glazed butte that had been the Cathedral of Learning, another climbing to the top of the Old Library, and the others taking positions to the south and east.

Altamont sat in silence, smoking his pipe and trying to form some conception of the wealth under that concrete floor. It was no use. Jim Loudons probably understood a little more nearly what those books would mean to the world of today, and what they could do toward shaping the world of the future. There was a library at Fort Ridgeway, and it was an excellent one—for its purpose. In 1996, when the rockets had come crashing down, it had contained the cream of the world's technical knowledge—and very little else. There was a little fiction, a few books of ideas, just enough to give the survivors a tantalizing glimpse of the world of their fathers. But now—

A rifle banged to the south and east, and banged again. Either Murray Hughes or Birdy Edwards—it was one of the two hunting rifles from the helicopter. On the heels of the reports, they heard a voice shouting: "Scowrers! A lot of them, coming up from the river!" A moment later, there was the light whip-crack of one of the long muzzle-loaders, from the top of the old Carnegie Library, and Altamont could see a wisp of gray-white smoke drifting away from where it had been fired. He jumped to his feet and raced for the radio, picking it up and bringing it to the bunker.

Tenant Jones, old Reader Rawson, and Verner Hughes had caught up their rifles. The Tenant was shouting, "Come on in! Everybody, come in!" The boy on top of the library began scrambling down. Another came running from the direction of the half-demolished Cathedral of Learning, a third from the baseball field that had served as Altamont's point of reference the afternoon before. The fourth, Murray Hughes, was running in from the ruins of the old Carnegie Tech buildings, and Birdy Edwards sped up the main road from Shenley Park. Once or twice, as he ran, Murray Hughes paused, turned, and fired behind him.

Then his pursuers came into sight. They ran erect, and they wore a few rags of skin garments, and they carried spears and hatchets and clubs, so they were probably classifiable as men. Their hair was long and unkempt; their bodies were almost black with dirt and from the sun. A few of them were yelling; most of them ran silently. They ran more swiftly than the boy they were pursuing; the distance between them narrowed every moment. There were at least fifty of them.

Verner Hughes rifle barked; one of them dropped. As coolly as though he were shooting squirrels instead of his son's pursuers, he dropped the butt of his rifle to the ground, poured a charge of powder, patched a ball and rammed it home, replaced the ramrod. Tenant Jones fired then, and then Birdy Edwards joined them and began shooting with the telescope-sighted hunting rifle. The young man who had been north of the Cathedral of Learning had one of the auto-carbines; Altamont had providently set the fire-control for semi-auto before giving it to him. He dropped to one knee and began to empty the clip, shooting slowly and deliberately, picking off the runners who were in the lead. The boy who had started to climb down off the library halted, fired his flintlock, and began reloading it. And Altamont, sitting down and propping his elbows on his knees, took both hands to the automatic which was his only weapon, emptying the magazine and replacing it. The last three of the savages he shot in the back; they had had enough and were running for their lives.

So far, everybody was safe. The boy in the library came down through a place where the wall had fallen. Murray Hughes stopped running and came slowly toward the bunker, putting a fresh clip into his rifle. The others came drifting in.

"Altamont calling Loudons," the scientist from Fort Ridgeway was saying into the radio. "Monty to Jim; can you hear me, Jim?"

Silence.

"We'd better get ready for another attack," Birdy Edwards said. "There's another gang coming down from that way. I never saw so many Scowrers!"

"Maybe there's a reason, Birdy," Tenant Jones said. "The Enemy is after big game, this time."

"Jim! Where the devil are you?" Altamont fairly yelled into the radio, and as he did, he knew the answer. Loudons was in the village, away from the helicopter, gathering tools and workers. Nothing to do but keep on trying.

"Here they come!" Reader Rawson warned.

"How far can these rifles be depended on?" Birdy Edwards wanted to know.

Altamont straightened, saw the second band of savages approaching, about four hundred yards away.

"Start shooting now," he said. "Aim for the upper part of their bodies."

The two auto-loading rifles began to crack. After a few shots, the savages took cover. Evidently they understood the capabilities and limitations of the villagers' flintlocks; this was a terrifying surprise to them.

"Jim!" Altamont was almost praying into the radio. "Come in, Jim!"

"What is it, Monty? I was outside."

Altamont told him.

"Those fellows you had up with you yesterday; think they could be trusted to handle the guns? A couple of them are here with me," Loudons inquired.

"Take a chance on it; it won't cost you anything but my life, and that's not worth much at present."

"All right; hold on. We'll be along in a few minutes."

"Loudons is bringing the helicopter," he told the others. "All we have to do is hold on here, till he comes."

A naked savage raised his head from behind what might, two hundred years ago, have been a cement park bench, a hundred yards away. Reader Stamford Rawson promptly killed him and began reloading.

"I think you're right, Tenant," he said. "The Scowrers

have never attacked in bands like this before.'' They must
have had a powerful reason, and I can think of only one.''

"That's what I'm beginning to think, too,'' Verner
Hughes agreed. "At least, we have eliminated the third of
your possibilities, Tenant. And I think probably the second,
as well.''

Altamont wondered what they were double-talking about.
There wasn't any particular mystery about the mass attack of
the wild men to him. Debased as they were, they still possessed speech and the ability to transmit experiences. No
matter how beclouded in superstition, they still remembered
that aircraft dropped bombs, and bombs killed people; and
where people had been killed, they would find fresh meat.
They had seen the helicopter circling about and heard the
blasting; every one in the area had been drawn to the scene as
soon as Loudons had gone down the river.

Maybe they had also forgotten that aircraft also carried
guns. At least, when they sprang to their feet and started to
run at the return of the helicopter, many did not run far.

Altamont and Loudons shook hands many times in front of
the Aitch-Cue House, and listened to many good wishes, and
repeated their promise to return. Most of the microfilmed
books were still stored in the old church; they were taking
away with them only the catalog and a few of the more
important works. Finally, they entered the helicopter. The
crowd shouted farewell, as they rose.

Altamont, at the controls, waited until they had gained five
thousand feet, then turned on a compass-course for Colony
Three.

"I can't wait till we're in radio range of the Fort, to report
this, Jim,'' he said. "Of all the wonderful luck! And I don't
yet know which is more important; finding those books, or
finding those people. In a few years, when we can get them
supplied with modern equipment and instructed in its use—''

"I'm not very happy about it, Monty,'' Loudons confessed. "I keep thinking about what's going to happen to
them.''

"Why, nothing's going to happen to them. They're going to be given the means of producing more food, keeping more of them alive, having more leisure to develop themselves in—"

"Monty, I saw the Sacred Books."

"The Deuce! What were they?"

"It. One volume; a collection of works. We have it at the Fort; I've read it. How I ever missed all the clues—you see, Monty, what I'm worried about is what's going to happen to those people when they find out that we're not really Sherlock Holmes and Doctor Watson."

Introduction to "The Keeper"

This is the last of the Terro-Human Future History stories set at the time of the far-distant Fifth Galactic Empire. It takes place on a much older Terra, scarred by war and glaciation. With its strong sense of mood and color, it is the most enigmatic story in Piper's history of the future, and maybe the best.

THE KEEPER

WHEN HE HEARD THE DEER crashing through brush and scuffling the dead leaves, he stopped and stood motionless in the path. He watched them bolt down the slope from the right and cross in front of him, wishing he had the rifle, and when the last white tail vanished in the gray-brown woods he drove the spike of the ice-staff into the stiffening ground and took both hands to shift the weight of the pack. If he'd had the rifle, he could have shot only one of them. As it was, they were unfrightened, and he knew where to find them in the morning.

Ahead, to the west and north, low clouds massed; the white front of the Ice-Father loomed clear and sharp between them and the blue of the distant forests. It would snow, tonight. If it stopped at daybreak, he would have good tracking, and in any case, it would be easier to get the carcasses home over snow. He wrenched loose the ice-staff and started forward again, following the path that wound between and among and over the irregular mounds and hillocks. It was still an hour's walk to Keeper's House, and the daylight was fading rapidly.

Sometimes, when he was not so weary and in so much haste, he would loiter here, wondering about the ancient

buildings and the long-vanished people who had raised them.
There had been no woods at all, then; nothing but great
houses like mountains, piling up toward the sky, and the
valley where he meant to hunt tomorrow had been an arm of
the sea that was now a three days' foot-journey away. Some
said that the cities had been destroyed and the people killed in
wars—big wars, not squabbles like the fights between
sealing-companies from different villages. He didn't think
so, himself. It was more likely that they had all left their
homes and gone away in starships when the Ice-Father had
been born and started pushing down out of the north. There
had been many starships, then. When he had been a boy, the
old men had talked about a long-ago time when there had
been hundreds of them visible in the sky, every morning and
evening. But that had been long ago indeed. Starships came
but seldom to this world, now. This world was old and lonely
and poor. Like poor lonely old Raud the Keeper.

He felt angry to find himself thinking like that. Never pity
yourself, Raud; be proud. That was what his father had
always taught him: "Be proud, for you are the Keeper's son,
and when I am gone, you will be the Keeper after me. But in
your pride, be humble, for what you will keep is the Crown."

The thought of the Crown, never entirely absent from his
mind, wakened the anxiety that always slept lightly if at all.
He had been away all day, and there were so many things that
could happen. The path seemed longer, after that; the land-
marks farther apart. Finally, he came out on the edge of the
steep bank, and looked down across the brook to the familiar
low windowless walls and sharp-ridged roof of the Keeper's
House; and when he came, at last, to the door, and pulled the
latchstring, he heard the dogs inside—the soft, coughing
bark of Brave, and the anxious little whimper of Bold—and
he knew that there was nothing wrong in Keeper's House.

The room inside was lighted by a fist-sized chunk of
lumicon, hung in a net bag of thongs from the rafter over the
table. It was old—cast off by some rich Southron as past its
best brilliance, it had been old when he had bought it from
Yorn Nazvik the Trader, and that had been years ago. Now

its light was as dim and yellow as firelight. He'd have to
replace it soon, but this trip he had needed new cartridges for
the big rifle. A man could live in darkness more easily than he
could live without cartridges.

The big black dogs were rising from their bed of deerskins
on the stone slab that covered the crypt in the far corner. They
did not come to meet him, but stayed in their place of trust,
greeting him with anxious, eager little sounds.

"Good boys," he said. "Good dog, Brave; good dog,
Bold. Old Keeper's home again. Hungry?"

They recognized that word, and whined. He hung up the
ice-staff on the pegs by the door, then squatted and got his
arms out of the pack-straps.

"Just a little now; wait a little," he told the dogs. "Keeper'll get something for you."

He unhooked the net bag that held the lumicon and went to
the ladder, climbing to the loft between the stone ceiling and
the steep snow-shed roof; he cut down two big chunks of
smoked wild-ox beef—the dogs liked that better than smoked
venison—and climbed down.

He tossed one chunk up against the ceiling, at the same
time shouting: "Bold! Catch!" Bold leaped forward, sinking
his teeth into the meat as it was still falling, shaking and
mauling it. Brave, still on the crypt-slab, was quivering with
hunger and eagerness, but he remained in place until the
second chunk was tossed and he was ordered to take it. Then
he, too, leaped and caught it, savaging it in mimicry of a kill.
For a while, he stood watching them growl and snarl and tear
their meat, great beasts whose shoulders came above his own
waist. While they lived to guard it, the Crown was safe. Then
he crossed to the hearth, scraped away the covering ashes,
piled on kindling and logs and fanned the fire alight. He lifted
the pack to the table and unlaced the deerskin cover.

Cartridges in plastic boxes of twenty, long and thick; shot
for the duck-gun, and powder and lead and cartridge-
primers; fills for the fire-lighter; salt; needles; a new file. And
the deerskin bag of tradetokens. He emptied them on the
table and counted them—tokens, and half-tokens and five-

tokens, and even one ten-token. There were always less in
the bag, after each trip to the village. The Southrons paid less
and less, each year, for furs and skins, and asked more and
more for what they had to sell.

He put away the things he had brought from the village,
and was considering whether to open the crypt now and
replace the bag of tokens, when the dogs stiffened, looking at
the door. They got to their feet, neck-hairs bristling, as the
knocking began.

He tossed the token-bag onto the mantel and went to the
door, the dogs following and standing ready as he opened it.

The snow had started, and now the ground was white
except under the evergreens. Three men stood outside the
door, and over their shoulders he could see an airboat
grounded in the clearing in front of the house.

"You are honored, Raud Keeper," one of them began.
"Here are strangers who have come to talk to you. Strangers
from the Stars!"

He recognized the speaker, in sealskin boots and deerskin
trousers and hooded overshirt like his own—Vahr Farg's
son, one of the village people. His father was dead, and his
woman was the daughter of Gorth Sledmaker, and he was a
house-dweller with his woman's father. A worthless youth,
lazy and stupid and said to be a coward. Still, guests were
guests, even when brought by the likes of Vahr Farg's son.
He looked again at the airboat, and remembered seeing it,
that day, made fast to the top-deck of Yorn Nazvik's
trading-ship, the *Issa*.

"Enter and be welcome; the house is yours, and all in it
that is mine to give." He turned to the dogs. "Brave, Bold;
go watch."

Obediently, they trotted over to the crypt and lay down. He
stood aside; Vahr entered, standing aside also, as if he were
the host, inviting his companions in. They wore heavy garments of woven cloth and boots of tanned leather with hard
heels and stiff soles, and as they came in, each unbuckled and
laid aside a belt with a holstered negatron pistol. One was
stocky and broad-shouldered, with red hair; the other was

slender, dark haired and dark eyed, with a face as smooth as a woman's. Everybody in the village had wondered about them. They were not of Yorn Nazvik's crew, but passengers on the *Issa*.

"These are Empire people, from the Far Stars," Vahr informed him, naming their names. Long names, which meant nothing; certainly they were not names the Southrons from the Warm Seas bore. "And this is Raud the Keeper, with whom your honors wish to speak."

"Keeper's House is honored. I'm sorry that I have not food prepared; if you can excuse me while I make some ready . . ."

"You think these noblemen from the Stars would eat your swill?" Vahr hooted. "Crazy old fool, these are—"

The slim man pivoted on his heel; his open hand caught Vahr just below the ear and knocked him sprawling. It must have been some kind of trick-blow. That or else the slim stranger was stronger than he looked.

"Hold your miserable tongue!" he told Vahr, who was getting to his feet. "We're guests of Raud the Keeper, and we'll not have him insulted in his own house by a cur like you!"

The man with red hair turned. "I am ashamed. We should not have brought this into your house; we should have left it outside." He spoke the Northland language well. "It will honor us to share your food, Keeper."

"Yes, and see here," the younger man said, "we didn't know you'd be alone. Let us help you. Dranigo's a fine cook, and I'm not bad, myself."

He started to protest, then let them have their way. After all, a guest's women helped the woman of the house, and as there was no woman in Keeper's House, it was not unfitting for them to help him.

"Your friend's name is Dranigo?" he asked. "I'm sorry, but I didn't catch yours."

"I don't wonder; fool mouthed it so badly I couldn't understand it myself. It's Salvadro."

They fell to work with him, laying out eating-tools—there

were just enough to go around—and hunting for dishes, of which there were not. Salvadro saved that situation by going out and bringing some in from the airboat. He must have realized that the lumicon over the table was the only light beside the fire in the house, for he was carrying a globe of the luminous plastic with him when he came in, grumbling about how dark it had gotten outside. It was new and brilliant, and the light hurt Raud's eyes, at first.

"Are you truly from the Stars?" he asked, after the food was on the table and they had begun to eat. "Neither I nor any in the village have seen anybody from the Stars before."

The big man with the red hair nodded. "Yes. We are from Dremna."

Why, Dremna was the Great World, at the middle of everything! Dremna was the Empire. People from Dremna came to the cities of Awster and fabulous Antark as Southron traders from the Warm Seas came to the villages of the Northfolk. He stammered something about that.

"Yes. You see, we . . ." Dranigo began. "I don't know the word for it, in your language, but we're people whose work it is to learn things. Not from other people or from books, but new things, that nobody else knows. We came here to learn about the long-ago times on this world, like the great city that was here and is now mounds of stone and earth. Then, when we go back to Dremna, we will tell other people what we have found out."

Vahr Farg's son, having eaten his fill, was fidgeting on his stool, looking contemptuously at the strangers and their host. He thought they were fools to waste time learning about people who had died long ago. So he thought the Keeper was a fool, to guard a worthless old piece of junk.

Raud hesitated for a moment, then said: "I have a very ancient thing, here in this house. It was worn, long ago, by great kings. Their names, and the name of their people, are lost, but the Crown remains. It was left to me as a trust by my father, who was Keeper before me and to whom it was left by his father, who was Keeper in his time. Have you heard of it?"

Dranigo nodded. "We heard of it, first of all, on Dremna," he said. "The Empire has a Space Navy base, and observatories and relay stations, on this planet. Space Navy officers who had been here brought the story back; they heard it from traders from the Warm Seas, who must have gotten it from people like Yorn Nazvik. Would you show it to us, Keeper? It was to see the Crown that we came here."

Raud got to his feet, and saw, as he unhooked the lumicon, that he was trembling. "Yes, of course. It is an honor. It is an ancient and wonderful thing, but I never thought that it was known on Dremna." He hastened across to the crypt.

The dogs looked up as he approached. They knew that he wanted to lift the cover, but they were comfortable and had to be coaxed to leave it. He laid aside the deerskins. The stone slab was heavy, and he had to strain to tilt it up. He leaned it against the wall, then picked up the lumicon and went down the steps into the little room below, opening the wooden chest and getting out the bundle wrapped in bearskin. He brought it up again and carried it to the table, from which Dranigo and Salvadro were clearing the dishes.

"Here it is," he said, untying the thongs. "I do not know how old it is. It was old even before the Ice-Father was born."

That was too much for Vahr. "See, I told you he's crazy!" he cried. "The Ice-Father has been here forever. Gorth Sledmaker says so," he added, as though that settled it.

"Gorth Sledmaker's a fool. He thinks the world began in the time of his grandfather." He had the thongs untied, and spread the bearskin, revealing the blackened leather box, flat on the bottom and domed at the top. "How long ago do you think it was that the Ice-Father was born?" he asked Salvadro and Dranigo.

"Not more than two thousand years," Dranigo said. "The glaciation hadn't started in the time of the Third Empire. There is no record of this planet during the Fourth, but by the beginning of the Fifth Empire, less than a thousand years ago, things here were very much as they are now."

"There are other worlds which have Ice-Fathers," Salvadro explained. "They are all worlds having one pole or the other in open water, surrounded by land. When the polar sea is warmed by water from the tropics, snow falls on the lands around, and more falls in winter than melts in summer, and so is an Ice-Father formed. Then, when the polar sea is all frozen, no more snow falls, and the Ice-Father melts faster than it grows, and finally vanishes. And then, when warm water comes into the polar sea again, more snow falls, and it starts over again. On a world like this, it takes fifteen or twenty thousand years from one Ice-Father to the next."

"I never heard that there had been another Ice-Father, before this one. But then, I only know the stories told by the old men, when I was a boy. I suppose that was before the first people came in starships to this world."

The two men of Dremna looked at one another oddly, and he wondered, as he unfastened the brass catches on the box, if he had said something foolish, and then he had the box open, and lifted out the Crown. He was glad, now, that Salvadro had brought in the new lumicon, as he put the box aside and set the Crown on the black bearskin. The golden circlet and the four arches of gold above it were clean and bright, and the jewels were splendid in the light. Salvadro and Dranigo were looking at it wide-eyed. Vahr Farg's son was open-mouthed.

"Great Universe! Will you look at that diamond on the top!" Salvadro was saying.

"That's not the work of any Galactic art-period," Dranigo declared. "That thing goes back to the Pre-Interstellar Era." And for a while he talked excitedly to Salvadro.

"Tell me, Keeper," Salvadro said at length, "how much do you know about the Crown? Where did it come from; who made it; who were the first Keepers?"

He shook his head. "I only know what my father told me, when I was a boy. Now I am an old man, and some things I have forgotten. But my father was Runch, Raud's son, who was the son of Yorn, the son of Raud, the son of Runch." He went back six more generations, then faltered and stopped. "Beyond that, the names have been lost. But I do know that for a long time the Crown was in a city to the north of here, and before that it was brought across the sea from another country, and the name of that country was Brinn.''

Dranigo frowned, as though he had never heard the name before.

"Brinn." Salvadro's eyes widened. "Brinn, Dranigo! Do you think that might be Britain?''

Dranigo straightened, staring. "It might be! Britain was a great nation, once; the last nation to join the Terran Federation, in the Third Century Pre-Interstellar. And they had a king, and a crown with a great diamond. . . .''

"The story of where it was made,'' Raud offered, "or who made it, has been lost. I suppose the first people brought it to this world when they came in starships.''

"It's more wonderful than that, Keeper,'' Salvadro said. "It was made on this world, before the first starship was built. This world is Terra, the Mother-World; didn't you know that, Keeper? This is the world where Man was born.''

He hadn't known that. Of course, there had to be a world like that, but a great world in the middle of everything, like Dremna. Not this old, forgotten world.

"It's true, Keeper,'' Dranigo told him. He hesitated slightly, then cleared his throat. "Keeper, you're young no longer, and some day you must die, as your father and his father did. Who will care for the Crown then?''

Who indeed? His woman had died long ago, and she had given him no sons, and the daughters she had given him had gone their own ways with men of their own choosing and he didn't know what had become of any of them. And the village people—they would start picking the Crown apart to sell the jewels, one by one, before the ashes of his pyre stopped smoking.

"Let us have it, Keeper,'' Salvadro said. "We will take it to Dremna, where armed men will guard it day and night, and it will be a trust upon the Government of the Empire forever.''

He recoiled in horror. "Man! You don't know what you're saying!'' he cried. "This is the Crown, and I am the Keeper; I cannot part with it as long as there is life in me.''

''And when there is not, what? Will it be laid on your pyre, so that it may end with you?'' Dranigo asked.

''Do you think we'd throw it away as soon as we got tired looking at it?'' Salvadro exclaimed. ''To show you how we'll value this, we'll give you . . . how much is a thousand imperials in trade-tokens, Dranigo?''

''I'd guess about twenty thousand.''

''We'll give you twenty thousand Government trade-tokens,'' Salvadro said. ''If it costs us that much, you'll believe that we'll take care of it, won't you?''

Raud rose stiffly. ''It is a wrong thing,'' he said, ''to enter a man's house and eat at his table, and then insult him.''

Dranigo rose also, and Salvadro with him. ''We had no mind to insult you, Keeper, or offer you a bribe to betray your trust. We only offer to help you fulfill it, so that the Crown will be safe after all of us are dead. Well, we won't talk any more about it, now. We're going in Yorn Nazvik's ship, tomorrow; he's trading in the country to the west, but before he returns to the Warm Seas, he'll stop at Long Valley Town, and we'll fly over to see you. In the meantime, think about this; ask yourself if you would not be doing a better thing for the Crown by selling it to us.''

They wanted to leave the dishes and the new lumicon, and he permitted it, to show that he was not offended by their offer to buy the Crown. He knew that it was something very important to them, and he admitted, grudgingly, that they could care for it better than he. At least, they would not keep it in a hole under a hut in the wilderness, guarded only by dogs. But they were not Keepers, and he was. To them, the Crown would be but one of many important things; to him it was everything. He could not imagine life without it.

He lay for a long time among his bed-robes, unable to sleep, thinking of the Crown and the visitors. Finally, to escape those thoughts, he began planning tomorrow morning's hunt.

He would start out as soon as the snow stopped, and go down among the scrub-pines; he would take Brave with him, and leave Bold on guard at home. Brave was more obedient, and a better hunter. Bold would jump for the deer that had been shot, but Brave always tried to catch or turn the ones that were still running.

He needed meat badly, and he needed more deerskins, to make new clothes. He was thinking of the new overshirt he meant to make as he fell asleep. . . .

It was past noon when he and Brave turned back toward Keeper's House. The deer had gone farther than he had expected, but he had found them, and killed four. The carcasses were cleaned and hung from trees, out of reach of the foxes and the wolves, and he would take Brave back to the house and leave him on guard, and return with Bold and the sled to bring in the meat. He was thinking cheerfully of the fresh meat when he came out onto the path from the village, a mile from Keeper's House. Then he stopped short, looking at the tracks.

Three men—no, four—had come from the direction of the village since the snow had stopped. One had been wearing sealskin boots, of the sort worn by all Northfolk. The others had worn Southron boots, with ribbed plastic soles. That puzzled him. None of the village people wore Southron boots, and as he had been leaving in the early morning, he had seen Yorn Nazvik's ship, the *Issa*, lift out from the village and pass overhead, vanishing in the west. Possibly these were deserters. In any case, they were not good people. He slipped the heavy rifle from its snow-cover, checked the chamber, and hung the empty cover around his neck like a scarf. He didn't like the looks of it.

He liked it even less when he saw that the man in sealskin boots had stopped to examine the tracks he and Brave had made on leaving, and had then circled the house and come back, to be joined by his plastic-soled companions. Then they had all put down their packs and their ice-staffs, and advanced toward the door of the house. They had stopped there for a moment, and then they had entered, come out again, gotten their packs and ice-staffs, and gone away, up the slope to the north.

"Wait, Brave," he said. "Watch."

Then he advanced, careful not to step on any of the tracks until he reached the doorstep, where it could not be avoided.

"Bold!" he called loudly. "Bold!"

Silence. No welcoming whimper, no padding of feet, inside. He pulled the latchstring with his left hand and pushed the door open with his foot, the rifle ready. There was no need for that. What welcomed him, within, was a sickening stench of burned flesh and hair.

The new lumicon lighted the room brilliantly; his first glance was enough. The slab that had covered the crypt was thrown aside, along with the pile of deerskins, and between it and the door was a shapeless black heap that, in a dimmer light, would not have been instantly recognizable as the body of Bold. Fighting down an impulse to rush in, he stood in the door, looking about and reading the story of what had happened. The four men had entered, knowing that they would find Bold alone. The one in the lead had had a negatron pistol drawn, and when Bold had leaped at them, he had been blasted. The blast had caught the dog from in front—the chest-cavity was literally exploded, and the neck and head burned and smashed unrecognizably. Even the brass studs on the leather collar had been melted.

That and the ribbed sole-prints outside meant the same thing—Southrons. Every Southron who came into the Northland, even the common crewmen on the trading ships, carried some kind of an energy-weapon. They were good only for fighting—one look at the body of Bold showed what they did to meat and skins.

He entered, then, laying his rifle on the table, and got down the lumicon and went over to the crypt. After a while, he returned, hung up the light again, and dropped onto a stool. He sat staring at the violated crypt and tugging with one hand at a corner of his beard, trying desperately to think.

The thieves had known exactly where the Crown was kept and how it was guarded; after killing Bold, they had gone straight to it, taken it and gone away—three men in plastic-

soled Southron boots and one man in soft boots of sealskins,
each with a pack and an ice-staff, and two of them with rifles.

Vahr Farg's son, and three deserters from the crew of Yorn
Nazvik's ship.

It hadn't been Dranigo and Salvadro. They could have left
the ship in their airboat and come back, flying low, while he
had been hunting. But they would have grounded near the
house, they would not have carried packs, and they would
have brought nobody with them.

He thought he knew what had happened. Vahr Farg's son
had seen the Crown, and he had heard the two Starfolk offer
more trade-tokens for it than everything in the village was
worth. But he was a coward; he would never dare to face the
Keeper's rifle and the teeth of Brave and Bold alone. So,
since none of the village folk would have part in so shameful
a crime against the moral code of the Northland, he had
talked three of Yorn Nazvik's airmen into deserting and
joining him.

And he had heard Dranigo say that the *Issa* would return to
Long Valley Town after the trading voyage to the west. Long
Valley was on the other side of this tongue of the Ice-Father;
it was a good fifteen days' foot-journey around, but by
climbing and crossing, they could easily be there in time to
meet Yorn Nazvik's ship and the two Starfolk. Well, where
Vahr Farg's son could take three Southrons, Raud the Keeper
could follow.

Their tracks led up the slope beside the brook, always
bearing to the left, in the direction of the Ice-Father. After an
hour, he found where they had stopped and unslung their
packs, and rested long enough to smoke a cigarette. He read
the story they had left in the snow, and then continued, Brave
trotting behind him pulling the sled. A few snowflakes began
dancing in the air, and he quickened his steps. He knew,
generally, where the thieves were going, but he wanted their
tracks unobliterated in front of him. The snow fell thicker and
thicker, and it was growing dark, and he was tiring. Even

Brave was stumbling occasionally before Raud stopped, in a hollow among the pines, to build his tiny fire and eat and feed the dog. They bedded down together, covered by the same sleeping robes.

When he woke, the world was still black and white and gray in the early dawn-light, and the robe that covered him and Brave was powdered with snow, and the pinebranches above him were loaded and sagging.

The snow had completely oblitereated the tracks of the four thieves, and it was still falling. When the sled was packed and the dog harnessed to it, they set out, keeping close to the flank of the Ice-Father on their left.

It stopped snowing toward midday, and a little after, he heard a shot, far ahead, and then two more, one upon the other. The first shot would be the rifle of Vahr Farg's son; it was a single-loader, like his own. The other two were from one of the light Southron rifles, which fired a dozen shots one after another. They had shot, or shot at, something like a deer, he supposed. That was sensible; it would save their dried meat for the trip across the back of the Ice-Father. And it showed that they still didn't know he was following them. He found their tracks, some hours later.

Toward dusk, he came to a steep building-mound. It had fared better than most of the houses of the ancient people; it rose to twenty times a man's height and on the south-east side it was almost perpendicular. The other side sloped, and he was able to climb to the top, and far away, ahead of him, he saw a tiny spark appear and grow. The fire could not be more than two hours ahead.

He built no fire that evening, but shared a slab of pemmican with Brave, and they huddled together under the bearskin robe. The dog fell asleep at once. For a long time, Raud sat awake, thinking.

At first, he considered resting for a while, and then pressing forward and attacking them as they slept. He had to kill all of them to regain the Crown; that he had taken for granted from the first. He knew what would happen if the Government Police came into this. They would take one Southron's

word against the word of ten Northfolk, and the thieves
would simply claim the Crown as theirs and accuse him of
trying to steal it. And Dranigo and Salvadro—they seemed
like good men, but they might see this as the only way to get
the Crown for themselves. . . . He would have to settle the
affair for himself, before the men reached Long Valley town.

If he could do it here, it would save him and Brave the toil
and danger of climbing the Ice-Father. But could he? They
had two rifles, one an autoloader, and they had in all likeli-
hood three negatron pistols. After the single shot of the big
rifle was fired, he had only a knife and a hatchet and the
spiked and pickaxed ice-staff, and Brave. One of the thieves
would kill him before he and Brave killed all of them, and
then the Crown would be lost. He dropped into sleep, still
thinking of what to do.

He climbed the mound of the ancient building again in the
morning, and looked long and carefully at the face of the
Ice-Father. It would take the thieves the whole day to reach
that place where the two tongues of the glacier split apart, the
easiest spot to climb. They would not try to climb that
evening; Vahr, who knew the most about it, would be the last
to advise such as risk. He was sure that by going up at the
nearest point he could get to the top of the Ice-Father before
dark and drag Brave up after him. It would be a fearful climb,
and he would have most of a day's journey after that to reach
the head of the long ravine up which the thieves would come,
but when they came up, he could be there waiting for them.
He knew what the old rifle could do, to an inch, and there
were places where the thieves would be coming up where he
could stay out of blaster-range and pick them all off, even
with a single-loader.

He knew about negatron pistols, too. They shot little
bullets of energy; they were very fast, and did not drop, like a
real bullet, so that no judgment of range was needed. But the
energy died quickly; the negatrons lived only long enough to
go five hundred paces and no more. At eight hundred, he
could hit a man easily. He almost felt himself pitying Vahr
Farg's son and his companions.

When he reached the tumble of rocks that had been dragged along with and pushed out from the Ice-Father, he stopped and made up a pack—sleeping robes, all his cartridges, as much pemmican as he could carry, and the bag of trade-tokens. If the chase took him to Long Valley Town, he would need money. He also coiled about his waist a long rawhide climbing-rope, and left the sled-harness on Brave, simply detaching the traces.

At first, they walked easily on the sloping ice. Then, as it grew steeper, he fastened the rope to the dog's harness and advanced a little at a time, dragging Brave up after him. Soon he was forced to snub the rope with his ice-staff and chop steps with his hatchet. Toward noon—at least he thought it was noon—it began snowing again, and the valley below was blotted out in a swirl of white.

They came to a narrow ledge, where they could rest, with a wall of ice rising sheerly above them. He would have to climb that alone, and then pull Brave up with the rope. He started working his way up the perpendicular face, clinging by the pick of his ice-staff, chopping footholds with the hatchet; the pack and the slung rifle on his back pulled at him and threatened to drag him down. At length, he dragged himself over the edge and drove the ice-staff in.

"Up, Brave!" he called, tugging on the rope. "Good dog, Brave; come up!"

Brave tried to jump and slipped back. He tried again, and this time Raud snubbed the rope and held him. Below the dog pawed frantically, until he found a paw-hold on one of the chopped-out steps. Raud hauled on the rope, and made another snub.

It seemed like hours. It probably was; his arms were aching, and he had lost all sense of time, or of the cold, or the danger of the narrow ledge; he forgot about the Crown and the men who had stolen it; he even forgot how he had come here, or that he had ever been anywhere else. All that mattered was to get Brave up on the ledge beside him.

Finally Brave came up and got first his fore-paws and then his body over the edge. He lay still, panting proudly, while

Raud hugged him and told him, over and over, that he was a good dog. They rested for a long time, and Raud got a slab of pemmican from the pack and divided it with Brave.

It was while they rested in the snow, munching, that he heard the sound for the first time. It was faint and far away, and it sounded like thunder, or like an avalanche beginning, and that puzzled him, for this was not the time of year for either. As he listened, he heard it again, and this time he recognized it—negatron pistols. It frightened him; he wondered if the thieves had met a band of hunters. No; if they were fighting Northfolk, there would be the reports of firearms, too. Or might they be fighting among themselves? Remembering the melted brass studs on Bold's collar, he became more frightened at the though of what a negatron-blast could do to the Crown.

The noise stopped, then started again, and he got to his feet, calling to Brave. They were on a wide ledge that slanted upward toward the north. It would take him closer to the top, and closer to where Vahr and his companions would come up. Together, they started up, Raud probing cautiously ahead of him with the ice-staff for hidden crevasses. After a while, he came to a wide gap in the ice beside him, slanting toward the top, its upper end lost in swirling snow. So he and Brave began climbing, and after a while he could no longer hear the negatron pistols.

When it was almost too dark to go farther, he suddenly found himself on level snow, and here he made camp, digging a hole and lining it with the sleeping robes.

The sky was clear when he woke, and a pale yellow light was glowing in the east. For a while he lay huddled with the dog, stiff and miserable, and then he forced himself to his feet. He ate, and fed Brave, and then checked his rifle and made his pack.

He was sure, now, that he had a plan that would succeed. He could reach the place where Vahr and the Southrons would come up long before they did, and be waiting for them. In his imagination, he could see them coming up in single file, Vahr Farg's son in the lead, and he could imagine

himself hidden behind a mound of snow, the ice-staff upright
to brace his left hand and the forestock of the rifle resting on
his outthrust thumb and the butt against his shoulder. The
first bullet would be for Vahr. He could shoot all of them, one
after another, that way . . .

He stopped, looking in chagrined incredulity at the tracks
in front of him—the tracks he knew so well, of one man in
sealskin boots and three men with ribbed plastic soles. Why,
it couldn't be! They should be no more than half way up the
long ravine, between the two tongues of the Ice-Father, ten
miles to the north. But here they were, on the back of the
Ice-Father and crossing to the west ahead of him. They must
have climbed the sheer wall of ice, only a few miles from
where he had dragged himself and Brave to the top. Then he
remembered the negatron-blasts he had heard. While he had
been chopping footholds with a hatchet, they had been
smashing tons of ice out of their way.

"Well, Brave," he said mildly. "Old Keeper wasn't so
smart, after all, was he? Come on, Brave."

The thieves were making good time. He read that from the
tracks—straight, evenly spaced, no weary heel-dragging.
Once or twice, he saw where they had stopped for a brief rest.
He hoped to see their fire in the evening.

He didn't. They wouldn't have enough fuel to make a big
one, or keep it burning long. But in the morning, as he was
breaking camp, he saw black smoke ahead.

A few times, he had been in airboats, and had looked down
on the back of the Ice-Father, and it had looked flat. Really, it
was not. There were long ridges, sheer on one side and
sloping gently on the other, where the ice had overridden
hills and low mountains, or had cracked and one side had
pushed up over the other. And there were deep gullies where
the prevailing winds had scooped away loose snow year after
year for centuries, and drifts where it had piled, many of
them higher than the building-mounds of the ancient cities.
But from a distance, as from above, they all blended into a
featureless white monotony.

At last, leaving a tangle of cliffs and ravines, he looked out across a broad stretch of nearly level snow and saw, for the first time, the men he was following. Four tiny dots, so far that they seemed motionless, strung out in single file. Instantly, he crouched behind a swell in the surface and dragged Brave down beside him. One of them, looking back, might see him, as he saw them. When they vanished behind a snow-hill, he rose and hastened forward, to take cover again. He kept at this all day; by alternately resting and running, he found himself gaining on them, and toward evening, he was within rifle-range. The man in the lead was Vahr Farg's son; even at that distance he recognized him easily. The others were Southrons, of course; they wore quilted garments of cloth, and quilted hoods. The man next to Vahr, in blue, carried a rifle, as Vahr did. The man in yellow had only an ice-staff, and the man in green, at the rear, had the Crown on his pack, still in the bearskin bundle.

He waited, at the end of the day, until he saw the light of their fire. Then he and Brave circled widely around their camp, and stopped behind a snow-ridge, on the other side of an open and level stretch a mile wide. He dug the sleeping-hole on the crest of the ridge, making it larger than usual, and piled up a snow breastwork in front of it, with an embrasure through which he could look or fire without being seen.

Before daybreak, he was awake and had his pack made, and when he saw the smoke of the thieves' campfire, he was lying behind his breastwork, the rifle resting on its folded cover, muzzle toward the smoke. He lay for a long time, watching, before he saw the file of tiny dots emerge into the open.

They came forward steadily, in the same order as on the day before, Vahr in the lead and the man with the Crown in the rear. The thieves suspected nothing; they grew larger and larger as they approached, until they were at the range for which he had set his sights. He cuddled the butt of the rifle against his cheek. As the man who carried the Crown walked under the blade of the front sight, he squeezed the trigger.

The rifle belched pink flame and roared and pounded his shoulder. As the muzzle was still rising, he flipped open the breech, and threw out the empty. He inserted a fresh round.

There were only three of them, now. The man with the bearskin bundle was down and motionless. Vahr Farg's son had gotten his rifle unslung and uncovered. The Southron with the other rifle was slower; he was only getting off the cover as Vahr, who must have seen the flash, fired hastily. Too hastily; the bullet kicked up snow twenty feet to the left. The third man had drawn his negatron pistol and was trying to use it; thin hairlines of brilliance were jetting out from his hand, stopping far short of their mark.

Raud closed his sights on the man with the autoloading rifle; as he did, the man with the negatron pistol, realizing the limitations of his weapon, was sweeping it back and forth, aiming at the snow fifty yards in front of him. Raud couldn't see the effect of his second shot—between him and his target, blueish light blazed and twinkled, and dense clouds of steam rose—but he felt sure that he had missed. He reloaded, and watched for movements on the edge of the rising steam.

It cleared, slowly; when it did, there was nothing behind it. Even the body of the dead man was gone. He blinked, bewildered. He'd picked that place carefully; there had been no gully or ravine within running distance. Then he grunted. There hadn't been—but there was now. The negatron pistol again. The thieves were hidden in a pit they had blasted, and they had dragged the body in with them.

He crawled back to reassure Brave, who was guarding the pack, and to shift the pack back for some distance. Then he returned to his embrasure in the snow-fort and resumed his watch. For a long time, nothing happened, and then a head came briefly peeping up out of the pit. A head under a green hood. Raud chuckled mirthlessly into his beard. If he'd been doing that, he'd have traded hoods with the dead man before shoving up his body to draw fire. This kept up, at intervals, for about an hour. He was wondering if they would stay in the pit until dark.

Then Vahr Farg's son leaped out of the pit and began running across the snow. He had his pack, and his rifle; he ran, zig-zag, almost directly toward where Raud was lying.

Raud laughed, this time in real amusement. The Southrons had chased Vahr out, as a buck will chase his does in front of him when he thinks there is danger in front. If Vahr wasn't shot, it would be safe for them to come out. If he was, it would be no loss, and the price of the Crown would only have to be divided in two, rather than three, shares. Vahr came to within two hundred yards of Raud's unseen rifle, and then dropped his pack and flung himself down behind it, covering the ridge with his rifle.

Minutes passed, and then the Southron in yellow came out and ran forward. He had the bearskin bundle on his pack; he ran to where Vahr lay, added his pack to Vahr's, and lay down behind it. Raud chewed his underlip in vexation. This wasn't the way he wanted it; that fellow had a negatron pistol, and he was close enough to use it effectively. And he was sheltered behind the Crown; Raud was afraid to shoot. He didn't miss what he shot at—often. But no man alive could say that he never missed.

The other Southron, the one in blue with the autoloading rifle, came out and advanced slowly, his weapon at the ready. Raud tensed himself to jump, aimed carefully, and waited. When the man in blue was a hundred yards from the pit, he shot him dead. The rifle was still lifting from the recoil when he sprang to his feet, turned, and ran. Before he was twenty feet away, the place where he had been exploded; the force of the blast almost knocked him down, and steam blew past and ahead of him. Ignoring his pack and ice-staff, he ran on, calling to Brave to follow. The dog obeyed instantly; more negatron-blasts were thundering and blazing and steaming on the crest of the ridge. He swerved left, ran up another slope, and slid down the declivity beyond into the ravine on the other side.

There he paused to eject the empty, make sure that there was no snow in the rifle bore, and reload. The blasting had stopped by then; after a moment, he heard the voice of Vahr Farg's son, and guessed that the two surviving thieves had advanced to the blasted crest of the other ridge. They'd find the pack, and his tracks and Brave's. He wondered whether

they'd come hunting for him, or turn around and go the other
way. He knew what he'd do, under the circumstances, but he
doubted if Vahr's mind would work that way. The Southron's might; he wouldn't want to be caught between blaster-
range and rifle-range of Raud the Keeper again.

"Come, Brave," he whispered, looking quickly around
and then starting to run.

Lay a trail down this ravine for them to follow. Then get to
the top of the ridge beside it, double back, and wait for them.
Let them pass, and shoot the Southron first. By now, Vahr
would have a negatron pistol too, taken from the body of the
man in blue, but it wasn't a weapon he was accustomed to,
and he'd be more than a little afraid of it.

The ravine ended against an upthrust face of ice, at right
angles to the ridge he had just crossed; there was a V-shaped
notch between them. He turned into this; it would be a good
place to get to the top . . .

He found himself face to face, at fifteen feet, with Vahr
Farg's son and the Southron in yellow, coming through from
the other side. They had their packs, the Southron had the
bearskin bundle, and they had drawn negatron pistols in their
hands.

Swinging up the rifle, he shot the Southron in the chest,
making sure he hit him low enough to miss the Crown. At the
same time, he shouted:

"Catch, Brave!"

Brave never jumped for the deer or wild-ox that had been
shot; always for the one still on its feet. He launched himself
straight at the throat of Vahr Farg's son—and into the muzzle
of Vahr's blaster. He died in a blue-white flash.

Raud had reversed the heavy rifle as Brave leaped; he
threw it, butt-on, like a seal-spear, into Vahr's face. As soon
as it was out of his fingers, he was jumping forward, snatch-
ing out his knife. His left hand found Vahr's right wrist, and
he knew that he was driving the knife into Vahr's body, over
and over, trying to keep the blaster pointed away from him
and away from the body of the dead Southron. At last, the

negatron-pistol fell from Vahr's fingers, and the arm that had
been trying to fend off his knife relaxed.

He straightened and tried to stand—he had been kneeling
on Vahr's body, he found—and reeled giddily. He got to his
feet and stumbled to the other body, kneeling beside it. He
tried for a long time before he was able to detach the bearskin
bundle from the dead man's pack. Then he got the pack open,
and found dried venison. He started to divide it, and realized
that there was no Brave with whom to share it. He had just
sent Brave to his death.

Well, and so? Brave had been the Keeper's dog. He had
died for the Crown, and that had been his duty. If he could
have saved the Crown by giving his own life, Raud would
have died too. But he could not—if Raud died the Crown was
lost.

The sky was darkening rapidly, and the snow was whiten-
ing the body in green. Moving slowly, he started to make
camp for the night.

It was still snowing when he woke. He started to rise,
wondering, at first, where Brave was, and then he huddled
back among the robes—his own and the dead men's—and
tried to go to sleep again. Finally, he got up and ate some of
his pemmican, gathered his gear and broke camp. For a
moment, and only a moment, he stood looking to the east, in
the direction he had come from. Then he turned west and
started across the snow toward the edge of the Ice-Father.

The snow stopped before he reached the edge, and the sun
was shining when he found a slanting way down into the
valley. Then, out of the north, a black dot appeared in the sky
and grew larger, until he saw that it was a Government
airboat—one of the kind used by the men who measured the
growth of the Ice-Father. It came curving in and down toward
him, and a window slid open and a man put his head out.

"Want us to lift you down?" he asked. "We're going to
Long Valley Town. If that's where you're going, we can take
you the whole way."

"Yes. That's where I'm going." He said it as though he were revealing, for the first time, some discovery he had just made. "For your kindness and help, I thank you."

In less time than a man could walk two miles with a pack, they were letting down in front of the Government House in Long Valley Town.

He had never been in the Government House before. The walls were clear glass. The floors were plastic, clean and white. Strips of bright new lumicon ran around every room at the tops of all the walls. There were no fires, but the great rooms were as warm as though it were a midsummer afternoon.

Still carrying his pack and his rifle, Raud went to a desk where a Southron in a white shirt sat.

"Has Yorn Nazvik's ship, the *Issa,* been here lately?" he asked.

"About six days ago," the Southron said, without looking up from the papers on his desk. "She's on a trading voyage to the west now, but Nazvik's coming back here before he goes south. Be here in about ten days." He looked up. "You have business with Nazvik?"

Raud shook his head. "Not with Yorn Nazvik, no. My business is with the two Starfolk who are passengers with him. Dranigo and Salvadro."

The Southron looked displeased. "Aren't you getting just a little above yourself, old man, calling the Prince Salsavadran and the Lord Dranigrastan by their familiar names?" he asked.

"I don't know what you're talking about. Those were the names they gave me; I didn't know they had any others."

The Southron started to laugh, then stopped.

"And if I may ask, what is your name, and what business have you with them?" he inquired.

Raud told him his name. "I have something for them. Something they want very badly. If I can find a place to stay here, I will wait until they return—"

The Sothron got to his feet. "Wait here for a moment, Keeper," he said. "I'll be back soon."

He left the desk, going into another room. After a while, he came back. This time he was respectful.

"I was talking to the Lord Dranigrastan—whom you know as Dranigo—on the radio. He and the Prince Salsavadran are lifting clear of the *Issa* in their airboat and coming back here to see you. They should be here in about three hours. If, in the meantime, you wish to bathe and rest, I'll find you a room. And I suppose you'll want something to eat, too . . ."

He was waiting at the front of the office, looking out the glass wall, when the airboat came in and grounded, and Salvadro and Dranigo jumped out and came hurrying up the walk to the doorway.

"Well, here you are, Keeper," Dranigo greeted him, clasping his hand. Then he saw the bearskin bundle under Raud's arm. "You brought it with you? But didn't you believe that we were coming?"

"Are you going to let us have it?" Salvadro was asking.

"Yes; I will sell it to you, for the price you offered. I am not fit to be Keeper any longer. I lost it. It was stolen from me, the day after I saw you, and I have only yesterday gotten it back. Both my dogs were killed, too. I can no longer keep it safe. Better that you take it with you to Dremna, away from this world where it was made. I have thought, before, that this world and I are both old and good for nothing any more."

"This world may be old, Keeper," Dranigo said, "but it is the Mother-World, Terra, the world that sent Man to the Stars. And you—when you lost the Crown, you recovered it again."

"The next time, I won't be able to. Too many people will know that the Crown is worth stealing, and the next time, they'll kill me first."

"Well, we said we'd give you twenty thousand trade-tokens for it," Salvadro said. "We'll have them for you as soon as we can draw them from the Government bank, here. Or give you a check and let you draw them as you want them." Raud didn't understand that, and Salvadro didn't try to explain. "And then we'll fly you home."

He shook his head. "No, I have no home. The place where you saw me is Keeper's House, and I am not the Keeper any more. I will stay here and find a place to live, and pay somebody to take care of me . . ."

With twenty thousand trade-tokens, he could do that. It would buy a house in which he could live, and he could find some woman who had lost her man, who would do his work for him. But he must be careful of the money. Dig a crypt in the corner of his house for it. He wondered if he could find a pair of good dogs and train them to guard it for him . . .

H. BEAM PIPER

FAFHRD AND THE GRAY MOUSER SAGA

☐ 79175	**SWORDS AND DEVILTRY**	**$1.95**
☐ 79156	**SWORDS AGAINST DEATH**	**$2.25**
☐ 79184	**SWORDS IN THE MIST**	**$1.95**
☐ 79165	**SWORDS AGAINST WIZARDRY**	**$2.25**
☐ 79223	**THE SWORDS OF LANKHMAR**	**$1.95**
☐ 79168	**SWORDS AND ICE MAGIC**	**$1.95**

Available wherever paperbacks are sold or use this coupon

Ursula K. Le Guin

10705	**City of Illusion**	$2.25
47806	**Left Hand of Darkness**	$2.25
66956	**Planet of Exile**	$1.95
73294	**Rocannon's World**	$1.95

Available wherever paperbacks are sold or use this coupon

POUL ANDERSON

MORE TRADE SCIENCE FICTION

Ace Books is proud to publish these latest works by major SF authors in deluxe large format collectors' editions. Many are illustrated by top artists such as Alicia Austin, Esteban Maroto and Fernando.

Robert A. Heinlein	Expanded Universe	21883	$8.95
Frederik Pohl	Science Fiction: Studies in Film (illustrated)	75437	$6.95
Frank Herbert	Direct Descent (illustrated)	14897	$6.95
Harry G. Stine	The Space Enterprise (illustrated)	77742	$6.95
Ursula K. LeGuin and Virginia Kidd	Interfaces	37092	$5.95
Marion Zimmer Bradley	Survey Ship (illustrated)	79110	$6.95
Hal Clement	The Nitrogen Fix	58116	$6.95
Andre Norton	Voorloper	86609	$6.95
Orson Scott Card	Dragons of Light (illustrated)	16660	$7.95

Available wherever paperbacks are sold or use this coupon.

ACE SCIENCE FICTION
P.O. Box 400, Kirkwood, N.Y. 13795

Please send me the titles checked above. I enclose _____.
Include 75¢ for postage and handling if one book is ordered; 50¢ per book for two to five. If six or more are ordered, postage is free. California, Illinois, New York and Tennessee residents please add sales tax.

NAME_____

ADDRESS_____

CITY_____STATE_____ZIP_____